*The car roared and bucked* with heart-thumping power. The motor had a mind of its own, a beast of metal and explosive gases in eight cylinders. I screeched onto a paved street in third gear. The big steering wheel felt alive in my clenched hands, silhouetted against the yellow light on the dashboard. The speedometer needle climbed to twenty-five, then thirty. In third gear, the Chevy cut through the night like a charging army. I drove for three blocks consumed with the thrill before it occurred to me that I'd stolen the stranger's car.

5-25-2017

Happy Birthday Jennifer
♡ Love Mom ♡

You can take the girl out
of Montana but never take
Montana out of her heart.
Deer Lodge was a
great place to grow up!

Also by Kevin S. Giles

.

*Jerry's Riot:*
*The True Story of Montana's 1959 Prison Disturbance*

*Flight of the Dove:*
*The Story of Jeannette Rankin*

*Forthcoming:*
*An expanded edition of the Jeannette Rankin biography*

Kevin S. Giles

# *Summer of the Black Chevy*

Sky Blue Waters Press

Published by BookLocker.com, Inc., Bradenton, Florida, U.S.A.

Printed on acid-free paper.

Sky Blue Waters Press
2015

First Edition

*To the Hooligans.*

*You know who you are.*

# Homeward

*My dying mother's eyes flamed* with denial. "Paul, no, not you, it was Louie!" she whispered, her failing heart allowing nothing more. Then she was gone, slipping away from me and all I had hidden from her. I had just begun to tell her a secret haunting me since 1965, my first year as a teenager. Now she would never know the depth of my regret.

The wind blew mournfully that night in Montana. I sat on the porch of my childhood house watching a magnificent Halloween moon crawl over the sky. Its blue light, deathly as my mother's skin, washed into the shadows. Fallen leaves rustled over the road. The coroner had come. He reeked of Lucky Strikes and overheated coffee. Being a man accustomed to examining the dead, he probed casually at her with scabbed fingers and laid his ear to her mouth and shook his head as I knew he would. "No surprise?" He nodded to himself, anticipating my answer. Then he pulled her eyelids down and whistled his way to his car for a body bag to carry away what was left of my mother.

My trip from Oregon had commenced on a whim. It's always best that a man moves quickly when he plunges into the heartache of his past. I didn't want to drive the Chevy. It would have roared up the highway, turning heads, and in some strange way distracted me from my mission. I knew I didn't have much time. The rental place found me a fast Jeep Cherokee, made for mountain driving, and put me on the road on a Tuesday morning in late October. I arrived in my hometown of Deer Lodge the next afternoon to find my mother's life ebbing under a pile of blankets in her bedroom. Regrettably I hadn't seen her for three years. Mom looked much older than she deserved.

My sister Sally, hearing of our mother's sudden decline, had arrived a few days earlier to take stock of an impossible situation. She began a storm of cleaning that uncovered liquor bottles of various quantities that Mom had used to wash down her heart medications. In tandem those substances had bleached away her youthful beauty and worse yet, stole her heart.

I tried to make my confession after Sally left for a drive home to seek peace in solitude. Mom, shivering, interrupted to say she was cold. I searched the closet in my old bedroom and found a sleeping bag she and Dad had given me for my first Cub Scout camping trip. It was a good memory of our young family, held dear before the trouble started. I unrolled it over her and when she smiled I held her hand and, finally, began choking out my secret. She spoke those few words of denial and died.

She had waited for me to admit what I had done because she wanted me to know she didn't believe a word of it. She wanted that understanding between us. She had followed life's trail to an improbable end, just as had so many others I had known and loved, especially Louie.

# Blue and Max

*Blue tugged on my tie* until he strangled the daylights out of me. I watched him in the bathroom mirror as he cinched me like he did Old Betsy in the corral.

"Blue! You're choking me!"

"You've got to plan for equipment failures during the ride, Paul," he told me, using his best John Wayne voice. "We can't have the tack coming loose."

Blue was in a phase where he liked to talk like a cowboy because of westerns we had seen at the Rialto. His dad owned a few acres in the foothills east of Deer Lodge, a railroad and prison town. He kept Betsy pastured in a grove of trees. For two summers we rode our bikes out there to see the old mare until Blue's fantasy to ride into the Old West began to unravel. More and more he made excuses to watch girls at the soda fountain downtown. I burned through quarters like crazy helping Blue hold vigil at the counter. After we each spent our allowance we'd head back out to see Betsy.

She grazed in a meadow at Zosel's Grove where in summer we walked in sagebrush and mountain wildflowers that grew to our knees. Betsy mellowed under the warm sun but when the weather turned cold and raw so did her temper. One autumn day she bucked Blue into a fencepost. He stood up crying and looking pitiful and holding his arm. The bones in his wrist pointed up, like when the gunslingers on television snap open a double-barrel shotgun to push shells into the chamber. He vowed he was done with Betsy but began to see renewed value in the cowboy life when girls at school clustered around him to autograph his cast. Blue had those movie hero good looks that drove girls wild. He wasn't short on confidence either. His black hair, longer than most boys in school, resembled Frankie Avalon in the beach movies when he cavorted with Annette Funicello. Blue liked winking at girls with his snapping blue eyes. I pictured myself in the same regard but Blue didn't hold out much hope.

"You look like a real idiot, Paul. You can't expect to hustle girls looking like you're fitted for a hanging noose. Put the knot in front why don't you."

"If you pull any harder you're going to kill me anyway." I watched him in the bathroom mirror as he leaned over my shoulder, laughing through his blazing smile. He tugged this way and that until he was satisfied. Blue bummed me out sometimes, to tell you the truth. He was the bossy type.

"At least now you don't look like some old lady down at the dime store dressed you. Go to the junior high dance looking like you got a hall pass from the mental hospital and they won't let you near the girls."

"Funny, Blue. What a comedian." He did make my tie look good but I wasn't going to tell him that. Blue had an ego the size of Montana. Give him one little compliment and around he'd go swelling up and telling me it's about time I noticed. He punched me in the gut one time to show off for girls. I was bent over trying not to throw up all over my black tennis shoes while he stood there flexing his bicep for Rhonda Lou Bessett and her big sister, the high school cheerleader. I was so mad I didn't talk to him for a week. One night after school Blue came over to my house to give me his souvenir from Philadelphia as a peace offering. It was a silver model of the Liberty Bell that stood about eight inches tall. I figured he paid three bucks for it, maybe five, when his family took a summer vacation in 1963. It was his most favorite possession. He shoved it into my hands and started talking like the punch to the gut never happened. That's Blue.

His real name was Bobby Taylor. To the teachers he was Bobby and to his mother he was Robert. To me he was Blue, a nickname I gave him way back in grade school. I met him in second grade when we started messing around one afternoon recess at old Central School. He dared me to climb the fire escape. It was an enclosed slide standing two stories high, a metal caterpillar stinking like pee and rusty aluminum. Bare feet were required to shinny clear to the top to the wooden door that connected to the school auditorium. We left our shoes in the sand and crawled upward in the dark tube to the top. There we sat, satisfied at our conquest, until a pretty face poked into the white opening far below us.

"You boys come down from there right now!" That was the sweet voice of Miss O'Leary, our teacher. Blue squinted down at the sun-bronzed goddess in the yellow dress. "Stay still," he whispered. For an instant we hid in our lair, pressing into the dark. Then Blue, leaning forward for a better look at Miss O'Leary, slipped. He shot forth on his stomach in the second that I came to remember how many Saturday afternoons I'd brought sheets of wax paper borrowed from my mother's kitchen to polish the tube for a fast ride. Head first he went, silently but at astonishing speed, toward Miss O'Leary's peering face. Blue must have launched out of the fire escape like a human cannonball because when I slid down after him, bracing my descent with my toes, I found him lying on top of our teacher in the dirt, his face only inches from hers.

I have to admit this incident started some wishful talk when we got older but by that time Miss O'Leary had gone off to Missoula to learn something new, or so we were told, and after that she married somebody and changed her name and we bragged she did it for good reason. Looking back, I can't say for sure Blue embarrassed Miss O'Leary when he knocked her flat on her back. Even with her glasses hanging from one ear, and her dress knotted above her knees and old Blue aboard, she was a dignified peach of a thing. In the seconds that it took me to get a good look, more and more little legs gathered around the fallen couple. Miss O'Leary told Blue to get off. He rolled aside like a spent lover, smiling at the attention. Our teacher stood up looking no worse for it. She smoothed her dress with sand-stained fingers before grabbing our collars. Off we marched to the principal, shuffling through the ranks of our playground admirers. The principal warned us to stay out of the fire escape unless we saw flames in the building. Then he sent us outside to bang chalkboard erasers on the school's weathered brick walls as punishment. We managed introductions in a cloud of blue powder.

"Name's Bobby," my new friend offered.

"You look blue. It's all over your face."

He drew a finger over his cheek and smiled. "Blue for sure. Maybe I'm blue all over."

"Then I'll call you Blue."

"My name's Bobby."

"Blue's good enough for me. Easier to remember too."

"You?"

"It's Paul. I go by Paul." First names were enough then. "Crazy ride you took down the fire escape."

"Bet Miss O'Leary won't forget that, huh?"

You'll understand why young boys take things in stride, even when required to slap erasers for falling on top of gorgeous young Miss O'Leary. Life was a freewheeling joy without burden. *I feel no pain. I'm a child.* In those young years I thought that we would go on forever being boys, me and Blue and our new friend who moved to Deer Lodge from Butte when we were in the fourth grade.

Max was a big kid. He loved marble games and liked to play for keeps. Max went around coaxing kids into playing their best marbles before he smashed them to bits with a steely, a shiny silver ball bearing I swear was as big as a baseball. This was fair game on the playground because Max set the rules when he brought his steelies to school. If you hit his steelie with your glass marble he would give you a marble in return. If he won, smashing your marble into bits, he threatened to pound you if you didn't give him a new one. You then were out two marbles. Max liked to choose the marble he wanted from the selection in the leather pouches that hung from our belts. Usually it was the other boy's most prized cat eye, sometimes even a rainbow or a clearie. When a boy refused, Max would size him up. "I won you fair and square," he'd say, clenching his fists. That was warning enough, as we all knew, because Max came from Butte. Everyone understood the Mile High mining city bore its kids fight-ready from the womb. When Max squared up, his eyes full of temptation on the dusty playground, the other boy always forked over a new marble to keep his teeth intact.

I wouldn't say Max was a bully. I was just a little afraid of him. When we got older he told me that boys who lived in Walkerville up the hill from Butte robbed workers of their lunch pails as they walked to work at the Mountain Con mine. Boys robbing men. I couldn't see Max doing that but he had an edge about him that came from living in a tough neighborhood in a city that had a reputation for hard times. Max and Blue shared the same instincts. They played hard the way boys do when they're set deep in their passions, headstrong and decisive.

I saw things more creatively. Mom advised me of that three times a year when she got home from parent-teacher conferences at school. "Paul, your teacher says you won't get anywhere by daydreaming. She says you need to buckle down and work. You've got brains but you've got to apply yourself." It was a familiar speech, full of arching voice inflections and stern references to test failures and other examples of my sloth. I can think of no better example of my undoing than when our fifth grade teacher, Mr. Klung, instructed us to build world maps on scraps of plywood. I volunteered for Italy. We had to build the country out of a mixture of salt, water and flour. I tasted the concoction before it congealed into a rock, ruining my fascination for the assignment. The salt left me thirsty for a week. The idea was to learn something about geography by constructing topography. I formed mountains with my fingertips and sculptured Italy the way it looked on a map. Then I painted a deep blue Mediterranean around Italy and turned in my masterpiece. Mr. Klung wasn't impressed. It turns out that we had a sea without Sicily, and this was an assignment where attention to detail was paramount in his mind.

So it went as Blue pushed my skinny bespectacled face in front of the bathroom mirror in May 1965. "What girl is going to dance with you looking like a roped calf? Paul, you've got to fix that thing."

Blue tended to worry about matters of appearance. No friend of his was going to the gymnasium for our first school dance looking like an idiot. Sometimes Blue stood for hours in front of the mirror combing his thick black hair. I swear to it. We endured a whirlwind week as our gym teachers coached us through dance etiquette. On cue, we recited, "May I please have this dance?" It seems funny to think of it now, but Max and I took that instruction like commandments from Moses. Blue had his doubts. He figured the girls would come to him instead.

Blue came to my house that night in a new black suit straight from the Toggery downtown. His head glistened with Vitalis, his heart raced with impending romance. When he saw my tie he acted like I was going to ruin whatever chances he imagined that night with girls.

"Look, it's all crooked and everything." He tugged and prodded at the thin fabric tied around the collar of my white shirt until it resembled a black pencil hanging to my belly. Then he cinched it good, like I'd seen him saddle his mare Betsy until her eyes bugged out and she swung her head around to try to nip him. I felt like doing the same.

When my tie met Blue's satisfaction we slapped on a gallon of Dad's aftershave lotion and adjourned to the living room where my parents looked us over. Dad always got a kick out of seeing me in a suit. He leaned back in his recliner, tapping tobacco smelling like cherries into his pipe. "You'll be a hit with the girls tonight, Bubby." That was a dreaded nickname. Dad was always pulling stunts like that in front of my friends. I kept telling him what it was like being a teenager. He acted like he didn't know anything about it.

Mom waved him off. "Frank, don't encourage Paul. He shouldn't be going to dances in the first place. He's too young." Mom knitted away on a sweater for yet somebody else in the family. I had a drawer full of them. She was younger than Dad by seven years. While he had grayed at the temples, her bountiful hair was red and thick. Tonight she had it pulled into a ponytail. She always looked like she would bounce up any moment to cheer for the high school football team.

"Mom, all the kids are going."

Dad came to my defense, waving his pipe for emphasis. "Paul is going into eighth grade in the fall, Martha. It's time the boy learned his way around the opposite sex. Can't have him sitting at home while Blue's out grabbing all the pretty girls."

"I don't care, Frank. He's barely a teenager right now and needs to act like it. He'll have plenty of time for girls when he's in high school." Having her say, she turned back to her knitting. I felt Blue tugging at my coat sleeve.

"That was embarrassing," I told him when we got outside.

Sure enough, he started laying it on me. "Going to kiss a girl tonight, Bubby?"

I gave him a hard shove. "Hey, careful of the suit." Blue got sore about things like that.

"How would you like it if I called you Bobby all the time? Then we could be Bobby and Bubby."

"Sounds like an English assignment, Bubby. Tales of Bubby and Bobby. Too bad your hair isn't red. We could be Red and Blue."

I balled up my fist. "How about Black and Blue?"

Having worn out that conversation, we walked silently down the dirt road into town. I lived in a 1912 farmhouse at the edge of town, where the scattered neighborhoods of Deer Lodge ended and the vast treeless foothills began. We had a real barn behind the house, its hip roof still proud and strong, but Dad didn't farm on the place. I knew only that somebody had bought most of the land long before we moved in, turning Herefords loose in the sagebrush. From one side of the house we saw empty land and the Deer Lodge Mountains. To the other we saw town, where occasional paved streets dissected orderly blocks of houses. Beyond our little town, Mount Powell loomed over the wide valley.

Blue and I hurried along in silence until we reached the chipped sidewalk in front of Mr. Pearson's house. Green buds peered from the weeping willow in his yard. He was a war hero who flew an American flag every holiday. Mr. Pearson never talked to me, or anyone else, either. Shell shock, I had heard somebody say about him. Whatever that was. It was Friday evening but the streets were quiet. Black and white television images flashed behind windows as we walked toward the school.

"You never know about these girls," Blue announced.

I wished he hadn't said that. I was already nervous at going to my first dance. Soon summer would come and then baseball. Dancing with girls scared me. They would come

11

wearing pretty dresses and eye makeup and we'd hardly recognize them. I wasn't confident like Blue. Maybe that's why I hung around with him.

"Paul, you listening?"

"Maybe so."

"They want to hold hands and kiss as much as we do, right? So how come they're going to stand on one side of the gym while we stand on the other? And why do we have to go back to our own sides after every dance?"

"Because the teachers told us to, that's why." That seemed reason enough to follow the rules. Blue lived to protest authority. Since that collision with Miss O'Leary he didn't spend much time in the principal's office but I could tell he was eager to make his own way in life. Problem was, he was only thirteen, like me.

We met Max at the gym. "I've been inside," he told us right away, nodding his fresh crew cut at the Alamo-like facade. He squeezed his broad face into a worried expression. Looks like a carnival midway in there." Max tended to exaggerate but you had to admire his capacity for description.

The three of us hurried up creaking stairs into the old gymnasium. It smelled of ancient wood and stale laundry. I thought of our jockstraps tangled on the floor in the locker room downstairs after gym class. Every boy in school wondered if the girls threw their bras in a heap in their own locker room. For about two weeks straight it was the only topic during lunch hour.

I hardly recognized the place. The basketball floor was dark except for orange light bulbs and flickering candles. A bowl of punch waited in one corner, a hi-fi with a stack of records in another. Streamers in our school colors, orange and black, fluttered above the dance floor. Some of the younger teachers from the junior high school came to chaperone. They herded girls to one side, boys to the other. None of us were allowed to cross the glistening wood floor until the signal was given. The boys stood around on their side, making jokes and bragging about their intended conquests. The girls waited demurely in folding chairs like a row of piano keys, a few dark dresses accentuating the light ones, blanching at us as if we were an attacking army preparing to assault the castle.

"You scared, Paul?" Max looked at me for affirmation. He didn't dare ask Blue. We both knew Blue wouldn't let on anyway, but Max and I were different. Max was a tough kid but not around girls. I steadied him with a reassuring grip on his wide shoulder. "Sure, Max, sure I am."

When the teachers put the needle to "Little Old Lady from Pasadena," about half the boys breeched the great divide toward the waiting girls. The bold excursion prompted a few others to follow.

I shot forward with the first wave. To my right, Max charged ahead like a blocking back for Blue, who twisted and turned behind him as if evading tackle. It soon became apparent that the fastest boys found the prettiest girls. Boys collided and pushed. I aimed for Marcy Kersher, who wrote me long letters of endearment when she sat behind me in English class, but I got shoved sideways into a girl who offered a hand soggier than a wet tuna sandwich. Boys and girls reeled and swerved all around us, attempting the "Swim" and the "Monkey" and other corny dances we learned in gym class. I heard Blue whoop. Max stumbled around underneath the basketball hoop with a sad-faced girl, trying to keep time to the song. They looked everywhere but at each other. I didn't recognize the girl. Her expression suggested she didn't want Max to know her either.

"You dance good!" my partner shouted through lips brimming with bubblegum. Someone at the beauty parlor had entwined her locks in enormous swirls. As she rocked to Jan and Dean I thought the weight of it would topple her to the floor. I pranced around on my toes with a dancing style I made up on the spot until I lost my balance and fell. I caught a quick look up her dress at a pair of thunderous white thighs before she stormed away in disgust.

Blue came by to console me. "Smooth move, Ex-Lax!" he shouted over the music, reminding me again: "You look like a real idiot!"

I retreated to the sidelines to hang out with the wimps, feeling sorry for myself, while Blue hopped and kicked like Betsy in springtime and Max snared the waif for a second dance. A boy next to me picked his nose. The boy next to him drank punch. There we stood, satisfied at our fraternity, until a skinny kid known as Nick the Stick hurried off the floor to let a rank one rip. He ran back to his girl, trailing a ghastly odor behind him. That seemed like a good time to clear out. When I saw Marcy standing alone I made a break for her.

I tried out my new etiquette. "Marcy, may I have this dance?" She looked at me with inquiring eyes. *So cute, she digs me.* I think we both felt embarrassed that we had exchanged glances in class but never had a real conversation.

"*Paauul.*" That's what she said, dragging it out, as if she had expected me all along. A white ribbon tied back dark chestnut hair streaked with blonde, different from all the other girls. It was a new daring look and I liked it. I sensed a hint of perfume. Unlike most of us, she didn't wear glasses, and she looked back at me from pools of green eyes. My glasses weighed at least five pounds and kept slipping down my nose but she didn't seem to mind. We held hands and danced slow, standing two feet apart and trying hard to avoid stepping on each other's feet. At the start of each dance I hurried across the floor to ask Marcy and she always said yes but little else. This continued until the music stopped for good, announcing an end to whatever love was being forged in the sunset of our evening. Somebody switched on the bright gymnasium lights, shattering our close feelings, while a few eager parents bunched at the door to gawk at our pubescent behavior.

We looked around at one another in our unfamiliar costumes. After two boys who were clowning around knocked over the punch bowl and were made to mop the hardwood floor with threadbare towels from the showers downstairs, the teachers ushered us toward the door. I walked Marcy outside where her mother waited in a Buick station wagon that coughed gray smoke. "I had a good time, Paul. Really I did. What was your favorite dance?" Shaking, I leaned forward to kiss her. Instead she squeezed my hand and hurried away. I saw her shining face under the dome light for a second. *I'm in love.* The Buick turned and groaned into the night.

Blue and Max and I assembled outside the gym. I checked my watch. It was an hour before midnight. Except for the floodlights from the prison three blocks away the night was dark and still. We stood in front of the gym, watching everyone go.

Blue turned to us, looking urgent. "We don't have much time."

"To get home?" Max inquired. He looked concerned.

I knew what Blue meant. "Girls? School will let out in a few months and then we won't see them all summer. I don't even know where Marcy lives."

"Hey, cowboy, better get a rope on that gal."

Max looked perplexed, which wasn't unusual. "What are you guys talking about?"

Blue smiled. "Max buddy, I see you had one on the line. Did you kiss her?" He snickered. "Could you even find her lips? She's a skinny one."

Max looked dejected. "I wanted to, but she had to go home."

"You wanted to what? Find her lips?"

"Knock it off, Blue. Yours wasn't so hot either." Blue laughed again.

"Paul?"

"Same deal."

"Same deal what? You couldn't find her lips?"

"I wanted to make out but she had to go home."

Blue decided to rub it in. "You losers missed out. I kissed two girls tonight."

"Liar!" Max alleged. Then, "How was it, Blue?"

I didn't believe Blue for a minute. He was a big talker, full of razz. I wanted to hear more because he might give me courage to kiss Marcy. I had to kiss a girl sometime. I hoped it would be her.

"You sad cases want to know, huh? Well, I knew what I was doing the whole way. They kissed back too."

"Did they slip you the tongue?" Max seemed eager to know.

"Me to know and you to find out, Maxy." Blue was on a roll.

"Well, Blue, who were they? Name them." I knew I had him with that one.

"Not telling. They asked me not to tell." Blue acted like the matter was closed. Knowing him, he'd bring it up again at school when he had an audience. I didn't care if he was telling a big story. It was fun to think about kissing a girl. Marcy, maybe. If not her, somebody. Soon. Every boy in school had kissed girls. They all said so. *Hope I'm not a nerd all my life.*

We turned toward home. A gentle wind blew the sweet scent of spring snow off Mount Powell. Stars sprayed across the sky. Living in Deer Lodge, Montana, was the best. School would end soon. Then came summer vacation and baseball and swimming lessons at the old pool and riding bikes to the river to fish for rainbow trout. Blue was right. We wouldn't have much time for girls this summer.

We stepped onto a dirt road that ran between the gym and the darkened field where our high school team, nicknamed the Wardens in recognition of the prison downtown, played football. We fell silent for a moment, each of us thinking about the dance. We would see the girls at school on Monday. I never thought I'd look forward to school that much except for going to shop class where we could cut up boards on machines. Our shop teacher, Mr. Melvin, liked to see joints planed to perfection where not even a sliver of daylight showed under the T-square. Mr. Melvin was a Ford guy. When you messed up he'd lay you low with one of his car jokes. "Fits like the door on a Chevy," he'd say, before sending you back to whittle your board until it resembled a toothpick.

Blue broke the silence. "Sure is quiet out here. What we saw tonight was just a taste of things to come, boys." We walked side by side, the three of us, flush with romance. Blue and Max were my best friends in the whole world. I admit that I looked up to them in some unexplainable way. It didn't matter what. That's the thing about being best friends. You don't go around making excuses.

As we walked home, gravel crunching under our feet, I wondered what Marcy would write to me in her next locker note. Would she say she loved me? *Dear Paul, I think you are the best boy ever in the seventh grade. Would you like to kiss me?*

Out of nowhere a roaring motor invaded the night. Headlights shot in front of us. Our shadows loomed like giant men. We turned to see an intruder of light and noise bearing down on us. I jumped to the left, Blue and Max to the right. A gleaming black sedan, horn blaring and dust roiling in its wake, shot between us.

"What the hell?" That was Blue, yelling his head off. Furious, surprised that I wasn't dead, I reached for the largest rock I could find and flung it at the vanishing car. I should explain. In Little League they put me in centerfield because I could throw a mile. It's true that my accuracy was in dispute, but I once threw the ball from centerfield right over the backstop. Nobody could say that I didn't have an arm. It's just that I couldn't hit a target.

Now why did I throw the rock with perfect accuracy? Just as the car surged beneath a streetlight, giving me a clear view, the rock whacked the windshield. The driver slammed to a stop, then kicked the car in reverse, showering gravel from the rear tires. It streaked backward toward us with frightening urgency. Blue and Max disappeared down the path that led to the football field. Blue yelled my name, hoping I would follow. I tried but the car stormed between us, a black thundering menace in the night. I ran away from the road toward the school. I would get home safe to where Mom and Dad would be waiting in the living room watching the late news from Butte.

The driver spun the car and gunned it and he was after me again. A loafer flew from my churning feet. I shot into a grove of pine trees near the gym. I stumbled and fell in the gloom, rolling to my knees in the branches. A car door wrenched open behind me.

"Somebody help!" Was that me or did I just think it? The gym was dark. Everyone had gone home.

The maniac stepped out of his car and headed for me in the trees. I couldn't see his face. His long muscular arms, bare to his shoulders, looked blue in the moonlight. A cigarette glowed orange. He said nothing, as if the rumbling car spoke for him. Blue and Max called to me but I couldn't see them. If we were together they would at least throw up their fists to fight. The dark figure crept through the trees. Would he murder me? What would Marcy think about that? All the magic of the dance was gone. I waited for the first blow. A soothing wind feathered through the trees. I smelled beer. It was a ripe odor, like when Dad came home from the bar downtown.

Maybe the stranger wouldn't murder me. Just beat me to a pulp. He was a big man, a monster out of control, raging and ruinous. He would pound me before branding my forehead with his cigarette. I would lay in the dark on a Friday night until Mom called the police and the single cop on duty in Deer Lodge found me bloody with a brand to warn all the other kids to never throw rocks at cars. The stranger would smash my glasses. It would take weeks to get a new pair and I had trouble seeing without them. He thrashed through the pine boughs. The glow on his cigarette grew brighter when he stopped to inhale. *Never be afraid of the dark, just what it covers up.*

"Hurry up!" yelled a girl in green pants. I saw her now, waiting in the headlights of the black car that still rumbled on the road, its driver door yawning open. She didn't look anything like the girls at the dance. She was tougher, more grown up. I saw enough of her to decide that a pretty face hid beneath all that makeup. She was an old lady of maybe sixteen.

"Don't hurt him," she called to the stranger, who now was close enough to touch me.

"Shut up, Faye." He was on me in an instant. Instead of killing me he lifted me off the ground and dragged me to the car. I was afraid to look at him. He shoved me into the driver's seat and pointed to the broken windshield. Fear brings oddities. I looked past the crack to Faye, her denim jacket flapping open to reveal a memorable plunging cleavage. I didn't know what I should respect more, my criminal act in breaking a windshield or this sudden appearance of the lovely Faye.

The stranger's hand shot out to grab my tie. I wished Blue hadn't cinched it so tight. It was choking me now. The stranger's grip felt like iron. He twisted me around, banging my head against the steering wheel.

"Let go! I can't breathe!" I felt like bawling. He was going to hurt me bad. I wanted to explain to him that I threw the rock because he nearly ran me over, but Faye yelled at him again.

"Louie! Let him go!"

The stranger released me. Faye stepped out of the headlights to swear at him. They began to argue.

There I was, sitting behind the wheel in an idling car. I remember the day Dad allowed me to drive his old Ford pickup to the city dump. "Hell, you'll have to learn how sometime," he said, a few minutes after Mom left for the store with Sally, my sweet sister. He taught me how to release the clutch and shift through the gears. We jerked to a stop again and again until I got the hang of backing the clutch pedal out while depressing the gas pedal at the same time.

This car, a rumbling mean Chevy I now realized, had a steering column with three on the tree. It would be easy after what Dad showed me to do. Work the column shift with the clutch. Down and close, up and away, down and away. It was clear to me now. Get away before they dumped my body in some lonely ditch in the country. I whipped the shift handle into first gear, hit the gas and felt the motor roar. The car shot ahead, past the dark stranger and the curvy girl. The door beside me slammed shut as I gained speed. They chased me in the red flare of the tail lights until I dropped the transmission into second gear. The car burst ahead, leaving them in the night.

If this guy Louie caught me now I'd be dead for sure. I managed to weave the car through the school playground without hitting a tetherball pole that loomed from the shadows. The car roared and bucked with heart-thumping power. The motor had a mind of its own, a beast of metal and explosive gases in eight cylinders. I screeched onto a paved street in third gear. The big steering wheel felt alive in my clenched hands, silhouetted against the yellow light on the dashboard. The speedometer needle climbed to twenty-five, then thirty. In third gear, the Chevy cut through the night like a charging army. I drove for three blocks consumed with the thrill before it occurred to me that I'd stolen the stranger's car.

If the police didn't find me, this guy Louie would. I wondered which would be worse. At the corner near the Catholic Church I spun left and shot down Montana Avenue, nearly hitting Blue and Max. They ran, but I pulled over and jumped out and yelled to them.

"We thought you were dead," said Max, all out of breath. I told him that was still a possibility.

"You stole his car?" Blue was incredulous. "He's going to kill you."

"You mean my dad?"

"Geez, Paul, that guy you stole the car from. He'll kill you and then your dad will and then the police will send you to prison." Blue sounded a little riled. It wasn't much like him but none of us had stolen a car before either.

Blue and Max climbed into the front seat beside me. For a moment they seemed in awe that I was capable of driving but then Max turned his interest to the Chevy's mechanical ability. "What's this got in it?" he asked, showing sudden interest in the rumbling motor. When I figured we were a safe distance from the school I pulled over quick and we popped the hood and bent over for a look.

"This guy knows what he's doing," Blue observed in great reverence, although none of us knew for sure. We couldn't see much in the dark and, except for Max, didn't know anything about engines anyway.

After a brief inspection, we climbed back into the car and headed down the street. A faded green sedan crossed in front of us, creeping into the night. Blue fiddled with the radio dial. The Rolling Stones burst into the front seat. He couldn't find much but KXLF out of Butte and some big rock and roll station way down in Omaha, a thousand miles away, which faded every time we turned a corner.

Max asked if he could drive. "This is stupid!" I told them, feeling a sudden impulse of conscience. "We're in big trouble!"

"At least you are, Paul." That was Blue, stating facts.

I drove to an alley a few blocks from where Max lived. When I killed the engine the car fell silent with a whimper, sorry to see us go. A big moon emerged over the mountains, shining a great wash of light over our criminal undertaking. Blue wanted to throw the keys in the bushes. I put them on the floorboard beside the gas pedal instead. Maybe Louie would find the Chevy and drive off and forget about me. *I'm just a boy.*

We slipped to our houses through backyards, under clotheslines and around garages, sometimes hearing a dog's low growl. When we parted I stuck to the deep shadows. I felt some relief at seeing the porch light burning at my house until I met my mother, a sentry in curlers, waiting at the kitchen table with a look that would set fire to an igloo.

"Where have you been, young man? We both know the dance got over a long time ago." I knew by her curt tone of voice how the line of questioning would go.

"I was out walking around with Blue and Max." It was better not to offer details when making up a lie. Otherwise the conversation would become longer and more involved.

"What possibly could you be doing in Deer Lodge until this time of night?" She arched her eyebrows at our orange wall clock for emphasis. She loved orange. Everything in that kitchen was orange, even the phone, but she'd never use it to call anyone past ten o'clock. That's how I knew she didn't have anything on me like some parents did when they checked around and gave their kids the business after catching them in a lie. Max got the belt once when his old man found out he smoked cigarettes in Terry Musselman's garage. Max told me he almost fell over after taking the first puff but that was nothing compared with what happened when his parents found out. His old man smacked him hard. Then he pulled out a pack of unfiltered Camels and made Max smoke four or five of them at the kitchen table. Max puked all night.

"Not too bad once you get the hang of it," Max reported to me and Blue the next day at school.

I felt obliged to follow my mother's eyes to the clock, given her preoccupation with it. I was surprised to see it was after midnight. I guess we had put some miles on that Chevy.

"Well, we walked some girls home and got to talking and stuff." Telling a lie like that felt wise in light of the evening's developments. I wondered what Marcy would think if she saw me tooling around in that stolen Chevy, black as midnight.

"Uh-huh. And where is your shoe?" My foot hurt but I wasn't going to admit it.

"We were horsing around walking home and it fell off someplace in the dark."

Mom watched me like she wasn't buying any of it. She acted like having a teenage boy in the house was new trouble. Sometimes I understood her and sometimes I didn't. She stood, glancing again at the clock and pulling her bathrobe tighter around her throat. "You're an hour past your curfew, young man," she hissed in a low voice as the rest of our family slept. "Wait until your father hears about this tomorrow morning. Now get to bed and just be grateful you're not lying dead on a road somewhere." *Little did she know.*

For some reason Mom locked the back door, which I considered a blessing knowing that guy Louie was running loose out there. We never locked the back door. Then she stormed to bed. I didn't expect trouble from Dad on the kissing story. If anything he'd brag about it to his buddies down at the lumberyard that he owned. *Old Bubby, kissing girls and only thirteen.* No doubt some other dad would counter that his son had been kissing girls since he was twelve or ten. You know how it goes.

I crept into my tiny bedroom at the back of the house, at the back of our town, at our long-ago farmstead where the well water ran clear and cold from the faucet. A sliver of moonlight peeked under the shade. It was the same window I broke playing catch with Blue. *You can't see him in the dark. If he's out there, you won't know.* In the weak closet light I pulled off my tie and hung up my suit. I won't tell you that I fell asleep right away, or that I didn't dream of fast cars or awake in a sweat when my sleeping mind encountered an angry face. I won't tell you that at all. Somehow a boy who's thirteen thinks the bright light of morning chases away phantoms of the night. Our little town of a few thousand people was the world, no smaller than everything else outside of it. I was sure nothing ever changed in Deer Lodge. It didn't occur to me that my car theft would divert my boyhood the way that a fallen riverbank changes a stream for the course of time.

"He'll never find me," I whispered as I curled deeper into my blankets, far away from the shadowy stranger named Louie.

# Stranger

*A sharp knock came* at the back door. House slippers shuffled across the kitchen linoleum. Then came a male voice. I cringed under my covers.

Mom pushed my bedroom door open. "It's Blue," she informed me, bobbing her head as if pointing to him. "At least somebody can get up in the morning instead of gallivanting around Deer Lodge at all hours of the night. I don't know what I'm going to do with you, Paul, honestly I don't."

She gave me a final glare, as if she'd scheduled my public execution for noon, and cleared out. Blue stepped into the room looking like he was going to burst.

"Wild ride last night, huh, Paul?"

"Blue! Not here!" I hurriedly pulled on a pair of blue jeans and my favorite striped t-shirt. I threw my jacket on, turning the collar up, and rummaged around the closet until I found my maroon Little League cap with the "I" for Indians on it. It made good sense for a car thief to disguise himself. Laughter floated from the living room where my sister watched Woody Woodpecker on the Saturday morning cartoons. Mom was off somewhere, fussing with housework, and I supposed Dad

27

had left for work at the lumberyard. It was almost nine o'clock and the sun was high and bright.

Blue and I, anxious to talk, stuffed some deep-fried donuts in our pockets and headed outside just as Max arrived on his bicycle. Blue had ridden his over, too, so I went into the barn to get mine. The dew still lay heavy on the grass. We wheeled our bikes out to the dirt road and pedaled away from town, eager to examine the night's developments.

Blue talked first. "Who was that guy?" He seemed curious as much from wonder as from fear. That's Blue for you, a wannabe rebel. He probably saw something in that stranger that he admired although I reminded Blue that I was lucky he didn't kill me.

"Still will. Maybe worse." Max, his stocky legs churning on a battered Schwinn missing the front fender, acted like he had it all figured out. "My cousin told me that one of the worst things you can do over in Butte is steal somebody's car. He said they'll throw you down a mine shaft and nobody will bother to look for the body."

He scared me with that. "I didn't know what was going to happen. I had to get away." I told them how the stranger pushed me right behind the steering wheel like he was inviting me to drive and left me there while he went to argue with the girl in green pants. They pressed for a full description. I embellished my observations a little, at one point calling her "a hot chick," which didn't fool Blue at all.

"You had time to fall in love with this girl while her boyfriend planned to kill you?" That's Blue, always sizing things up. While he was at it, he told me that when I was running from the car I looked like a skittish filly at a firecracker festival.

"How could you tell? I didn't see you guys hanging around."

Max looked skeptical. "Why didn't you just haul off and punch him?"

"Why didn't you guys come help me?"

They fell silent. I could tell they felt bad and decided to lay off. "You guys couldn't have done anything anyway." Blue left that alone.

We pulled up in the middle of a field where cattle once grazed. It was full of sagebrush and tangles of old brown barbed wire. Somebody had dug a hole big as a house, leaving the earth piled in a weed-covered mound. Whatever dream was planted there died years ago. Maybe the hole was somebody's basement. Since we were old enough to ride we had pushed our bikes to the top of this mound, a good fifteen feet high, and coasted down into the pit over rocks and broken beer bottles past the car axle with two rotting tires. It was a wild ride. Max broke a tooth one day when he collided with the axle. Seeing his heels in his air, his rider-less bike following, I knew it wouldn't be good. Max was all banged up, his chin bleeding, his bicycle bent. After the doctor stitched Max up he swore he was done riding bikes.

"Just because of that old axle?"

"Darn near killed me."

"Why didn't you ride around it?"

"I dunno."

That was Max. He never was one to make a big deal out of anything, unless it was watching *Gunsmoke* on television. He loved watching Marshal Dillon shoot the bad guys. Guns and justice appealed to his sense of adventure.

A few days later Max came back from the dentist with a gold tooth right in front. I hurt his feelings when I told him he looked like one of those old lady fortunetellers when the carnival came to town. He looked for a minute like he would slug me.

Blue took pity. "You can pick up girls with that. I wish I had a gold tooth." Max smiled again.

We labored to pedal our bikes through the field, soft from melting snow, and rolled into the pit through puddles of rainwater. That done, we straddled our bikes and ate donuts.

"So, Paul, were you crying and everything?" Blue always wanted to know your private business.

"I was pretty scared but I didn't bawl like a baby."

"Who is he?"

"I don't know. I didn't get a good look at him. The girl he was with called him Louie."

"I don't know anybody named Louie. Max?"

"I remember somebody by that name once." Max sat cross-legged on the ground, playing with an iron-on patch on the knee of his jeans where the corners had come loose. Blue and I scooted up close.

Max looked indifferent." It couldn't be him. The Louie I heard of lived over in Butte and he was older than us. He's probably an old man by now."

"That's no help," Blue said.

I thought of the shadowy face and the steel biceps the night before. "Max, how much older would you say he was than you?"

"I don't know, maybe five years, I guess."

"How do you know him?"

"When I lived in Butte he drove his motorcycle around scaring people. He wasn't even old enough to drive one. He'd come up to where we lived in Walkerville when my mom was hanging clothes in the backyard." Max laughed, tipping his face to the sun. "He came through one day tearing her blouses and even her bras right off the line and then took off. She chased him until he turned around and came right back at her with the motorcycle and then she ran into the house, slamming the door and swearing about those damn wops causing trouble all over Butte."

"What's a wop?" Blue asked.

I remembered a movie I saw on television. "Somebody from Italy, I think. So, did she call the cops?"

"Nobody calls the cops in Butte unless you're dead. And then you get hauled off to somebody's living room where they stretch you out on a door they take off the hinges. People drink beer and look at you and tell sad stories and stuff."

Blue snapped a look at me, his eyes showing that his mind was turning. "Do you think it's him?"

///// 

At dinner that night Mom did her best to get Dad riled about my rampaging around town after the dance. "If they only knew," I thought. It did cross my mind that Louie might call the cops to report his stolen car. The thought of both Louie and the town police officer, Charlie, coming to the house worried me. The way I saw it the cop would handcuff me and then Louie would drag me behind the Chevy and my mother would wave at my heels bouncing in the dust and tell me to be home by ten.

"Frank, you just don't know what this boy was up to last night." She clucked on and on, trying to rile my father.

"Leave the boy alone," Dad finally said. We all fell quiet at hearing this rare directive from Dad. He didn't talk much about his own boyhood. I figured maybe he did a thing or two that got him into trouble and he suspected the same about me. Maybe Dad understood that boys couldn't grow into men if they stayed home all the time to read books and do dishes and make sure their mothers never worried.

Steam from the boiled potatoes fogged the kitchen windows. A car passed our house slowly, then turned up the road and gained speed. Mom's meatloaf tasted delicious. "Pass the catsup?" I requested.

Sally broke the silence. "There goes that car again," she said to no one in particular. She pointed to the window, nearly spilling my milk. Sally could be an awfully annoying nine year old.

"What car?" Mom asked, trying hard to show interest.

"That black car out there that keeps driving back and forth. There he goes again."

"Must be lost," Dad muttered. It was Saturday night. We all wanted to finish dinner to get out to the living room to watch a new episode of *Bewitched*. I didn't even mind doing the dishes to avoid watching *The Lawrence Welk Show* that came first. Sitting through the champagne bubbles was agony. "A-one and a-two and a…"

I won't try to fool you. Sally's observation nailed me right to my orange wooden chair. I kept watching the street but saw nothing through the thin cotton curtains but the wind-churned branches of our golden willow trees. It wasn't dark yet and I had a clear view of the street. The car was gone.

Sally and I stacked dirty dishes in the sink while our parents settled in the living room to watch the final moments of Welk and his orchestra. I turned on the hot water and leaned over to her. "So what did you see?"

"What do you mean?"

"You know, the car?"

"Just somebody driving around."

"What kind of car?"

"A black car."

"You don't know what kind of car it was? Like a Ford or a Chevy?"

"How do I know? I'm nine. It was black and shiny is all."

"Who was driving?"

"Why do you want to know all this?"

"Sally, don't be a brat. I have my reasons. Help me out here."

"Cost you a dollar."

"A whole buck? Who's got that kind of money?"

Sally squirted soap in the sink and started washing. I stood with a dishtowel, waiting to dry. "Okay, a dollar."

"Go get it first."

Now I was going to lose money and miss the beginning of my favorite show. I rummaged around in my dresser until I found five dimes and two quarters. Sally plunked them in her pocket. "It's old Mr. Danielson."

"You mean the guy at church?"

Sally looked at me like she couldn't believe I needed confirmation. "Mr. Danielson got a new car."

I was taken and out a buck besides. "So why's he driving past our house all the time then? He lives, what, a couple of blocks away?"

"Daddy says Mr. Danielson is driving around to put some miles on his new motor. What do you care anyway?"

I was really sore at Sally. First she scared me and then she tricked me into giving up a buck. That was the price of a movie down at the Rialto and a plate of fries at the 4Bs afterward. I wanted to sound off but thought better of it. Sally would only go blab about it. Mom already was gunning for me. I figured I had better lay low.

We finished the dishes just as I heard the opening music for *Bewitched*. I hurried to the living room, my wet towel still in hand, to see Samantha wiggle her nose to create magic. It wasn't as good as seeing Matt Dillon gunning down a crook in Dodge City in a quick draw but you had to love a pretty witch.

Dad left for the bar afterwards. He never drank much that I could tell but liked to catch up on town gossip. It was late when he came home and I was in bed, relieved that Mom hadn't said another word about my night on the town. I heard the old pickup slide through the gravel to a familiar stop. Dad dropped his keys on the kitchen counter, clicked the light off, and the house fell silent.

///// 

The next morning, as Mom popped toast, Dad told us he'd heard a thing or two at the bar.

"Frank, it's Sunday and we've got church." She didn't want any bar talk in the house under those circumstances.

"The police had some trouble the other night."

With that Mom turned away from the toaster, suddenly impressed. "What kind of trouble, Frank?" She wiped her hands on her apron, the one with red trim and patterns of pears.

"Seems somebody forced a driver out of his car and then took off with it," Dad related. "The thief just about ran the owner down getting away. Sounded like a bad deal."

Dad filled his coffee cup from the tin pot on the stove. "I heard it happened near the school Friday night. The cops found the car in an alley down by the ballpark."

Mom shot me a sharp glance. "Who was involved, Frank?"

"I didn't hear," Dad said.

I stared at my cereal bowl, intent on finishing my oatmeal, actually quite relieved at the prospect of going to the Presbyterian Church for a change. At least the sermon delivered wouldn't be from Mom. At least then, but she took full advantage of the closing minutes of breakfast before I could escape to my bedroom to polish my shoes. It was a Sunday ritual in the Morrison household to polish shoes, using black paste from a little tin. You don't want to go around with unpolished shoes in my mother's church.

"Paul, this is exactly why you were supposed to be home on time. You don't know what kind of trouble you'll find when you're running around after curfew doing who knows what."

*She knows.* Mom was pretty smart. She carried on about stuff, like when I got "Glad All Over," my first Dave Clark Five record, and played it about a thousand times until she couldn't stand hearing it anymore. She hid it from me between her winter sweaters in her dresser. Or maybe she doesn't suspect the real story Friday night, but she doesn't know how close she came to knowing, either, if that makes sense.

When Blue came to church that morning with his parents, he and I slid into a pew near the back. We bent our heads at the opening prayer. It was the perfect chance to tell him what Dad heard at the bar.

"That guy's going to kill you for sure," Blue reminded me. I told him I was tired of hearing about my impending death. I had visions of a funeral in the church where the minister droned over my coffin and people looked at my pasty face and sniffled and then came to our house to eat ham. It felt a bit like Easter without the bunny. *I'm too young to die.* Then it hit me.

"Blue, we've got to find this guy so I can tell him I'm sorry before he kills me."

Blue chewed on that. "He might find you first and kill you and then you won't have to apologize."

That was worth considering. I didn't know which was worse, facing Louie like a man or being pounded into the ground like a fencepost. He was a demon of the night. It was a good thing we were in church. I began to see the value of prayer.

"How about this?" I dropped my voice to a whisper after heads turned. "Let's you and me and Max go find Louie and when we do I'll say I'm sorry for stealing his car and I'll bet he'll say he's sorry for almost killing us."

Blue frowned. "He's about as likely to apologize as old Betsy after she broke my wrist that time. Besides, we don't even know where he lives."

"We'll look around until we do."

"What if he lives in Butte or Anaconda? Even if we got a ride over there we'd be dead for sure."

I didn't argue that point. Max told us enough about Butte to make me scared to even get out of the car when we went shopping over there. Anaconda was no better, full of kids who would beat your brains out if they caught you looking at them. Just like that. If you were lucky to escape a fight they'd razz you about being a sissy.

"Maybe if this guy Louie doesn't live in Deer Lodge he won't come back again." That was my best idea at the moment.

"What did the license plates say?" Blue whispered. Each county had different numbers. Butte was one, Anaconda was thirty and Deer Lodge was twenty-eight.

"Blue, I didn't think about checking license plates."

"Well, you were driving the car around like you owned it." He glared at me like I had really screwed up. It's true that looking at the plate would have been a simple matter if I'd thought of it. I was always doing stupid things like riling my mom and forgetting to check license plate numbers.

With one jarring shuffle of feet and fabric everybody stood to sing a hymn. It was something about glory and God. Anyone watching Blue and I in the kaleidoscope of light from the stained glass windows wouldn't suspect us as car thieves at all. Choirboys, maybe, adorned with our bowties and our hair cropped close with straight-arrow parts. Like every other boy in school we carried black plastic combs in our hip pockets to make sure we looked cool all the time.

The worshippers around us warbled like birds with a respiratory illness. I'll bet even God said a prayer of thanks when the music ended.

"Okay, I'm in," Blue finally whispered. That didn't surprise me. I knew I could count on Blue. We'd round up Max after church to break the news that we were looking for my probable killer. I was pretty sure he wouldn't mind.

Sure enough, Max saw my notion as an adventure. "Maybe if he doesn't dump your body down a mine shaft we can ride in that car again." I didn't understand why cars thrilled Max because his older brother Kenny missed a curve on the old highway south of town one night. He smashed into a tree that didn't yield an inch. They found him at the break of dawn, crumpled under a heaved-up dashboard, his left arm hanging outside the car like he was cruising Main on a sweet summer night. After the funeral Max didn't talk much. Blue and I went with Max to see the smashed Oldsmobile. It helped us understand that Kenny wasn't coming back. Max cried when he saw one of Kenny's shiny black shoes pinned under the crumpled brake pedal. Dried petals of a white carnation lay with the shattered glass in the front seat. It was hard to grasp why Kenny never came home from the prom that night. His date, a pretty girl named Cindy, died too. I won't go into it. It's just too sad for words.

The fascination Max had for cars scared me a little. If this guy Louie gave Max a chance he'd climb behind the wheel of that Chevy and have it rocking to seventy in no time flat. Max told me he'd never once driven. After Kenny wrecked the Oldsmobile, the only vehicle left in the Jorgenson family was the tow truck. Mr. Jorgenson used it to haul cars to his garage behind the house and to drive Mrs. Jorgenson to the grocery store. They seemed to find reasons to make sure Max didn't wind up like his brother. I kind of wished that I'd let Max drive that rumbling Chevy the night I stole it.

The sun came full and bright that afternoon. After changing out of our Sunday clothes we pushed off aboard our bikes in search of Louie the stranger. This idea might be smart or it might be stupid. It felt a lot like inviting a dog to bite.

We rode a couple of blocks before Max asked where we were going. Blue pulled over, looked around, licked his finger and held it to the wind. "That way," he pointed, his finger wagging in the direction of Main Street.

Max didn't see the wisdom in that. "Bluesy, that's stupid. That's not going to help us find him." Blue allowed Max and me the privilege of this variation on his nickname. We were, after all, involved in each other's business from breakfast to bedtime. Blue said nothing, stood on the pedals and got his bike moving again. He veered through a mud puddle, splashing brown water all over us before heading downtown. We followed, Max on his banged-up bike and me on my new one, gaining speed on the gentle decline down Milwaukee Avenue. If you were careful to avoid the potholes you could coast all the way without steering. Like every paved street in Deer Lodge, this one looked like a minefield with patches on top of patches and holes in between. I was thankful for the dirt roads up on The Hill where Blue lived. I should explain. To kids like us Deer Lodge was separated into four parts. Many of the town's newer houses were up on The Hill, a kind of mesa several blocks wide that really was an extension of the foothills on the valley's east side. Down The Hill meant the older neighborhoods below The Hill on three sides. That's where Max lived, not far from our house on the outskirts of town. Then there was the West Side across the tracks where the North Coast Limited and Milwaukee Road passenger trains roared through town. We learned early that it wasn't a good idea to go to the West Side unless we wanted trouble. And then there was downtown with frontier buildings that looked like sets in western movies.

We shot onto the broad sidewalk along Main Street, weaving between the parking meters. Being a Sunday and all, nobody was around. A town cop, his hat tipped up, walked from one store to another, rattling doors. I'd never talked to a cop except old Charlie. I heard they liked to check to make sure the town was locked up tight.

Back and forth we went. Missing the parking meters without steering off the curb took such concentration that I almost forgot our mission. It really didn't matter because the street was mostly empty. A farmer passed in a battered truck full of clanking metal objects. Then came a little red sedan that huffed and puffed to a halt at the only working stoplight on Main Street. A tiny woman gray to the core stared at us through the steering wheel. "This is no good," I said. "We're not going to find him this way."

Blue looked concerned. "I thought for sure we'd see him cruising the drag. Maybe get a good look at the redhead, huh, Paul? Think she would blow you a kiss?" He shivered and pulled on his jacket. Dark clouds moved off the mountains, promising rain. We rode around but saw nothing that resembled a black Chevy without chrome trim.

Then the rain fell. We pedaled fast as we could for The Hill, churning hard for the climb, barely making the top without having to walk. Max as usual shot ahead, propelling his old bike like a madman, sprocket wailing and tires wobbling under the power of his stocky legs. He waited for Blue and I to join him before pointing out that we had arrived at the very spot where Louie had tried to run us down near the gym where we danced. The ruts where those tires had spun lay before us, gathering rainwater.

"Let's get out of here," I suggested to nodding heads. We flew through the downpour to Blue's house, where Max and I shouted our goodbyes. The rain fell with a fury and thunder rumbled across the valley. It looked like spring came early. I parked my bike in the barn and ran inside the house, where I found Dad napping in his favorite chair.

///// 

School came Monday morning. Blue and Max, snapped into denim jackets, trooped over to meet me like they always did. The rain had stopped but fog draped the valley and the air felt cool and clean. Finishing the breakfast dishes, a duty for which I was paid a dollar a month, I collected my history and math books from the table where they'd sat untouched since school let out Friday. Off we went.

Students milled through the hallways, slamming locker doors and hurrying to class when the first bell rang. Miss the second bell and you were dead. My first class was science, where Mrs. Klingensmith took roll, then shut off the lights to show a procession of filmstrips purporting to teach us about biology. The filmstrip ritual predictably followed with a series of questions directed to the least interested among us, including me. She ignored students who raised their hands, opting instead for Blue and me and other miscreants who sat near the back of the classroom admiring the skeleton. It was missing an arm and hanging from a noose-like metal hook.

"How come this skeleton doesn't have a penis?" Blue whispered to me.

"Maybe she's a girl," I whispered back.

41

"Or maybe a boy who had an unfortunate accident."

"Why would a skeleton have a penis anyway?"

"Don't be stupid, Paul. That's why they call it a boner. The guy who hooked this skeleton's bones together forgot the arm and the penis."

We were attracting some attention. A few boys next to us snickered.

"Hope it didn't hurt," Blue said.

"I doubt it. You got to be dead if you're a skeleton."

Mrs. Klingensmith overheard us. She shut off the machine that cast grainy illustrations of amoebas and other mysteries of science on the wall. She leaned against her desk, arms crossed over her white lab coat. My classmates, expecting to see my public beheading, fell silent.

"What do you boys hope to do when you grow up?" she said in an onerous tone that told me a lecture was coming. I slipped lower in my seat. Being a mining engineer in Butte would be fun. I could crawl around caves like Tom Sawyer. Maybe I could play baseball for money and travel in a bus with the team name painted on the side. Or run a lumberyard like my dad, measuring boards all day and inhaling the sweet aroma of sawdust. For that reason, sawing pine boards gave me a thrill, and you have my word on that. But Mrs. Klingensmith didn't give me a chance to answer.

"What I think," she intoned, pausing a few seconds for effect, "is that boys who don't pay attention in science class will wind up digging potatoes in Idaho or oiling gambling machines in Nevada. And that's not even the worst that can happen." I felt only mildly concerned at this prediction, given that I was a seventh grader and wanted to kiss a girl before I saw the world. Such dire warnings, intended to shape us into capable citizens someday, puzzled me. I'd heard that potato growers made good money in the valley. By oiling slot machines did she mean gambling? School confused me sometimes. It was full of references to a world most of us had never seen. Just because an astronaut might land on the moon didn't bring it any closer to Deer Lodge. I was quite sure that I never would see cities of colonial fame like Boston and Philadelphia, which seemed fitting in our history books but didn't register to me in real life. Sure, my parents drove us to the ocean near Seattle once and a few times we took the train all the way east to North Dakota, but I'd never been south to Wyoming or north to Canada. To me western Montana was a sprawling wonder unto itself. Mountain ranges bunched together like folds on a smoky blue blanket. Capes of snow lasted long into summer. Creeks brimming with clear frigid water tumbled from the canyons.

To young boys like me and Blue and Max, Deer Lodge was the center of the universe. It was a boys' paradise. Max even quit his bragging about Butte, a sure sign. At night our sky stretched tight over the big valley and the mountains framed the valley. The moon looked down on us and felt like ours alone.

Mrs. Klingensmith made fools of Blue and me, calling us to the front of the class to share what we knew about amoebas. Blue, being a natural brain, mustered a few facts that got him by. I stuttered and stammered until Mrs. Klingensmith shook her head in disgust. The next parent-teacher conference wouldn't be good. *Why should I care what the teacher says?* My troubles in science made me forgot all about Marcy Kersher until English class when she understood from my stares that I was hot for her. Marcy soon addressed the matter in a note I found pushed through the air vents of my locker. She looped her words in green ink on lined notebook paper. A faint scent of her perfume rose to my nostrils.

"Dear Paul," it began, "I had fun at the dance and hope you did too. I saw you watching me this morning. Does that mean you like me? Some of the other girls said you must because you asked me to dance so many times Friday night. Did you enjoy the dance? My mother asked what I liked most about it and I said dancing with Paul. She asked who you are so I told her a boy who I think is cute. I hope you don't mind...."

I didn't have time to read it all because the bell rang again, but I jumped to the last line: "Will you walk me home after school?"

I broke the news to Blue and Max in the lunch line. Blue and I ate from the mysteries of the kitchen, filling our plastic trays as we passed a row of big lunch ladies in hairnets who ladled from silver pots the size of washing machines. Max brought his lunch, usually peanut butter and jelly on rye, in a brown paper bag from home. Sometimes he brought an onion that he ate like an apple. I asked about it once but he started on another Butte story. I'd heard a million of them.

Blue leaned across the table and grabbed my tray like he didn't want me to take another bite. "She wants to get serious, Paul."

"How do you figure?"

"Next thing you'll be carrying her books. After that she won't want you looking at another girl."

Max chimed in. "All that and you haven't even kissed her." He wiped peanut butter from his upper lip. "Sounds like Blue thinks you better watch yourself."

Blue wore his adult face for a moment. "So what are you going to do about this guy Louie? Who knows where he came from or where he'll show up?"

"He's so in love with Marcy he forgot all about Louie," said Max, needling me.

I scanned my tray. "Hey, who took my carrot sticks?"

"Who are you? Bugs Bunny?" Max held them out in his hand. It was doubtful that he had washed before lunch. When we dissected frogs in science class he came to the cafeteria reeking of formaldehyde. We made him sit by himself for three days after that.

"I don't want them now, Max. Help yourself." And then back to Louie: "I'll bet he's gone for good."

Blue seemed concerned. "What if he jumps you?"

"I've got you thumpers around to help." I pushed my eyeglasses higher on my nose.

"So all three of us are going to walk Marcy Kersher home?" Max sounded hopeful.

/////

After school, Marcy waited for me at her locker, just as I had asked in a reply note I scribbled between classes that afternoon. You didn't want to get caught writing in class. If the teacher read the note aloud you never lived it down. Boys got in fights behind the old swimming pool building over the ribbing they got because of mistakes like that.

I fidgeted while Marcy knelt in front of her locker, assembling her homework. Blue and Max made a point of cruising past to make faces and blow kisses, which I didn't appreciate, and in the bedlam of shouting and locker slamming she stood and said something to me.

"What?" I replied, shaken at the prospect of talking in person.

"I said I'm ready." She tossed her head and smiled. I was glad Blue and Max were gone because I heard myself offering to carry her books. We started down the hall, careful to stay side by side. I tried not to trip on my shoelaces. I hoped my pants were zipped but I was afraid to look. Marcy was hot stuff in her pink sweater and tan skirt and white knee socks. "This way," she pointed to the door down the stairs.

The fog had burned away. Now the sun shone on us from a cobalt-blue sky. It felt good being thirteen and in love. We strolled away from school, down the sidewalk past the grove of trees where that guy Louie had caught me. Then came the gym. She slipped her hand inside mine, coaxing me to a stop where we had parted after the dance. She came close and we kissed. It happened so fast and easy that I confess I felt no worry or fuss. My lips lingered on hers, trying to savor the sensation, while the books under my arm slipped and fell to the sidewalk. Her kiss shot through me like electric shock. At that moment the stranger didn't scare me. My encounter with the black Chevy had come and gone like all the trouble and triumphs in a boy's life, flown on the wind to the valley's farthest reaches, surrendered to a girl's touch. I was too young to understand how love lifts you out of trouble. I won't say that I forgot about the stranger right then and there. No, I won't say that at all. But I will tell you that love trumps fear.

Marcy lived a good five blocks from school, down The Hill and toward the park where I played baseball in the summer. We dawdled past the courthouse and the jail to Cottonwood Creek. Marcy pulled me toward a path that dipped to the bubbling water behind a grove of trees. She stepped over a log that sat alongside the creek like a bench. "Sit awhile, Paul? My friends and I, we came here last summer and told ghost stories when it got dark. Do you tell ghost stories, Paul?"

"We did all the time, me and Blue and Max I mean, until Kenny died. It's different when you know someone who could be a ghost."

"That was a terrible thing, Paul. Poor Max. I don't know him much except in class but everybody knows what happened to his brother."

"Marcy, how come you write me notes?"

She stayed quiet for a moment, plunking stones into the creek. "How come you read them, Paul?"

"Because, well, because I like you."

"Then you know why I write them, don't you?"

I know it was late when we encountered Marcy's mother walking to her car with keys in hand. She stopped, apron flapping, looking more relieved than annoyed.

"Marcy! Dinner's ready. I was worried." Marcy squeezed my hand and let go. "You remember Paul, Mother?"

Mrs. Kersher smiled. I thought she looked like Marcy, just an older version. She nodded and rubbed her bare arms. "It's getting chilly out here. Why don't we give Paul a ride home?"

Marcy and I sank into the front seat of the Buick. It rattled and fired and we were off. Halfway home I caught a glimpse of a sleek black Chevy that passed us. I heard its rumble and knew it was the one. *Thank you, Mrs. Kersher, for driving me home.* This was my moment, not his. Marcy's perfume filled the car.

# Hack Face

*The rains poured forth* in western Montana for the next couple of weeks, soaking Deer Lodge more than even the old timers at the barbershop remembered. Grass grew in great abundant waves. Craggy Mount Powell west of town turned whiter with fresh snow at its crown, while the Clark Fork River far below in the valley surged with brown water. Rain fell day and night, pounding the roof of our old house like a demon demanding to come inside.

We huddled close over fish sticks and green beans in the orange kitchen one evening in May while thunder boomed. The lights flickered off. While Dad fumbled around to find a flashlight, Mom pulled a red Christmas candle from the cupboard. On closer inspection it was her favorite Santa Claus. Soon five faces flickered around the table as we watched fire shoot out of Santa's head. His cap disappeared into a glob of shapeless wax. Mom looked sad. "Such a shame. I was saving this candle for a special occasion."

"When would that be, Martha?"

"Now, Frank, don't start." She didn't like to light her holiday candles. We all knew it. They'd appear at the table year after year like invited company, never introduced to the heat of a match.

We ate in silence, listening to the rain. "No TV tonight," Dad said, pointing in the direction of the darkened living room. "Bet a transformer blew somewhere. Hate to be out working on those poles in a storm like this. Damn rain never stops."

Flashes of lightning lit up the kitchen, freezing expressions on our faces. Water slapped hard against the windows. *The stranger, out there somewhere.* It seemed like a good time to think up a ghost story.

"If you think it's dark in here, imagine being out in the graveyard right now," I told Sally.

"Don't you dare!" Mom warned. She could see where I was headed, at least in intent. My sister looked worried.

"In the dark out there you can't see who is coming." Sally hid her eyes. "Out of the ground —."

"That's enough, Paul." Dad hid a smile. I could tell he was getting a kick out of it. He'd told me that when he was a boy he and some buddies went around town at Halloween tipping over outhouses and tying nerds to tombstones with clothesline rope. Other times he told me to ignore what he said because what he did was wrong. That was after Mom gave him the business for putting ideas in my head. I didn't know what to think. Tipping over outhouses sounded like fun but I saw only a couple of them around our town. Dad liked to tell stories about the olden days before we had Zenith television sets and transistor radios.

We nibbled on our fish sticks while the rain drummed on the roof. It poured off the eaves in silver sheets, falling into pools on the grass.

"So Bubby, got any new girlfriends?" That was Dad, shooting me a problem straight out of left field. Sure enough, Sally caught on.

"Paul already *has* a girlfriend," she said. Sally giggled. She was small for her age but hardly backed away from stirring up trouble.

"Now Sally —."

"Mom, I saw them. They drove right up to the house. Paul was sitting next to a girl."

"This girl was driving, Paul?" Mom was ready to kill the older girl with a driver's license, whoever she was.

Dad intervened. "How did you get hooked up with an older girl? Does she own that car?"

I dropped my fork. "No, for heaven's sake. She can't drive. Her mother gave me a ride home."

Mom leaned into the candlelight, suddenly oblivious to Santa's melting beard. "Who is this girl?"

"Her name is Marcy."

"Do I know her mother?"

"I don't think so."

"Is this the girl you were chasing all over town after the dance when you had a curfew of eleven?"

"Yeah, Paul."

Mom frowned at my sister. "Sally!"

I could see where my mother was headed, trying to catch me in a contradiction. Clever.

"She's a nice girl, Mom."

"Where does her dad work? Does her mother smoke? I don't want you seeing her if she's not a nice girl."

"Geez, Mom —."

Dad interrupted to save me. "I haven't heard another thing about that stolen car."

"Funny, you down at the lumberyard and all," Mom said, brushing loose strands of red hair from her eyes.

"I know. You'd think—."

"Not even who was involved, Frank?"

"No — yes — wait. I heard somebody mentioned but it wasn't a name I know."

I sat perched on my chair, ready to burst. Mom looked eager and Dad put down his coffee cup. Here it comes.

"Well, who was it, Frank?"

"Some kid named Louie owns the car. Nobody I know."

I chewed on that. Our town wasn't that big. Dad knew every man and boy who ever drove a nail or sawed a board in Deer Lodge, and most anyone else who didn't. Down at the lumberyard, a block off Main Street, men sat around on stacks of boards half the morning talking about politics and weather and fishing and hunting, cussing about this and that. They drank coffee out of a bottomless tank Dad set to brewing right after he arrived in his pickup when dawn rimmed the eastern mountains. On warmer days he'd swing open the big doors to the warehouse where lumber sorted by grade and dimension waited for customers. Sometimes on Saturdays I went with him, eager for the aroma of fresh pine that washed over me as I walked between the stacks, a bed of sawdust crumpling beneath my feet. The farmers came first, fresh from an early breakfast and morning chores. Then the carpenters arrived, eager to load and go because time was money, but never so much in a hurry that they failed to join the coffee drinkers for a cup or two. Finally came the home improvers, as Dad called them, many of them trying to make sense of how much lumber they needed to frame a shed or build a fence or straighten a sagging garage. Dad showed more patience than I ever saw at home. He'd pull a pencil from behind his ear and start calculating on a fold of blue paper he carried in his shirt pocket. After the pencil spun and scratched, he'd announce how many boards and nails were needed but to my knowledge he never once tricked a customer into buying more. "When you depend on your customers for your livelihood," he once told me, "you deal honestly with them straight to the cash register."

It was a bright blue Saturday morning like this, just a few weeks before school would let out for the summer, that Dad asked me to help him at the lumberyard. The torrential rains had gone, squeezing their last drops from a lead-gray sky that finally, after weeks of soggy downpour, retreated over the mountains and disappeared. The rain had hurt Dad's lumber business, bringing his usually brisk spring sales to a near standstill. I know because he came home early from work, his shoulders sagging. He spent many evenings at the kitchen table figuring numbers in his ledger. One night he called Mom out of the bedroom where she was sewing. He whispered but I heard enough to know it wasn't good. "Better hold off on that grocery shopping for a few more days, Martha," he told her, pointing to his figuring.

"But Frank, the pantry's almost empty." She stopped when she saw worry on his face and went back to mending clothes. After Dad turned in that night I went into the pantry to confirm this predicament. Most of the shelves were bare.

On the morning of the revival Dad made coffee first thing. He smiled at me like he knew a big secret. He even sang a few bars from "Battle Hymn of the Republic," roaring into the morning, while I pushed open the big doors on the warehouse. Dad walked into the mud outside the warehouse and looked to the big sky, spreading his arms wide as if trying to hug it all. "The Lord brought us a beautiful day, son!" It was good to see Dad like that even though we were broke. Mom was talking about selling some sweaters she had knitted to make a few bucks.

Somehow Dad knew that people spend money when the sun shines. Pickup after pickup rolled into the lumberyard where Dad and his faithful sidekick, Toby Milner, loaded lumber into tomorrow. An array of boots swung out of trucks. Big men with tape measures hooked to their belts tromped around, pulling boards from stacks and holding them like rifles, sighting down the full length. "No warped lumber here!" Dad called out. Shriveled old men driving Ramblers tied boards to luggage racks. One woman wearing green pedal pushers charged through the commotion looking for dowels for her garden. A farmer with bib overalls straining over a well-fed belly arrived in a popping, grinding farm truck. Hired hands jumped off to load several dozen rough-cut beams. Toby and a few customers caught the fever. Soon several men worked together and before long the farmer set to lashing the load with thick brown rope.

"Frank — don't sell out before I get my barn raised!" the farmer yelled to Dad. The old man eased the clutch out, shuddering the old truck into motion, as hired hands clung to the immense stack of lumber. It went like that well into the afternoon, first one load and then another. Dad handed me cash that I took to Edna McDougal, the old lady who ran the register on Saturdays. It rang and rang and rang, each tally ensuring more food for our pantry shelves.

About early afternoon Dad realized he was running short of lumber. The tall stacks, standing unsold through the drizzle of the previous month, had melted away like winter snow in a Montana Chinook. "Paul!" he bellowed. I dropped my baloney sandwich and ran out to where Dad shoveled boards into a waiting pickup. Beads of sweat wandered down his reddened face. He looked all out of breath. "Here's what I want you to do, son. Take the pickup to the sawmill." He stopped and pulled a dust-stained handkerchief from his pocket to wipe his face. "Bring back as many of those four by fours as you can. You know where to find 'em. Load 'em quick, got it?" He tossed me his key ring before turning away to manhandle another board. I couldn't believe it. Dad turning me loose to drive and I didn't even have a license.

"And Paul!" I turned at the door. "Stay on the back roads and don't hit anything."

With that advice I walked out to the round-nosed Ford, green like a forest, which sat waiting for me like an accomplice in the shade on the other side of the building. The sun felt hot. Before I turned the key I jerked the long black shift handle around, remembering how the gears progressed in the temperamental old pickup, and depressed the clutch pedal a few times to get the feel of it. I got the motor running but killed it trying to get the smooth motion of gas pedal in, clutch pedal out. After a few tries I got the pickup rolling through the train yards where the tracks and switches tangled in endless loops like untied shoelaces. Across the river I went, into the high foothills west of town where Hack Face O'Hanlon ripped logs into rough lumber.

You couldn't run a lumberyard without those four by fours. All the ranch people wanted them for corral posts and sheds and who knows what else. I knew just where to go, having spent many weekends helping Dad and Toby load lumber. Sometimes Blue and Max came too and we rode to the mill in the bed of the pickup, standing behind the cab to catch the wind in our faces. The ride was fun but pitching lumber began to feel like work after an hour or so. Dad threw us a few dollars here and there, and sometimes cracked a beer for me after work if he knew Mom wasn't around, but he said that if you had a family business everyone had to throw a shoulder into work without expecting money. Even Sally, someday, would be throwing lumber. Sally, bucking boards at Hack Face Heaven, as Dad called it. He'd get to joking about that, rocking with laughter.

Hack Face ran a saw big as a Ferris wheel, I swear, but by all accounts he did a good job cutting lumber to size in a flapping commotion of drive belts and pulleys. He powered the contraption with a roaring truck engine mounted in a shed, and if the huge hungry teeth on the saw weren't enough to scare you, the clamor from the shed would. Blue smoke poured through the cracks. On my first visit Dad warned me to stay far away from the saw, a cannibal device that churned sturdy logs into a spray of bark and sawdust and flying splinters. The source of Hack Face's nickname was clear at first glance. A flaming scar plowed diagonally from his right jaw to the left side of his forehead on a path between his eyes. The evidence indicated a terrible accident that could have been worse yet had the debris that kicked back from that saw hit him square in the eyes. As it was, Mr. O'Hanlon squinted a lot, each eye narrowed like it was cringing from the memory of that close miss.

I didn't know if Hack Face had a real first name. Dad warned me never to address him by anything other than Mr. O'Hanlon, first because I was a boy and second because we were his customers. Dad put a lot of stock in courtesy when it came to buying and selling. He gave me a lesson in economics, too. Turns out Hack Face sold Dad lumber for less than he sold to other people because Dad bought so much of it. Dad in turn sold that rough-cut lumber for the same price down at the lumberyard that anybody would pay if they drove clear up the mountain to Hack Face's sawmill. "Volume and convenience," Dad told me, explaining how he made a thin profit and kept Hack Face in business at the same time. Dad ordered his finish lumber out of the Missoula mills because it came clean and straight and satisfied the fussier customers.

The old pickup bucked and whined as I steered up the rough road, hardly more than a bulldozer's path. I killed the engine a couple of times when I braked at the deep puddles but noticed, with great pleasure, that I was getting the hang of the clutch. Soon I crested a bluff where the road dropped into a crease in the foothills. I followed the crease higher still, where the ramshackle mill sat on the fringe of the tree line at Elk Ridge. At first it looked deserted but then a white head bobbed in the shade of the shack and the old man stood and waved. I pulled in, spinning tires in the mud, to a stack of cut orange fir bleeding amber tar.

Hack Face came toward me, his bare arms swinging. "Sent the boy, huh?"

"Yes sir."

"Whaddya need?"

"Dad said load it up with four by fours."

"Big do'ins down in Fancyville?"

"Everybody and his brother."

Hack Face breathed deep like he was trying to inhale all of that spring day. It was a pretty sight up there all right if you looked past the junk cars congregated around his cabin and machinery parts poking everywhere from the meadow grass. "Rain ain't gone two days and already hot enough to fry eggs. I got that old saw goin' all morning and thought to myself that damn it's gettin' hot as a whorehouse in Butte and shut her ass down and had a smoke." He squinted at me, wiping sawdust from his eyes with hands as big as tree stumps. It was almost like he was pointing right to the ugly scar. I looked away. "You old enough to drive, boy?"

"No sir, Mr. O'Hanlon. My dad needed my help."

"I ain't tellin' nobody." He was big and wild, spitting tobacco through yellow teeth spaced as wide as pickets on a fence. In my thrill of driving the pickup I had forgotten I would be alone with the brute.

"You afraid of me, boy?" He didn't seem to care to know my name.

"Maybe some, sir."

"Hell, boy." Then — "No better man than your dad. Pays up honest like and brings me a coupla six packs on the Fourth of July and Christmas too. You don't needa worry about nothin'."

I guessed that on another day Dad would have thought twice about sending me up the mountain. I felt proud that Dad trusted me to help him on maybe his biggest day ever at the lumberyard. Too bad Blue and Max weren't there to see this. Before long Hack Face and I loaded the pickup. He did most of it, I admit, and then I sat with him in the shade to rest my aching arms. Up close I could see that he wasn't as old as he looked, maybe not much older than my dad, but the scar and his general ragged appearance combined to suggest a hard life. He leaned against the shed and pulled a bottle of brown liquid out of the grass.

"Want some, since yer old enough to drive a motor vehicle and all?" He waved the bottle under my nose. When I jerked my head back at the revolting stench he looked a little disappointed. "Whiskey," he explained. When he pulled the bottle away I breathed deep to clear the wretched odor from my nostrils. The wet earth, full of ruts and puddles, emanated a scent that wasn't unpleasant but more a message of impending summer. Across the meadow, a creek thrashed out of the forest. I heard it tumbling and longed to cast a line for trout. I sat there beside Hack Face, staring into the willow trees that drank from the stream, dreaming, when I began to take more notice of his tarpaper shack. A chimney leaned like a Friday night drunk and two tiny windows brown with mud stared at us, but otherwise the shack looked sturdy enough. An outhouse, just like Dad described from his hooligan days, stood out back.

Dad told me once that Hack Face invited him for coffee one morning but even in broad daylight it was hard to see his way around inside. They drank out of cracked plastic cups salvaged from the town dump and sat on crates for chairs. Dad said the shack was clean enough, all things considered. Being just a boy I didn't know much about why men lived like this but I had seen them all over in the hills around Deer Lodge. Dad explained to me that some of them hated other people. Most of them despised lawns and paved streets and neighbors crowding them. Some of them, he said, packed up and headed for the high country after they got into trouble with the law. I hoped he wasn't talking about Hack Face O'Hanlon, who looked like a lonely man. I understood the attraction of living near Elk Ridge when the land was bursting with new life, but why in winter, when snow drifted to the eaves of that shack?

"I'd better go, Mr. O'Hanlon. My dad's waiting." And then — "Was I supposed to bring money?"

"Nah, yer old man will take care of it. Tell him next time he's up. And to bring a carton of Camels, too, if'n he can."

With that Hack Face stood and walked to a pile of logs. He hoisted one onto his shoulder, grunting out his farewell. "See ya, boy." As I pulled away, the old pickup complaining at the weight of its load, Hack Face had the sawmill thundering like a calamity in progress. I watched the big saw turning in the rear-mirror. I thought of the whiskey. Dad said it was bad drink and put ugly thoughts in a man's head. "Cold beer ought to be good enough for any man," he said. I thought of Hack Face cutting trees into logs and logs into lumber that somebody would buy and drinking whiskey and beer and watching the sky. We never saw him around town. He just kept sawing those logs.

///// 

Down the road I went, keeping the motor growling in a low gear like Dad did. "You get going fast with a load like this, you'll lose control," he told me once. "Thing is, son, a good pickup can take a lot of punishment if you don't take chances with the brakes and springs and don't let the motor load up too much. You keep it geared down, see, keep the speed down with a big load. Remember that you've got the oil pan riding just a few inches above the road. When you get to driving on your own someday you'll have no problem."

With that advice, here I was, barely able to see over the hood. The pickup crept down the steep road, its nose poking skyward, remnants of a half dozen pungent fir trees stacked tall behind me. Now this was living. Too bad Marcy couldn't see me. Maybe she would sit next to me like high school girls did on dates. Blue told me that as soon as he bought a car he was going to find a girl to lean on him while he cruised the drag with his arm out the window. He said it would be great for making out. I'd driven a good mile, entranced with this idea, when a tremendous explosion jarred me back to matters at hand. The pickup shuddered and even at that slow speed the rear end swung side to side. My heart hammering in my throat, hands locked on the steering wheel, I stood on the brake to stop. Half of the lumber lay scattered along the road behind me. I quit the motor, swung the creaking door open, and stepped into the mud. Right away I saw the blown rear tire shredded on the rim.

I should have listened to Dad when he tried to teach me how to change a tire. The spare was looking right at me, mounted to the side of the box behind the cab. The jack, I knew, was stowed behind the seat, wrapped in a blue towel to keep it from rattling around. Dad was particular about things like that. I found the tire iron and got the spare off. Then I set to turning the lug nuts on the blown tire. It took me a good ten minutes to get the first two off but I couldn't budge the third. I just wasn't strong enough to yank it loose. Kneeling in the mud, I saw I had another problem. I couldn't get the jack under the rear bumper because the tailgate was down. The beams were too long. I'd have to unload the two dozen or so remaining in the bed of the pickup. I thought about walking back up the road to ask Hack Face O'Hanlon for help but I'd driven far enough that I couldn't even hear the racket anymore. The other way was a good three miles into town.

After trying again to turn the remaining lug nuts, I threw the tire iron in disgust and climbed back into the cab where a lingering odor of Dad's pipe smoke hung in the air. The seat's dusty old springs squeaked under me as I wondered what to do next. To fill up those useless minutes I found some twanging country and western music on the radio. It was a good idea to pretend you have other things to do when you're sitting with a flat tire on a sagging pickup halfway up a mountain while your dad is running out of lumber on his best sales day of the year. He'd be saying, "Where is that damn kid?" If I ever got the truck fixed I'd catch it when I got home.

Long about the third bar on a mournful slide guitar solo, a faint rumble of a vehicle came from below me, on the other side of a hill. Good, I thought. Dad sent Toby out to help. As the noise grew louder, sounding familiar from somewhere, I switched off the radio and waited. I wasn't feeling bad at all that Marcy wasn't with me. She'd probably laugh when I couldn't get the lug nuts loose. When Blue heard the story I'd get a lecture about my failure to impress girls.

The black Chevy burst over the hill. Even in the daylight I recognized it right away. It had that roaring, menacing presence from that night after the dance. How many nights had I stayed awake when the house was dark and silent, listening for strange noises? Some days I got to doubting that I'd stolen that car, like you doubt a bad dream and then forget it. As the weeks passed, Blue and Max and I talked less about the mystery car and more about girls. Blue had a couple of dates to the Rialto where he mashed with girls in the dark, or so he bragged. Max got locker notes from the waif he met at the dance. Old Max, that devil, spent more time using soap in the boys' washroom in case he got to hold hands with her.

With my friends busy, I paid more attention to Marcy. I couldn't walk her home in the pouring rain but sometimes we stayed after school to study together until her mother drove up. Now that we had girlfriends, even if we didn't confess to love, the testosterone was running high. I started talking tough about Louie with Blue and Max.

"You want to kick his sorry cowboy ass!" Blue whooped in his customary manner.

"Anytime. He got lucky."

"You weren't wetting your pants as bad as everybody thought, is that it?"

"No way," I lied. "Truth is, Blue, I liked it."

"Liked what? Almost getting pounded?"

"I mean the thrill of stealing that Chevy and driving it."

"Kind of like coming to the rodeo with the best girl while everybody else watches? Throwing a rope around her so everybody knows she's yours?"

"Blue, I'm talking about a car."

"I know. Feeling like a big deal, right?"

"Maybe like that."

Blue looked puzzled. "You mean this guy doesn't scare you? Paul! Don't joke around about that. He could have run over all three of us that night. We'd be all broken up and dead and people would be crying and stuff. Nobody would even know what happened. We got lucky, I'm thinking. You got lucky most of all."

We were talking about this one day as we walked down the hill to watch Max at track practice. They were teaching him to throw a shot put. Max tossed that thing a mile. We sat on the wet bleachers, less than a hundred feet where the black Chevy almost ran us down, while another dark rain cloud barreled toward us over Mount Powell.

I turned to Blue. "What I felt behind that wheel, it's something."

*/////*

When the car stopped next to me I figured I was dead. A chiseled face, hard as rock and framed between black sideburns, peered through the open window. *It's him, the stranger, looking right at me.*

"What the hell happened here?"

"Tire went flat." That's all my tongue would allow to explain.

"You old enough to drive?"

Here it comes, I thought. He knows.

"No."

"Then what you doing up here with lumber dumped all over the damn road?"

I slid backwards into the pickup just a bit. "Hauling it when the tire blew."

"Did you steal that lumber?"

"My dad buys lumber at Mr. O'Hanlon's place." I pointed up the road.

The stranger leaned farther out the window to survey the scattered posts. Then he took a good long look at the shredded tire. "What's the matter there?" He spoke past a cigarette bobbing on his lips. "Not strong enough, huh?" He cut the engine on the Chevy. "You gotta damn sorry mess, ain't you?"

I began to comprehend that he didn't recognize me. If he did he'd be choking me for sure. As he smoked he took out a comb to glide long strands of coal-black hair into place. He wasn't as old as he looked, I decided, maybe eighteen. With his hair in place, he swung open the door and dropped two black boots to the ground. They had silver chains across the back. He was "a long drink of water," as Dad would say. Biceps popped from his arms when he shrugged off his faded blue jacket to reveal a black t-shirt. "Warm day," he said. Louie leaned over and grabbed the tire iron off the ground. I cringed, sure now that I was wrong and that he recognized me after all and they would find my body in the ditch beside Hack Face's empty whiskey bottles. "No muscles, huh?" he repeated.

"I couldn't get the last ones."

"Takes some power. You're too damn skinny. Short, too." He looked me over. "Hell, how can you even see the road through those thick lenses? You could fry ants on the sidewalk with those glasses."

Insults over, he fitted the wrench onto the first nut and curled his arms. It snapped loose without complaint. I slipped out of the cab to watch him. "See, you gotta push on one side and pull on the other and lean your weight into it 'cause these nuts get locked tight as a choir lady's ass when they rivet them on with the air hose down at the garage." He loosened the others even while he was talking.

"You gotta spare that works?"

I rapped on the spare tire with my knuckles to make sure it was inflated.

"Least something's going well for you today, Ace." He stepped to the back of the pickup. "Now the jack. First these here timbers have to come out." He lifted two at a time, just like Hack Face did. I dragged one out, then another, trying to keep up with him. When the last timber was out he slammed the tailgate shut. He fitted the jack under the back bumper. Raising the back end in no time, he popped off the rim with the blown tire, replaced it with the spare and let the jack down. "Tighten these." He handed me the tire iron. While I leaned my weight into the turn as I'd seen him do, he loaded the timbers again and threw the shredded tire on top.

He broke out another cigarette and stepped back to survey the situation. "Smoke?" I was almost scared enough to take one, but shook my head. "Didn't think so. How old, you, anyway?"

"Thirteen."

"Hot shot junior high kid?"

"I'm in seventh grade."

"Ain't what I asked."

He took a long puff, staring past the pickup like he was remembering something far away. I was certain of it. He froze, holding his burning cigarette. I saw nothing on the grassy hillside or beyond that should capture his attention. He was lost someplace for a good twenty seconds, a long time to stand next to someone who could pound you to a pulp without a word going between you. He was a mysterious boy — or man. I couldn't decide which. I couldn't remember seeing anybody in Deer Lodge like him. He almost looked too old for his age. Something about him reminded me of high school boys when I was in kindergarten. That's when I slept in the covered porch of our old house down on California Avenue. I sat on my bed munching cereal from a red bowl in the mornings, watching them walk past on their way to school. Louie looked like those kids with their blue jeans rolled up but there was more to him, something fierce and confident and handsome. I had to admit that much.

"Gotta name?" He was back from wherever he had gone.

"It's Paul."

"Louie." He didn't bother to stick out his hand. "Good thing your old man trusts you even if you can't fix your own sorry mess."

"I-I appreciate your help. I was in a real bind."

"If you're gonna drive learn how to change a tire. And look here, maybe you'll see the road better if you get rid of those glasses."

The stranger named Louie bounced into his car and revved it up. "You're too damn young to know what the hell you're doin' but you're tryin', I give you that." He gunned the motor a couple of times. Then — "Somebody helps you, Ace, you help somebody else. My uncle appreciates your business."

Louie dropped the Chevy into gear and roared up the road. I watched him go.

# Louie

*I rolled into the lumberyard* just as Blue and Max arrived on their bikes. They watched with great interest as I backed into the warehouse while Dad shouted directions. *Turn left, turn right, don't hit anything!* Once parked, I lingered behind the wheel for effect. If I'd had a cigarette I might have put a match to it. I felt a moment of regret that I didn't bum one from Louie. My friends parked their bikes and came over to the pickup, envy glimmering in their eyes.

Max reached for the steering wheel, moving it back and forth to get the feel of it. Blue rested his foot on the running board and whistled. "Now it looks to me like you're driving everything you can get your hands on, son. First the Chevy, now your old man's Ford pickup." I heard reverence in Blue's voice.

Max interrupted. "Paul, you think your dad would let me drive? Just down the alley and back?"

"Ask him, Max."

"Nah, he looks kind of mad."

"No, he's —."

Dad shouted from somewhere in back of the pickup. "Paul, get this lumber unloaded, will you? Took you long enough. Time's money, boy, we have customers waiting." He sounded tired, maybe irritable, nothing like his cheerful demeanor when he opened the place in the morning.

I swung out of the cab and went to work. Blue and Max helped. When we were done I found Dad. "Should I take the pickup out and park it?" He looked around at the milling customers. "No, better not. Toby —!" After I handed Toby the keys, Dad asked why I took so long at the mill. When I told him about the blown tire, his face softened. "Glad I could rely on you, son. Go ahead with your buddies. The day's about done anyway and so am I. Trouble with making money is, it takes it all out of you sometimes. Tell your mother I'll be late. Got to do inventory and figure out how to get another load of mill wood over here from Missoula quick. And that rough cut you got from Hack Face will be gone by the time I close."

Blue and Max straddled their bikes in the sunshine, waiting for me. I got on my own and pedaled away with them, thinking Dad looked old and worn out. I wondered if I would look any better at forty-one than he did.

///// 

I never thought of a Montana winter as a time of hard living. While adults burrowed into their living rooms, cursing icy sidewalks and snow-clogged streets, we kids hit the sliding hill or the ice rink. One seemed as fetching as the other. During the day we'd rocket our wooden sleds down the hill and pull them back up until our socks and gloves sagged with snow and our bare ankles and wrists chaffed red. At night we'd hit the ice rink where it covered the old baseball field, skating in the dark and warming ourselves at a bonfire that nobody seemed to extinguish. We sat on logs, bundled in our stocking caps and bulky coats, watching water slide off our skate blades as we nudged our feet closer to the glowing coals.

It was here, in the night at a fire beside the town ice rink, where I first noticed Marcy Kersher. She skated with other girls, all of them holding hands. I was to discover that a boy's appetite for a pretty girl dressed in pink runs big. She never knew I was alive at first, I was sure of that. I watched her, firelight reflecting on the lenses of my glasses, as she twirled with her friends. They giggled and jabbered a blue streak as young girls do. I sat on a log with Blue, my usual companion at the rink, both of us silent but watching. Looking back, I think I emerged into my true appreciation of girls in the winter of 1965. I admit some boys started earlier. They call it puberty. Talk started in Grade 5, sure enough, but to me girls were classmates in dresses and knee socks, nothing more. Those nights at the rink told me something had changed. I was a seventh grader now, tingling in the presence of girls and not understanding why. Blue attempted to explain these new feelings to me. He rambled on about birds and bees getting horny, but I could tell he was confused himself. My parents didn't talk about birds and bees. I never understood what birds and bees had to do with admiring cute girls with gentle bumps in their sweaters.

Hardly a car passed the old rink after eight. The fire cracked and sputtered in the winter air. In the far corner of the rink stood the remains of a rickety wooden backstop for the baseball field. In summer the field went unused, probably because of all the ruts and gopher holes on the base path or because we played on the new fields at Jaycee Park. In winter the old green structure presided over the rink like an exclamation point. On the other end was the junior high school, strangely dark at night. We came to school one morning after a burglary when somebody cut the window out of the back door and pried a safe the size of a refrigerator out of the wall in the principal's office. The thief left a crow bar on the floor. I figured he maybe stole our lunch money. We didn't know what else the principal might have kept in there except maybe dirty magazines. Some of the boys claimed to have seen them.

Out on the rink, skating in the evenings after school, we talked about how much we hated seventh grade. We talked big but Blue and Max and I and all the other boys knew that school was the best place to meet girls. When school closed for the summer in Deer Lodge we'd see the town girls in their cutoff denims. If they didn't live on farms and ranches in the valley, they worked in their mothers' kitchens all day long in town. That's what Blue and I figured. Girls went to cooking school, Max told us, and when they weren't baking cookies they stayed at home to play the clarinet and learn manners. "Girls are like Catholics," he said, "going around to classes and meetings and keeping their hands clean and stuff like that." I didn't know what Max meant but it sounded right, even if he didn't have a sister to know for sure. Catholics in Deer Lodge had a big old academy where they went to pray. Blue, a true storyteller, said that after school they climbed something like six stories to an attic where they knelt and licked a cat's face and that's why they were called cat-lickers. I didn't know what to think. Old Blue knew these things somehow.

When I was young I wasn't sure girls could be Catholics. We were Presbyterians. Girls came to our church but you weren't supposed to talk to them. Nobody was supposed to talk in church or even look at each other. You just looked straight ahead at Reverend Bartlett. Even then he was a tottering old soul who spoke from the podium like a dead man, blowing the words forth from what seemed the hollows of the grave. We were pretty sure he'd never licked a cat's face because he was Presbyterian. Boys weren't allowed in the back parts of the church where Reverend Bartlett kept his office. Maybe he kept a cat and maybe he didn't. The church was a quiet place where it was considered bad manners to sneeze during a sermon or fart or show emotion of any kind. Blue and I got away with our whispering in the pews when the old tigers sang hymns, but that was about it.

It was easier to bargain out of an occasional church service after winter passed. Even the adults wanted to stay outside on a Sunday morning. When the snow melted and the ice disappeared, we dragged out our bicycles and baseball gloves. Blue and Max and I signed up for Little League baseball but we never played on the same team. Max was the best player I ever saw those summers long ago down at the ballpark. When he swung those beefy arms he hit the ball a mile. When Max wasn't playing ball in Deer Lodge he'd go to Butte to play with some old friends who laid out bases around the ore tailings in Finn Town. They tried to hit grounders instead of flies because between baseball seasons the outfield fell into a mining shaft. Max said somebody put a board fence around the hole but more of the ground kept disappearing until even the fence fell in. Blue played second base where he was quick as a cat, but he wasn't much better at batting than me. He swung like he wanted to kill the ball. I had a different problem. I just couldn't see the ball. It didn't dawn on me that a boy in thick glasses wasn't born to play baseball. I wanted to mimic my heroes Harmon Killebrew and Tony Oliva who swatted home runs for the Minnesota Twins, sending balls sailing over the fence in deep center. Down at Jaycee Park the outfield trailed off into crab grass and weeds. In the spring of my seventh grade year, I checked the bulletin board every hour for a week until I saw the postings. This summer I would play on the Giants. Blue made the Yankees, Max the Red Sox. I couldn't wait for summer, for the aroma of fresh-cut grass, for the crack of a bat on a hard-thrown ball.

/////

About a block from the lumber yard, when I figured there was no way Dad could hear us, I told Blue and Max about the adventure on the mountain. They couldn't believe Louie hadn't beaten me to a pulp. Max, who never turned away from a good fight, started with the questions first.

"So how come he didn't mess up your face?"

"I guess he didn't recognize me."

"Was he tough? I mean, is he from Butte like I thought?" Max thought everybody from Butte was tough. I guess he had reason to know.

"I wouldn't mess with him. You wouldn't either if you saw him."

Blue laughed. "He'd knock your glasses off and that would be it. You wouldn't see a thing and then he'd have you pinned on the ground with your face in the mud. You'd be whining like a stuck pig in a minute."

"You wouldn't be making fun if you saw him. He was standing right next to me."

"He's like what, a grownup?" Max again.

"Maybe like a senior in high school. I don't know. He might be a dropout. He looks like a hood." We knew it was dangerous to hang around hoods. They lived mean and carried knives for cutting. Hoods rumbled with chains and clubs. That's what we saw on television, anyway. I knew a few hoods who lived down the alley. They looked like they would give somebody the business if given good reason.

"Paul, you should tell your old man," Blue said, turning serious. "You don't want to keep running into this guy. I don't think he's anybody to mess around with."

"He left me alone, Blue."

"Only because it didn't occur to him that you took his car."

"I wasn't going to remind him."

"And he said Hack Face is his uncle?" Blue looked at me in disbelief.

"That's what it sounded like."

Max shifted on his bike. "You don't want to get old Hack Face gunning for you, too. That man is trouble. My pappy says Hack Face tore up the Corner Bar one night. Says he threw a farmer right over the bar and knocked another guy cold with one punch. Then he scooted out of there and went back to Elk Ridge and never comes down no more. The police figured on leaving him alone as long as he stayed up there, that's what Pappy says."

Blue kicked his bike into motion. "If you ask me, good place for both of them, out of our way."

We pedaled up Milwaukee Avenue under elm trees pregnant with budding leaves. A family played croquet in their yard, smacking wooden balls with mallets on the short grass, still fresh from an afternoon cutting. Across the street at a gray house, a man napped in a rocking chair on his covered porch while his wife chipped away with a hoe in their garden, kneeling in the damp soil on old knees. The bells at the Catholic Church told us it was five o'clock. Hearing that, Blue kicked his bicycle into overdrive.

Max yelled at the disappearing figure, his red shirt whipping in the wind. "What's the hurry, Bluesy? Time for bed?"

Blue slowed just long enough to fire off an explanation. "Dinner. My mother's fixing pot roast. See you losers later." Max and I watched him fly up the hill.

"Pot roast, Paul. Sounds damn good. Boiled potatoes too I'll bet."

I sometimes wondered if Max got enough to eat. I figured we were close to poor sometimes but we never went hungry. Mom always figured something out, scraping up miracles from the pantry where fat gleaming canisters held flour and sugar and other provisions that she baked when things went bad at the lumberyard. Some days we ate a lot of biscuits. Peanut butter too.

Max and his parents lived in a sagging house with long cracked windows. When winter came Max helped his pappy nail plastic over the glass. Then they split firewood and stacked it high against the garage out back where Mr. Jorgenson repaired cars. They had one wood stove in the house and another in the garage. That's how they stayed warm on winter days. A couple of times I saw them huddled around their small kitchen table, dividing a can of soup and a few slices of bread. I worried about Max, one of my two best friends in the whole world, but he didn't care much for pity. I couldn't understand how Max kept getting bigger when he got so little to eat. Even since Christmas, his arms strained at his shirt. His face looked fuller under that blond crew cut. Max was looking more and more like his pappy, a giant of a man with flapping ears who had toiled in the mines in Butte until he coughed black dust out of his lungs. He worked down in the stopes repairing motors on the tractors that hauled ore out of the belly of the earth. Once I watched Mr. Jorgenson carry a car engine across the garage, his mighty arms wrapped under the flywheel and the transfer case. He didn't scare me like Hack Face O'Hanlon but he was just as big as Hack Face and probably stronger.

I had an inspiration. "Wanna ride past Marcy's? I mean, unless you have to run off like Blue, why don't we go over there? I don't have to be home for another hour."

"Fine by me." Max looked at me with some disappointment. "Might as well go look at your girlfriend. I don't get to look at mine except when she's at school. You know, before she gets on the bus to go home." The girlfriend waif, Peg Ottaway, lived on a farm in the south valley. Max and Peg had been going together, at least hanging around together, since the dance. Blue teased Max by calling her Prudence or Prude for short. Max got hot about that. One day he turned on Blue, threatening him with a black eye, and with girls in the picture I felt something was different among us. I guess it meant we were growing up but I didn't like us turning on each other. Max became protective of Peg, as I did with Marcy, and it seemed strange that Blue was the one without a girlfriend. The girls flocked to him because he was one of the best-looking boys in school. He couldn't decide which one he wanted. To me Peg was a lot like Max. She didn't say much but she was loyal. She let Max follow her around. Sometimes they held hands before she boarded the orange school bus for some road out in the country. Max didn't know where she lived. We figured if we ever got our hands on that black Chevy we'd go find her. It was big talk, full of fantasy.

We spun past the high school and down Cottonwood Avenue past the jail. A fat woman once went berserk in there, Dad said, tearing the police chief's shirt off and throwing people around like they were rag dolls. Past the corner and across the creek, we found Marcy sitting on the front stoop, reading a book.

"Paul! Max!" She seemed happy to see us. She closed the book just a little. I couldn't read the small red writing on the cover, but the book looked suspiciously like homework. We sat there like two dummies looking at Marcy, who was wearing some nice cutoff jeans, a pink blouse, and white tennis shoes. She had rolled her socks down to the top of her shoes. All the girls did. I decided right then that Marcy had great legs, although I'd seen enough of her legs when she wore miniskirts to school to figure I was on the right track. I nudged Max, who was leering with his mouth hanging open. While he collected drool with the back of his hand I parked my bike and walked up to the porch.

"Did you guys come to study? I don't see your books." Marcy smiled and fussed with her streaked hair, fixed that way down at the beauty shop. All the rage in California, she had told me. "Really, Paul, we have that big test coming in English this week. Mrs. Miller said it might be an essay. Remember? Find a book in the library that we really like, read it and be prepared to talk about conflicts with the main character."

"Is that all you do is study?" Marcy could be a bummer sometimes. She was a brain for sure.

"Says the boy who always works." She smiled again.

"Is that the book you chose?" I felt stupid asking, since school was almost out and I'd probably carried that very book home for her ten times. Marcy stuck a bookmark between the pages. She held the book out for me to see. It had a sincere scholarly cover and looked new, too, nothing like the battered books I found in the school library that had been checked out to kids way back in the 1950s.

"*Keepers of the House*? What's it about?"

Marcy caressed the book. I understood why because that's what I did when I found a really good book, wanting to cherish each page after I became part of the story. "It's about a white woman in the South in the last century. Her family was respected until somebody found out her grandfather had a relationship with a housekeeper who was a Negro."

"What do you mean by relationship?" Max asked. He had parked his bike beside mine and now stood next to me, likely more interested in Marcy's bare legs than anything that remotely resembled homework.

"Well, boys," and she winked, "it means when a man and a woman, you know, get together." A naughty look passed over Marcy's face. She kept grinning, her teeth glittering in the late afternoon sunlight.

"Like sex, you mean?" It felt very odd mentioning that word to Marcy. It was an adult word, full of implications I didn't understand. My parents never spoke the word around the house. Blue's parents didn't either. His mother hid their weekly copy of LIFE magazine when the cover story was all about how babies were born. Blue faithfully waited for LIFE to arrive in the mailbox, as it always did, and when Blue's mother made some feeble excuse that the editors had skipped publication for a week he knew something was up. After he investigated under his parents' bed and rummaged through their closet (where he found his dad's loaded handgun), he turned to the hall closet, where it was folded into the sleeve of a winter coat. Blue brought it over to our hiding place in the field, where we learned a lot about babies as we leafed through the eye-popping pictures, but not much about sex. Back in the fourth grade I'd heard the word on the school playground and asked Mom for an explanation.

"Don't you ever speak that word again, young man." She threatened to wash my mouth with soap if she ever heard me talk about sex. That gave me pause, because she bought industrial-strength Lava, and the two times she gave me the mouth-washing treatment it felt like licking volcano rock. She wouldn't let me spit the soap out right away either. One time I glimpsed myself in the mirror. Gray suds foamed around my lips. I looked like a rabid dog.

And so it seemed completely out of order that I'd even bring up the word to my new girlfriend, probably within hearing distance of her parents who either were horrified or thought I was stupid.

Max interjected. "You're reading a sex book from school?" His eyes were wide open. I knew he was kicking himself for not going to the library more often.

"Silly boys." Marcy dismissed us with a wave. "The book is *literature*, you know? It has deeper meaning about the difference between people who are one color and people who are another —."

"We had those over in Butte," Max interrupted. "The Micks up in Dublin Gulch and the Bohunks and Krauts and them other kinds back in the olden days. That's what my pappy says."

"Not like that," Marcy corrected him. "Differences between black and white back when we were fighting the Civil War. There's a main character, see, named Abigail Howland, and she's really brave but spiteful too when the townspeople turn on her because her grandfather got involved with this black woman."

"Are we talking about getting it on again?" asked Max, who seemed to welcome the idea. Maybe it was my imagination but Marcy seemed to close her legs a little tighter. They were long and gaining shape.

"Max, we're talking about classic struggles between people. That's what we're writing about in this essay."

"So where did you get a new book, Marcy?" I pointed to the cover.

"It just came out this year. We bought it in Missoula. Mrs. Miller said it was okay if it didn't come from the school library. It won the Pulitzer Prize, you know." She caressed the cover again, lost with Abigail Howland in Alabama. "So Paul, when are you planning to read a book? I mean, we have to write the essay on Wednesday."

"I already did."

"You read a book already?" She looked at me, trying to hide her disbelief. "What's the title of this book?" She acted like she caught me there.

"It's about the Civil War. *The Little Shepherd of Kingdom Come*. It's about a boy named Chad raised in the wilderness of

Kentucky by a mountain family, but when the war comes all the people he's ever known in his life start taking sides."

"That sounds like a good one." Marcy crossed her legs. "Do you think maybe Chad and Abigail have a few things in common?"

I knew Mrs. Miller wanted us to think that way. She always talked about how we needed to understand the bigger world outside Deer Lodge. She was fond of saying that if we kept our minds in our tiny town we'd never leave it. I heard Mrs. Miller was from Minneapolis. Just what she was doing in Deer Lodge wasn't clear to any of us, but she sure was a good teacher.

I didn't know anything about people from the South. I'd never seen anybody with black skin in person. I liked reading about the Civil War but it seemed so long ago that it felt to me like fiction, full of romance about dying and honor and sacrifice. I didn't know much about death. When I was a young boy a neighbor tripped over a garden hose and fell headlong into a tree and died. Dad covered him with a blanket until the ambulance drove up. I didn't see anything except a lump under a sheet with an arm swinging free as the police chief rumbled the gurney over the gravel road toward the ambulance, nothing more than a blue Ford station wagon with a light on top. Such morbid excitement rarely came to Deer Lodge. As Mrs. Miller pushed us more and more into the library, I began to realize that Deer Lodge and the subjects of books had little in common.

Marcy turned to Max, who had settled beside her on the front stoop. "Max, you watching out for my boyfriend? When he's not working at the lumberyard he's got his mind in the

Civil War. I'm sitting here by the phone, pining away for Paul to call."

Max looked at Marcy, catching her meaning. His parents didn't have a phone. I knew how he longed to call his girlfriend in the country. He got up to leave, sensing Marcy's suggestion that she and I have some time alone. Good old Max, not wanting to mess things up for me. "Gotta go, time for dinner I bet." He hollered goodbye and pedaled off.

Marcy reached out her hand. I pulled her up and we kissed. I wanted to tell her about driving the truck to Hack Face O'Hanlon's and meeting Louie, but her mother appeared at the door, telling Marcy it was time to eat. A distinct aroma of venison floated from the kitchen.

///// 

That evening Dad cracked a Great Falls Select and walked out to the barn while Mom cleared the table after dinner and Sally spread out her arithmetic homework. I followed Dad. He loved his refuge, pungent with sawdust and grease and long-ago cattle, full of saws and grinders and lathes and other machines bolted to oversized benches he had built. A wood stove in the corner kept the place warm in winter but tonight he flung open several windows and the back door to let the evening come inside. School would be out in two weeks. I couldn't wait, because spring soon would ripen into summer.

Dad sat on his old work stool, which looked suspiciously like it came from the city dump. It had long chrome legs and a yellow plastic seat pimpled with brown cigarette burns. Mom wouldn't permit cigarette smoking in the house. She sniffed in disgust when Dad put a match to his pipe. It was a different story in the barn, where he kept a carton of unfiltered Camels, his favorite brand, in a cupboard. I found him sitting on his stool sorting nuts and bolts under the hot light of a battered metal lamp. He seemed to have no particular purpose in doing so. He looked more tired than usual.

Dad looked up when he heard my footsteps. "Mom thinks you did yourself in today," I told him, concerned for his appearance.

"Maybe, some." Dad didn't seem like he wanted to talk much.

"Dad, can I help at the lumberyard more? I mean, haul more lumber from the mill like I did today?"

"You can't be driving, Paul. You're only thirteen. If the cops saw you I could get pinched."

"You let me drive today."

"Today was different. I needed your help and you didn't let me down. We just can't make a habit of it." He took a swig of beer and then a puff from his smoldering Camel. "That tire—."

"I'm really sorry, Dad. I was being as careful as I could. That damn tire just blew."

Dad managed a laugh. "I guess it was a damn tire but you shouldn't be talking like that in case your mother hears you. But how did you get that tire changed all by yourself?"

"Somebody who was going up the mountain stopped and helped me."

"That's good. Whole damn tire is blown. Damn retreads." Then, "Anyone I know?"

"I don't know. He didn't look familiar to me."

Dad seemed satisfied with that explanation. I wanted to tell him about Louie and the black Chevy, and almost did, but he shifted to the bench again, turning over the rusted nuts and bolts in his calloused hands.

# Tommy

*I thought I'd be alone* at church Sunday morning but there sat Blue, full of pot roast and looking sad. He got that way when the sun shone and he wanted to cast a line on the Clark Fork River. "I tried to get out of coming today," he whispered to me as soon as Reverend Bartlett started his invocation. He looked pained at confessing his failed attempt. "I did too," I whispered back in a conspiratorial tone.

Blue slid closer. "I can't wait to get out of this monkey suit. Let's sneak out as soon as everybody falls asleep. I'm going to die if I can't go fishing. I hear those trout calling my name." I knew it would be easy. Our parents were sitting a few pews in front us, preoccupied with shuffling pages in the hymnals and checking their pockets and purses for money for the collection plate. They wouldn't even know we left. After church they would shake hands with everyone and walk over to the Christian Center next door for coffee and cupcakes. They knew I was going fishing with Blue and Max after church. They just didn't know we were plotting an earlier departure.

"Now?"

"No, wait until the sermon."

Our minister started explaining something called predestination in a halting voice. He stood at the podium in a black robe, ignoring the heat gathering in the church, while women fanned themselves with little paper programs. It was a sultry hot Sunday in late May, the kind to make you wish that school had ended and mothers forgot about church and we could hit the river early when the fish were feeding. I wouldn't know real humidity until years later, but the mountain air, usually dry as dust, felt heavy and close. Sweat trickled under my collar buttoned tight at the neck under a bowtie. An usher walked past us to prop open the outside door. Blue sat rigid in the pew, watching his father. When his father's eyes closed and his head nodded, Blue stooped low between the pews and signaled me to follow. We slipped outside in no time. I was betting that the few people who saw us leave, including the minister, wished they could go fishing too.

We ran most of the four blocks home. I changed out of my suit in record time, threw on an old pair of blue jeans and a red t-shirt, and met Blue at the corner. He dropped his tackle box beside mine in the wire basket on my bike and we rode over to get Max, balancing our fishing poles across the handlebars. We weren't much for doing anything but casting lures.

We surprised Max, who was still wearing his pajamas. His thick wrists stuck out of the sleeves. "Are those baby bears I see, Maxy?" Blue pointed to a pattern of brown animals marching across the front of Max's pajama top. Max turned red. "You're going to get it when we get down to the river," he growled at Blue.

After Max got dressed we headed for the river with Blue howling his head off over the pajamas. Max tried to ram Blue's bike a few times but Blue was too quick, spinning out of the way at the last instant. We kept out of sight of the church, crossed Main Street, flew past Morrison Lumber, and crossed the railroad tracks toward the river. Over the bridge we went. We had a secret fishing spot down the river about a mile, in a grove of willows where the Clark Fork fell into a deep pool before it eddied over a shelf of rocks. We filled our creels with rainbow trout last summer. The Clark Fork looked sickly in some places but our secret spot was the best. The river still ran high from the spring soaking but we didn't care. We figured the fish hid in there someplace.

"Wait!" Blue skidded his bike to a stop. "Let's try here first. I'll bet this stretch is full of trout." We disembarked at a little coulee near the road to Hack Face O'Hanlon's sawmill. Blue casted as many predictions as he did lures. He was always sure of himself.

"This is the West Side, you know." I felt it my duty to remind Blue and Max of that. Every kid in Deer Lodge knew about the West Side. It wasn't a place where you messed around if you lived east of the river. That is, if you weren't one of them.

The day was still and the sun was bright. I felt hot but no longer damp and confined like I had in church. It didn't seem right to make boys sit in church in coats and ties in warm weather when the weekend was too short anyway. I looked around, nervous at being in plain sight. I worried about things like that. Blue and Max didn't act like it was any big deal. Blue charged down to shore with his new rod and reel. A gold lure glimmered in the sunlight. He cast into the river, reeled in and cast again. Max moved down the river a couple dozen feet. He sat in the weeds, searching through his tackle box for a suitable lure. The river bubbled past, running deep in that spot.

"So Paul?"

"Yeah, what, Max?

"How come we don't fish with worms or flies?"

"Because it's boring fishing with worms unless you enjoy sitting for hours. Fly rods cost too much money."

"Ya gotta be rich?"

"I reckon so." I tried a small lure, red and white on one side and silver on the other, but on my first cast I shot over the narrow river to the other side and, to Blue's delight, snagged some tall grass.

"Hey, Bubby, this isn't Flathead Lake. See if you can hit the water next time." Blue cast into a gurgling rush. His line glistened and went taut. Then his pole whipped and he pulled against a couple of sharp snaps. "See how it's done, boys," he shouted to us. "While you two losers are snagging lures all over Deer Lodge I'm catching trout." Blue was never one for modesty. He splashed through the water, his blue jeans soaked to the knees, his handsome face intense with concentration. "Gotta watch for snags!" He maneuvered the line past a log and reeled in a fine rainbow trout. "That's gotta weigh two pounds," Max observed with no little reverence for Blue's fishing skills. Blue swung the fish onto shore, and when he did, it landed at the feet of the biggest bully in junior high school.

There stood Tommy Tucker, buck teeth sprouting from his mouth. A white shirt splashed with Kool Aid stretched over a torso built like a rain barrel. Tommy ran a grubby paw over his unkempt mop. "You girls don't belong over here, now do ya?" He spit for emphasis.

Tommy's fellow eighth graders gave him wide berth in the hallways. He liked to bump kids into the lockers, slam doors on their hands and throw them down the stairs. He terrified the seventh graders. I never had dealings with Tommy but I knew a few kids he pounded after school. Behind Tommy stood a boy who looked just like him, only bigger and with a flushed face. He looked like a sophomore or maybe a junior. His nose and eyes were buttons in a beach ball of flesh.

"So what we got here?" Tommy inquired, directing our attention to the flopping trout at Blue's feet. "The girl caught herself a little ole fish."

Blue reached down to scoop up his fish, still thrashing with the hook in its mouth. Tommy clamped a muddy tennis shoe over it. "Keep your hands off this, girlie. This here's a West Side fish. You pantywaists from across the tracks don't be fishing on our side." Blue backed away a step or two, sizing Tommy up. Max dropped his pole and moved toward us like a wary cat.

"Now how we gonna teach right from wrong here?" Tommy reached down and grabbed Blue's new rod and swung it in the air. The fish, covered in sand and weeds and mashed with a giant footprint, swung lifelessly.

"That's mine," I heard Blue say. Max was close. We knew Max was familiar with this kind of encounter. Nobody wanted trouble from Tommy. He talked like a huge chattering gopher. "Mmmmine?" he whined, mocking Blue. Tommy cocked his arm and heaved Blue's birthday rod and reel, fish and all, into the Clark Fork.

Blue shot ahead like I knew he would and the fight was on. For a while it was a scuffle, all heels and grunts, as each boy tried to throw the other to the ground. Tommy was strong but so was Blue. It's just that Tommy had a killer instinct and Blue didn't. So when Tommy pushed away, Blue dropped his hands. Tommy fired a punch right into Blue's nose. It hit with a sickening smack, like an ax handle clubbing a tree trunk. Blue fell backwards, hands locked on his face and fingers red with blood.

Max flew past me in a flash, his fists streaking. He hit Tommy five or six times, hammering him in the lips and eyes and ribs and throat. The bully fell to his knees and slumped forward into the weeds, out cold.

I took off my t-shirt and pressed it to Blue's nose as he lay on his back. "Oh, it hurts, Paul." Max stood his ground, his fists in the air. The big Tucker brother was coming at him now. Behind that brother stood a third, even larger and meaner than the first two. He waited about fifteen feet away to give the two combatants room. Tommy lay motionless. His toes touched inward and his fat rump aimed skyward. It wasn't a pretty sight.

"Pick on somebody your own size, why dontcha?" the second brother yelled. That statement made no logical sense, given that he loomed over Max and was at least three years older. He wore a ragged brown shirt with the sleeves cut off. His arms swung like slabs of ham.

Max landed the first blow. His fist smacked on Tucker's cheek with a thud. The bigger boy reeled backed, his eyes wide with surprise. I thought of Max's dad carrying that engine in the garage. I figured Max could do that someday. Max kept his fists close to his bobbing head. The brute clobbered Max in the head, then he charged. Max fell backwards under the boy's weight, recoiling under a pounding fist. They grappled in the mud near the water. Max fought like a Butte boy but I could see that he was losing. Tucker was just too big for him. The brute, breathless and bleeding, pinned Max with his knees and clubbed him in the face.

I wasn't any hero and knew it. When I tore into Tucker, locking my arm around his throat, he felt as strong as old Betsy in one of her snits. Fighting the Tuckers was a lot like getting thrown off Betsy. That's how Blue would describe the situation later. Tucker fell backward, squeezing the breath out of me, but Max wiggled free. In the seconds before my glasses fell off I saw Blue on his feet, pulling Max away. Tucker threw me to the ground. He stood to swing at Max again. When I tried to stop him a pair of hands clamped on my arm. It was the biggest Tucker, swearing at me through yellow teeth. He lifted me high enough that my tennis shoes dangled in thin air. The sky and ground spun until I crashed on the ground. My chin felt wet and hot.

Max yelled for help. I heard scuffling and got to my knees. I couldn't see much without my glasses except for the looming ugly face of the middle Tucker brother. He saw fit to take a swing at my head. Something hard hit me. I collapsed on the rocks, my brain numb.

///// 

Our gym teacher, Mr. Grant, taught us how to box. At least he showed us how much a punch hurt. He dragged out some tired old boxing gloves, arranged us in a circle on the gym floor, and traded me a pair of gloves for my glasses. Mr.

Grant probably figured that what we couldn't see wouldn't hurt us. Bucky Clover, another boy with thick glasses, got the other pair of gloves. The circle of boys in their red trunks closed around us, all of them eager to see how much damage we'd inflict on each other. I landed the first hit, square in Bucky's face. When I reared back to hit him again he socked me a good one in the left eye. We exchanged punches, each harder than the last, as our seventh-grade classmates roared and called for more. I heard Blue whooping somewhere in the background but without my glasses I couldn't be sure where. With each wallop to the head I felt more and more like I was riding a playground merry-go-round. The room turned at a furious pace. I circled to stay away from Bucky's wild swings. Each of us kept our right hands low and cocked. I tried hard to knock Bucky down. After Mr. Grant stopped the fight somebody pushed on my glasses while I staggered around trying to remember where I was. I'd never be Cassius Clay. We watched a few other fights but when two bigger boys drew serious blood Mr. Grant put away the boxing gloves for good. He was on his knees wiping evidence off the gym floor when I left for math class.

I trooped along to the classroom feeling like I left my brain in Idaho. I wanted to brag to Marcy but Blue and Max assured me I had no future as a boxing legend. Blue razzed me about how stupid I looked. Max coached me not to drop my hands and to hit fast, using both hands. Neither one got a chance to box in gym class. Blue might do well if his hair didn't get messed up. Max would clean somebody's clock. We never got a chance to find out. I figured some parents complained because we never saw the gloves again. Mr. Grant had us playing kickball instead.

"Mr. Morrison, can you solve this equation for us?" I squinted at the blackboard, straining to focus my eyes on the numbers in white chalk. Mr. Arnosen held the palms of his chalk-smeared hands in appeal. "What's the matter, Mr. Morrison? Not paying attention back there?" The room fell silent except for Blue's predictable snicker. Anyone who looked stupid in front of Blue would pay for it. Marcy sat right in front of me. I resented Mr. Arnosen's interruption. Marcy's bra strap was showing through her white cotton blouse. That I could see without difficulty. I tried to compute the numbers and letters visible near the clasp.

"Mr. Morrison, we don't have all day." I pushed my glasses against the bridge of my nose to see better but that didn't help. I felt Bucky's punches hitting me again and again. I simply couldn't understand what Mr. Arnosen was asking me to do.

Marcy's hand shot in the air. "Mr. Arnosen, I'm dying to answer this. It's—."

"Miss Kersher, I've asked Mr. Morrison."

"I know, sir, but I'm pretty sure that Paul isn't feeling well today."

"Then shouldn't Mr. Morrison go down to see the nurse?"

I grabbed my books and headed to the sick room. Marcy was swell. I should get her a promise ring.

/////

Blue and Max would say later that they never saw him coming. He appeared all of a sudden, whaling the daylights out of those big Tucker boys. I heard his arrival from somewhere deep in the buzzing cave where my mind had taken me. I heard squealing tires and a roaring motor and sliding gravel. I heard boots coming fast. It felt too strangely familiar. I knew without looking that it was Louie Moretti.

/////

Mom started on me even before Dr. Klaus finished stitching my chin back together. "Paul, you don't know how much of a scare you've put into your father and me with this stunt. And sneaking away from church and all—."

I shifted uneasily on the examination table, rustling the stiff white paper they pull out to make sure you don't bleed all over their furniture. Dr. Klaus bent over me, under a glaring white light, pulling thread through my chin. "Broke a tooth, too," he told Mom.

She leaned over me to get a look. "It's the front one, young man." Then, softer. "It's bad enough. I'm so glad it wasn't worse." Her voice sounded sad, far away. She grabbed my hand. *She really cares.*

"Where's Dad?"

"He was so shook up he had to go sit down. Your father's been much too tired lately." She ran her fingers through my hair, brushing out sand and grass.

"Just about done here," said Dr. Klaus, who no doubt didn't want to witness whatever punishment my mother was intending for me. He twirled silver instruments a few inches above my face. I felt a few tugs, then a snip. As he covered his handiwork with tape, Dad stepped into the room. He looked both worried and mad. I figured I would catch it when we got home.

"Doctor?" I heard him ask. Then to me, "Damn, son, looks like you tangled with a grizzly bear." He coughed.

"Frank, Martha, here's what we've got. Five stitches in the chin but nothing broken that I can find except that tooth. He's got a bruise near the ear here that's going to look and feel like a mule kicked him for about a week." I felt the doctor's velvet-soft fingers, smelling like antiseptic, probe high on my cheekbone. "Nothing broken but you'll need to watch him. It's this blow to the side of Paul's head that needs careful attention. No school until Wednesday. Bed rest for three days, aspirin every four hours, and if you notice anything out of the ordinary call me right away. Other than that, some cuts and bruises on his arms and legs but nothing that won't heal."

Dad and Dr. Klaus helped me off the table. I felt sore all over. My head pounded. "Blue and Max?" I had visions of them crumpled in the river brush, torn to bits by the marauding Tucker brothers.

Dr. Klaus spoke in a kindly voice. "Dr. Dennison is looking them over in the rooms next door, Paul. You get rested up and then you can compare notes." I couldn't see for sure without my glasses, but I swear Dr. Klaus shot my parents a knowing look.

I limped into the hallway, a parent's hand under each arm. When they opened the car door it struck me. "How did I get here?"

///// 

When Mom finally let me out of bed on Tuesday, Blue and Max raced over after school, breathless with desire to tell me about the fight. They told me together that Louie took on Tate Tucker first.

"Which one was Tate?" I asked Blue, who now seemed to have the scoop on the whole family of Tuckers. We sat in the grass in my backyard, still pungent from when Dad mowed it. Blue looked like a raccoon. Both of his eyes were black. A strip of white tape ran across his nose, an underline beneath two exclamation points. Blue was proud of having a broken nose from a big fight. It was a good bragging point with boys in school. Most of them shook at the prospect of fighting a Tucker. Good with the girls, too, once they got past how ugly we looked.

"The big one, you know, the biggest one. He —."

Max interrupted. "I saw that big old boy throw you like he was bucking bales. Old Blue here was bleeding like a stuck pig, and then both of them bigger Tuckers charged us."

"I thought we were dead," Blue interjected. No argument from any of us there.

"Then," Max continued, "that boy who looks like Elvis Presley comes barreling at them Tuckers like he's going to a fire. That big old Tate took a swing at him that could have smashed granite and missed and then Elvis —."

"Louie," I corrected, feeling some compassion for the stranger who had both scared me and helped me.

"So Louie drills Tate Tucker right in the gut and then a few times in the head and then —."

Blue jumped in, eager to tell his share. "Knocks him to the ground and puts the boots to him, kicking him a few times until Tony Tucker jumps him."

"Wait, which one is Tony?"

"He's the middle one who belted Blue," Max said. "Louie pounded him too. I haven't seen a street fight like that outside of Butte. Feet, elbows, boots, everything flying and the Tuckers crying."

"Max, you sound like a poet." Blue started to laugh but grimaced at the pain. Max smiled at the compliment.

I eased my head back into the grass. It felt good to lie down. "So what about Tommy Tucker? You really cold-cocked him, Max. I couldn't believe how you laid him out." I remembered why I'd always been half-afraid of Max, even though he was one of my two best friends in the whole world.

"When he woke up he ran away, the pantywaist," said Max, scorning Tommy for using that word to describe Blue.

"And then," said Blue, "Louie helped us all into the Chevy and drove us home."

"I got to sit up front," Max bragged. "Probably because he didn't want you two idiots bleeding all over the dashboard." Max had welts on his face and a black eye. That much I could see without my glasses. Little scabs covered his knuckles from plowing a volley of punches into Tony Tucker's fat face.

"I don't remember coming home. I don't remember anything about that."

Blue picked up the story. "No, Paul, he took us to my house and my folks had just come home from church. They called the doctor and told Louie to get us to the clinic. They went by Max's place and got your folks at the church."

"Blue's old man called the police," Max said. "My pappy was wanting to head over to the West Side to tear up that whole nest of them Tuckers but Mr. Taylor said no sir, let the police handle it. Got to be twenty Tuckers holed up over there, my pappy says."

Blue smiled, his white teeth contrasting with the mess on the upper half of his face. "Wait until you get back to school tomorrow, Paul. We're a big deal with people knowing we took on the Tuckers and all. Max even got to kiss the waif."

Max seemed confused whether he should be insulted or boastful, but he warmed quickly to the latter. "Damned good, too," he muttered. "Like kissing an angel." For once Blue shut up. There was new respect all around. A brown station wagon pulled to a stop alongside our house. "It's Marcy," Blue alerted me, aware finally that I couldn't see that far. I heard a car door slam, then another. She walked toward us in her usual pink shorts, her streaked hair bobbing in a ponytail. Blue and Max, sensing a private moment in the works, loped off toward home. I heard Marcy's mother chatting with my mine in hushed distressed tones at the back steps. Marcy knelt beside me on the lawn, her face cramped with confusion. Tears filled her eyes.

///// 

Dad was a better source of local news than the local *Silver State Post*, which he often said told us everything but what was going on. He got home from the lumberyard at five-thirty, just in time for dinner. Sally had the table set. An aroma of hamburger casserole filled the kitchen. "It's all over town," said Dad, who scrubbed his hands hard at the sink. "Everybody's talking about the big fight and those Tuckers skipping town."

Mom turned from the stove. "Leaving Deer Lodge, Frank?"

"That's what I hear. The cops went over yesterday to that Tucker shack on the West Side and rousted them out and said they were going to arrest the adult one who jumped the kids but the old man said he hoofed it to hell and beyond. And then I hear Chief Leary laid into the old man and promised an ass-kicking from here to Warm Springs if he didn't get a grip on those kids."

"Frank, not in front of the children." It was a mild reprimand. She wanted to hear more. We all did. "So that big bully left town?"

"All of them. Sometime last night they packed up and headed out. Leary went up there and found the place empty. Took off owing money all over town."

"To us, Frank?"

"Nah, I don't remember old man Tucker coming down to the lumberyard. If he did he'd get nothing on credit from me, I'll tell you that. Those Tuckers are trouble. I hear they got whupped pretty good though." Dad winked at me and slumped into his chair at the head of the table, weariness in his voice. "What a day at the yard, Martha. We didn't know whether we were coming or going, between all the gossip and questions about the fight and everybody needing lumber." He nodded in my direction. "Lots of concern about how the boys are making out."

"Dad, my face hurts some but I'm ready to go back to school and —."

Dad cut me off, brimming with a big smile. "Show off that pretty face to that cute girl with the funny brown and blonde hair you're running around with?"

"Frank, you mean Marcy," Mom said. "She's a nice girl, even if she's a bit unorthodox in her appearance."

"I don't doubt it." Dad massaged his tired neck with a blistered hand.

She put a plate of steaming casserole in front of him. He liked to drink coffee with dinner. She had that ready, too, in an orange-colored cup that matched the kitchen color scheme.

"And Frank?" She nodded her head at me. Sally caught her meaning. She brushed her red curls from her eyes. She was a miniature version of our mother.

"Is Paul getting in trouble now?" Sally had a bit of regret in her tone. I knew she was batting for me. She was pretty sharp for being a runt. I always figured that when she grew up she would have the smarts to become a lawyer or even president, except everyone knew that girls couldn't run for president.

"Hush, Sally, eat your dinner," Mom told her. I kept my head down. The dreaded punishment would come soon enough. I might be grounded until high school graduation, or Mom might bring that stick out of the pantry to whip me. Dad might make me join the Army before he let me drive again. It was a lot of aggravation for a boy of thirteen.

When Sally finished eating Mom sent her out to play. Mom and Dad shuffled in their chairs, bracing for a speech. I felt stupid sitting there with my chin bandaged and a bruise as big as a baseball on my cheek. I had spent the afternoon looking at my chipped front tooth in the bathroom mirror. I bet I went there a hundred times, examining the tooth from every angle and wondering whether Marcy would dump me for looking stupid. The left front one was broken off right at the corner, making kind of a triangle. With that and my banged-up face I looked like a truck had hit me. Only the Tuckers. They were bad enough.

"Paul —," Dad began. "You disappointed your mother and me when you left church and went fishing during the reverend's sermon. We're upset about that. The thing is, we're calling the shots. When we tell you we want something done, that's what we mean. It's an insult to us and to the good reverend, who put a lot of work into his message. You getting me, son?"

I nodded, waiting for the hammer to fall.

"Now this fight," he continued. "That was bad but it wasn't your fault. I was talking to Mr. Jorgenson who said you waded right into those Tuckers when they were whaling on Blue and Max. It takes a man to do something like that."

Mom turned to me. "What your father is trying to say, Paul, is that we're proud of you for helping your friends. That was the right thing to do. And Lord, I'm glad you weren't hurt any worse. It's bad enough." She choked up and began clearing plates and silverware. She wiped her eyes with her apron and tried to hide it.

Dad smiled and leaned across the table and spoke in a conspiratorial tone. "You thought you were getting another whupping, didn't you boy?" He let out a belly laugh and reached for his pipe.

I looked at Dad and then at Mom, incredulous. "You mean I'm not being punished?" I hated to ask, in case they changed their minds.

Dad pointed to my battered face. "That's punishment enough, don't you think?" He lit a match and held it to his pipe. "But one thing, Paul. I hear the young man who finished off those Tucker boys is Louie Moretti."

"That's what I hear, Dad."

"Isn't he the boy whose car was stolen a few months ago the night of your school dance?"

"I don't know." Dad's expression told me that he didn't realize I was involved.

"Well, mighty nice thing he did. If I ever see him I'll thank him. Who knows what might have happened —." His voice trailed off.

It was then, on the premise that my parents would extend their sympathy to a confession, that I told them about the chase after the dance and how I drove Louie's black Chevy to get away. Mom bolted for the pantry to get her whipping stick. Dad persuaded her to calm down. "The boy did what he could to escape trouble. Nothing wrong with that," he told her. Dad put his pipe on the table and looked me straight in the eye. "Of course, telling lies is another matter. I'm grounding you for a week for doing that. You come straight home from school, nothing doing this weekend."

"But Dad —."

"Paul, what if I lied to my customers down at the yard? How long before they figured that out? I wouldn't make a living and then where would we be?"

I tried to explain. "I thought he was going to hurt me and the car was running and I just drove it away. I was really scared." Now I was worried about Louie all over again.

Dad looked outside, not sure what to say. Sally, a true climber, disappeared into the golden willow tree outside the kitchen window. Seconds later she slid down the big rope I had tied high in the branches. "Still —." Dad started. I could tell he didn't know what to make of Louie any more than I did.

That night, lying awake in my bedroom, I thought of Chad Buford, the Little Shepherd of Kingdom Come. He was a boy caught in contradictions. He loved both the poor mountain girl Melissa and the rich city girl Margaret. Each girl touched a portion of his spirit. Then came the Civil War with its blue side and its gray side. Chad was both homespun simple and a complicated nobleman. He fought to survive and craved for love. He didn't fit into his world any better than Louie did in ours. I began to wonder if Chad, although a made-up person, was Louie, or Louie was Chad.

# Marcy

*Blue was right about us* being heroes in school. We got new respect, even from eighth graders. We didn't need to embellish details of the fight. Our bruised faces told it all. Blue bragged the most, Max the least, with me somewhere in between. Blue and I quit our bragging the second day I was back to school because it didn't seem right. Who knows what the Tuckers might have done to us if we'd gone fishing without Max, or if Louie Moretti hadn't arrived? It all seemed too much to understand. My face hurt. The eye doctor had sent the remains of my glasses to Helena for repair. It was embarrassing to go around squinting like an old man.

By the weekend word was getting around town that Paul Morrison was drifting into trouble. At least that's what my mother reported to me when she swept into the house with a sack full of groceries. I was sitting at the kitchen table writing my essay for English class. "I heard it at bridge club," she told me mournfully as if my rebel behavior had breached the last bastion of decency in Deer Lodge. "Some of the ladies said, 'Why, Martha, we are so very surprised that Paul would do something like this. He's always been such a good boy.' And I had to tell them, 'Yes, we're having some trouble with Paul but boys will be boys, you know,' and I was mortified to realize that those ladies are thinking poorly of this family, Paul. And with your father owning the lumberyard and all. What will people think?"

"Did you —?"

"And no, I didn't tell them about you cruising around at the wheel of a stolen car. Lord knows they've figured that out already. You just don't understand what people know in this town and gossip about." The grocery sack rustled as she put away her purchases.

"But —."

"Now Paul," she said, talking in a louder voice from the pantry, her unmistakable domain. "I'd like you to think long and hard about the trouble you've caused us this spring. This family has had enough of your teenage excitement, young man." I felt miserable enough being grounded while other kids were outside playing. Marcy had invited me to a hayride in the back of her dad's pickup. I felt sick at missing it and worried about who would take my place, all cuddled up next to her. Now, this. When Mom worked up a head of steam it was useless to reason with her. I squinted at my notebook where I had crafted a description of conflict between my fictional hero Chad Buford and those mean Dillon brothers who jumped him in the backwoods of Kentucky. I was seeing that story in a new light. The Dillons seemed every bit as mean and ugly as the Tuckers.

"And another thing, young man," Mom said, standing beside me while she folded the sack. Here it comes, I thought. She always called me that whenever she was upset. "Why can't you be more like Blue? He doesn't misbehave like this." Sometimes I wondered whether Blue was the apple of my mother's eye. A saint. I dreaded the "be more like Blue" speech. It was delivered in unctuous ceremonial tones, a companion to "Blue would never do that."

"I didn't —."

"Paul, I hope you're doing your best on that report," she said, stabbing a finger toward my notebook where I'd labored to write half a page in blue ink. I might be a social misfit but I at least had good penmanship. "All your teachers say that your biggest problem is that you don't apply yourself." I heard her retreating footsteps on the linoleum. The screen door slammed at the back of the house. A minute later the faucet squealed outside as she started the sprinklers. For a moment I sat there, trying to remember my train of thought. My favorite book lay on the table beside me. The gold title on the maroon cover beckoned like an old friend. Then it hit me. I started a new line in my notebook. "Sometimes conflict can happen in real life…," I wrote, full of enlightenment.

*/////*

Four days later I came home with a big "A!" marked on my English report. "Excellent job relating fiction to personal experience!" Mrs. Miller wrote beneath my grade. She made comments in the margins, too, congratulating me for little insights into conflicted relationships. In one place I had written, "Chad Buford grew up an orphan but experienced the same conflicts with his friends and fellow soldiers that he might have felt with his parents if they had lived. He felt resentment, betrayal and loneliness. Sometimes he felt love when he realized that people were trying to look out for him. So conflict can be both bad and good. I think Chad Buford found out the hard way. So did I …" Mrs. Miller knew all about the Tuckers. She probably didn't know that I was in hot water at home unless she played bridge with mothers whose tongues flapped like window shades in strong wind. I considered bragging to my parents about my grade but thought better of it. My essay suddenly seemed personal and private. I folded it twice and locked it in a silver metal box where I kept my treasures, including a clipping from the Butte paper of President Kennedy's assassination, my badges from Cub Scouts and a few baseball cards of my favorite Minnesota Twins. School ended for the summer two days later. Homework seems less important when the school closes. My parents got busy and never asked about the essay. I wouldn't see it again for thirty years.

"At least today you don't look like you're mixing it up with wildcats," Dad told me when I arrived at the lumberyard on Saturday morning. "Don't want to scare the customers, right? Milner, come look at my boy's face."

Toby sauntered over, thumbs hooked behind his belt. He was one of the tallest men I'd ever seen, towering at least a foot over Dad. Toby played for the Wardens when he was in high school, making a name for himself all over Montana. He scored thirty-five points, Dad said, when the Wardens lost the state title to Wolf Point by a single basket. Toby played for the Bobcats at the university in Bozeman for a couple of years until he broke his ankle when he fell on a player during a rebound. That's why he walked with a slight limp. Toby lifted his cap to scratch his balding head. "Looks like the boy is healing, Frank." I couldn't remember a time when Toby hadn't worked for my father. At Christmas he dressed as Santa Claus to bring us candy, but even Sally knew it was Toby because he reeked of sawdust. Toby once had a wife who disappeared. I asked Dad where she had gone but he said it was no one's business and warned me never to ask Toby.

Dad pinched my jaw, shifting my face toward light from the doorway. My face still hurt and the stems from my new glasses pressed into my skull behind my ears. Eye doctors enjoy torturing kids. "Damn kid took those Tuckers on," Dad magnified, his voice full of pride. I saw a flicker of doubt in Toby's face but Dad ignored him. "They tore open my kid's chin, hammered him on the head. He's still walking around to talk about it."

Toby peered closer, concerned eyes framed between a pair of thick brown sideburns. "When those stitches coming out?"

"Doctor said Monday," I replied through pursed lips. My father squeezed my face, evidently feeling he had bragging rights on the abuse I had taken. "Should have seen the other guys," I spit out. I tried to laugh.

Dad let go and turned to Toby.

"You laid eyes on this guy Louie Moretti?"

"I wouldn't know him if he was road kill."

"The boys say he kicked those Tuckers into tomorrow. Knocked the oldest one silly."

"Kid's got guts. Best to give those Tuckers some room but he did the right thing fighting for the kids, I'd say."

"I'd like to thank this Moretti boy."

"Frank, you don't know, he might be as bad as those Tuckers."

"I know, but still —." Dad and Toby walked away, haggling over details.

Dad had me working in the office with Edna for most of the day. Business was so-so. I didn't have much to do but I think Dad was afraid I might get hurt bucking boards in the yard. Even so, sitting beside Edna, it felt good being free from Mom's captivity at home and to have seventh grade behind me considering how the spring went. Blue and Max talked big about how we'd run the junior high school when we were eighth graders. Marcy had no time for that. "That's ridiculous," she told both of them as we walked out of school on the eve of summer vacation. "Nobody cares about that except dumb kids." They looked hurt.

Blue tried to reason with her. "Look here, Marcy. It's a privilege to ride the runts, you know. Part of growing up."

"So you're saying that's what the Tuckers were doing to you?"

Blue caught her meaning right away. "That was different. Nobody has the right to whale on kids half their size."

"So where do you stop then, when you're riding the runts?"

"Geez, Marcy, don't get all worked up about it."

"I don't like seeing people get hurt." Marcy tossed her ponytail and stalked off toward home. All three of us knew she meant us. Girls were sensitive that way. I had to run to catch up with her. She turned to me, still striding along, her arms conspicuously empty of books that she lugged home, or had me lug, after school. "So, tough guy, looking for another fight?"

"No, it marks up my pretty face."

She stopped and put up her fists but managed a smile.

"So Marcy, what was that about?"

"Someday you'll understand," she said, kissing me on the lips. I had to admit that a girl who kissed a banged-up face like mine wasn't half bad. After I walked her home her mother invited me to stay for dinner. Because school was finished my parents allowed me to stay out until eleven. I think they felt bad about grounding me. Mom told it this way to Mrs. Kersher over the phone: "We think that Marcy is a good influence on Paul." I heard it all. So after dinner Marcy and I played croquet in her backyard until sunset and then walked two blocks to Jaycee Park where we kissed under the stars on the ball diamond. Her mouth felt open and warm. I wondered what it would take to get her to first base.

There I sat on Saturday at the lumberyard, passing time with Edna and thinking about Louie, when an idea hit me. I waited until she knocked off at mid-afternoon, folding the remains of a chocolate donut in a slip of billing paper and stowing it in her purse. Edna always brought donuts on Saturday mornings. She nibbled at hers like a mouse. Dad and Toby wolfed theirs down, chugging dark coffee between bites. I ate mine more strategically by chewing the outside until just a rim of donut remained around the center hole. I can't tell you why I started that. Something to do, I guess. Anyhow, Edna took off her apron, turned the cash register over to me, and heaved a sigh in my direction. "Hope that face heals soon, honey." The door closed behind her, tinkling the little bell above it. Edna was swell, a grandma at the lumberyard. I watched her walk out to her Corvair, a pale green affair on little tires.

When Edna pulled away I picked up the phone. The black receiver felt heavy and oily in my hand and smelled of Edna's rose lipstick. After a moment of silence, the operator came on. "Number please?"

"One-three-six-six."

"One moment please." After a series of clicks came, "Hello?" It was Mrs. Kersher. I was thankful it wasn't Marcy's father, a gruff bear of a man who ran a barber shop. Fred Kersher scared me. I imagined him amputating my lips with his scissors if he knew I had kissed his daughter. For once I was thankful that Mom cut my hair, even when she trimmed my bangs to make me look like Pat Boone. She played his records all the time.

"Mrs. Kersher, is Marcy home?"

"Oh, it's you, Paul. Just a minute." Her voice sounded far away. I pressed the receiver tighter to my ear as boards clattered in the warehouse behind the office.

"Hello, Paul?"

"Hi Marcy, it's me."

"Are you working?"

"Sort of, I guess. I mean, Dad put me in the office today."

"So Edna went home and you're playing with the phone?" That Marcy, she was a sharp one.

"Marcy, I've got an idea."

"Is it a lawful one?" She sure knew how to lay it on a guy.

"Look. Would you like to ride to the sawmill with me?"

///// 

Talking Dad into letting me drive his pickup took some doing. I waited until he and Toby were working full tilt in the yard before I politely observed that he was running low on rough-cut timbers. "I'm not helping by sitting around," I told him. "Let me take the pickup up to Hack Face O'Hanlon's for a load?"

His expression told me no, but he reconsidered. "I guess you done it once." He reached in his pocket for the keys.

"You get another flat, it's your business. Can't expect somebody to come driving past every time. And lock up the cash register before you go." When Dad was busy at work he talked harsher than he did at home. Nervous, maybe. *Pushed like a man trying to work beyond himself.* I worried about him but that lumberyard was his domain. Nobody, not even Mom or Toby, tried to tell him how to run his business. Dad swiped his shirtsleeve over his forehead. "You be careful, boy. We gotta get you a license someday." I figured in two years, when I turned fifteen.

I didn't wait too long in the pickup before Marcy arrived and parked her bicycle in the shade behind the warehouse. It all seemed too perfect. I had wheels and a girl. She opened the passenger door and climbed into the front seat, frowning at the layer of dust on the faded black vinyl. She looked at me with eyes full of fear. "If my parents find out they'll kill me," she said right away. "I was worried my mom would overhear this stupid plan of yours."

At first that sounded like a harsh assessment but I had to admit I would suffer the same fate if Dad saw me driving off with Marcy. I eased the clutch out, more skillfully than before, and we rattled off. Through the train yards we went, then over the Clark Fork to the sawmill road. When we passed the clearing at the river where the fight took place, I took a long look, hoping Marcy would notice. Instead she stared straight ahead.

"Paul, why are we going up here?"

"To get a load of lumber for my dad."

"And he said I could go along?"

"He didn't say one way or the other."

"Then you didn't ask him, did you?"

I changed the subject. "I'm hoping to see somebody up here."

"This Hack Face O'Hanlon man? He sounds scary, Paul. I'm staying in the truck."

"He's all right. Just don't call him Hack Face to his face. It's his nephew."

"What about his nephew?"

"He drives the black Chevy."

Marcy glared at me, those deep green eyes wide with surprise. "What's he doing up here?"

"I think he lives up here."

"Stop right now, Paul." I knew from her hard look that I had better not mess around. Dust on the gravel road curled around us when I braked the old Ford to a stop. The dust tasted sweet on the tongue, then gritty. Marcy threw the door open and stomped down the road toward Deer Lodge. I honked the horn but she ignored me. "Just great," I said to myself, my date to the sawmill ruined.

I watched Marcy in the mirror, hoping she'd come back. She walked about fifty feet. Then she stopped, her shoulders heaving. She was crying. I shut off the motor and walked back to her. I didn't know what to say. I'd never had a girl bawling on me before.

"Marcy, what's the matter?" She sure was blubbering a lot. I'd never seen her like this.

She wiped her eyes with the back of her hand. "What is it with you getting mixed up with these people who go around fighting and chasing people?" She wiped some more. "And pulling me into the middle of it?"

"I just want to see," I told her, feeling lame.

"Why did you invite me along then?"

"Because I wanted you to ride with me."

She shot me a quick glance. "At least you can sound sincere about it."

"I wouldn't risk getting in trouble if I wasn't."

"You could have come over to my house instead."

"I wanted you to see Louie because I'm, well, mixed up."

"What about?

"I don't know if I should be thanking him or running from him."

Marcy got that brainy look like she did in school. "You've got reason for both. If we go up here you think you'll find an answer?"

"Hoping so."

"And then we'll go home?"

"Promise."

"Truth?"

"Truth. Hey, you want to sit beside me?" Marcy scooted into the pickup like we were on a real date. The high school kids down on Main Street cruised the drag from the fairgrounds at the north end of town clear down past the prison to the old rest home and then turned around again. It didn't matter much to me that we were driving Dad's old Ford to see Hack Face O'Hanlon and his wild nephew. All of a sudden Marcy didn't seem to care either. I didn't really understand why Marcy made such a fuss. Girls are funny that way. She sat close with her knees on either side of the floor shift. I kept my hand on the knob between gears, holding it there just inches from her bare legs. Blue and Max would never believe this.

When we rolled up to the mill, Hack Face O'Hanlon waved a greeting from inside a cloud of wood chips while the saw wailed its way through a log. By the time I pulled over he had cut the power. "Oh my," Marcy whispered, watching him walk our way. Sawdust powdered his face except for sweat trickling from his eyes. Hack Face looked like a crying clown.

"Hey boy!" Marcy jumped when Hack Face pounded a meaty hand on the hood. "Got yourself a sweet little gal there?" He leaned in the window to get a better look. Marcy shrunk behind me when I introduced her to Mr. O'Hanlon, but he quickly turned his attention to my bruised face. "Hell, boy, looks like you tangled with a mean old dog." He looked hard at me, the swollen scar arching between his eyes before he smiled through random teeth to show his approval. "Drivin', fightin' and cattin'. Hell, boy, you'll be like my nephew someday."

"Is he—?"

"So your old man's aching for some of my cut-up logs, is that it?" He eased his shaggy head out of the cab, leaving a tornado of whiskey breath behind him. He turned toward the shack and boomed. "Louie! Get your sorry ass out here and help these here kids. I got cuttin' to do." With that he pounded the pickup again, yelled goodbye, and fired up the saw. Marcy gripped my arm. "Is it safe up here, Paul? That man scares me. What if he tells your dad that I came along with you?"

I hadn't considered that. "Go easy. He won't do anything bad." I stepped out of the pickup. Marcy hesitated before following me. She looked around, her pretty eyes appraising the scene around her. That was Marcy for you. She was too darn curious. "I didn't know this was up here. Paul, you never tell me anything."

"I—."

"And look down there. Deer Lodge looks tiny in that big valley." To kids like us, the town seemed big until we got outside of it. Quilts of farms and ranches stretched south all the way to Anaconda where the smelter smokestack loomed. We could see that far from Hack Face's sawmill even though it took half an hour of highway driving to get to Anaconda from Deer Lodge. Mom took us over there every August to buy new leather shoes for school. The female clerks, pencils stuck in their beehive hairdos and cat eye eyeglasses hanging from cords around their necks, called me Honey. They reminded me of Edna.

"Well, look here," came a voice from behind us. "You're gettin' to be a habit, Ace."

There stood Louie. Sure enough, he looked like Elvis Presley. Not the Elvis we saw singing and kissing and driving convertibles in movies down at the Rialto. Louie looked like the earlier Elvis when he was younger and wilder, his collar turned up and his hair greased back and a sneer planted on his face, like he was informing everyone around him that he was The King. Marcy shuffled near me, her eyes locked on Louie's chiseled face, and for a moment I felt a pang of jealousy. I had to admit he was loaded with cool looks. He acted like he didn't have a care in the world, and Marcy knew it.

Louie wore a faded red shirt with the sleeves torn off at the shoulders but the collar turned up. His overalls were rolled up at least six inches above his black boots. A chain of some sort hung from his pocket. I doubted if Louie had taken a single punch from the Tucker brothers. I didn't see a mark on his face.

"I hear you pounded those Tuckers to a pulp." I had to know.

He looked pleased. "Kicked those sorry Tucker asses into tomorrow, or so I'm told. Didn't stay around to nursemaid them fat boys. And look 'atcha with them bruises." Louie studied my face. "You get a lick in, Ace?"

"I tried. I think so. The big one threw me and then another one hit me good."

Louie shifted his attention to Marcy. "Who's the doll?"

"This is Marcy, my girlfriend." I might have put a bit too much emphasis on that last point, but he got my drift.

"I never mess around with a man who fights for his girl, Ace. Shame, she's a pretty thing." Marcy blushed. "Thank you," she said.

I saw my chance. "Say … Louie?"

"Yeah?"

"I want to thank you for what you did. Pounding those Tuckers and all. If you hadn't come —."

Louie waved a hand to stop me. "You three adolescents would have beat those fat boys into beggin' for a diaper change. Hell, you had them boys whimperin' by the time I showed up." Tommy Tucker wasn't around to tell it different. Blue and Max and I wondered where those Tuckers had gone and whether they'd slip back into town and jump on us someday. Dad said no, those boys were long gone and could expect serious trouble if they ever came back. I don't know what he meant by that, but it suited me just fine if they stayed away for good.

"So —?"

"No thanks necessary. Let's say you owe me one. Make that two considerin' the flat tire I changed." *If he remembers that I stole his car, I thought, he'll want a lot more than that.* Louie hoisted three beams all at once from the woodpile. He had the same rugged build as Hack Face but a smaller, more refined version. Years and hard drinking had overtaken Hack Face. Louie was slim and fibered like tough rope. His muscles rippled when he shoveled the timbers over the tailgate into the bed of the pickup.

"This what you wanted, Ace?"

"As many as will fit is what my dad wants."

"You gonna stand there modelin' for your girlfriend all day or show her how a man works?" He winked at Marcy. I leaned into the stack, grabbing one of the timbers. It felt slippery with sap. Dad said that Hack Face had no method of drying them, like the big mills in Missoula and Columbia Falls did, but that didn't matter anyway. Farmers and ranchers didn't care if the timbers cracked and twisted as they seasoned. They just wanted sturdy wood to frame barns and other outbuildings. The fir and pine that Hack Face cut managed to do that just fine.

"So what name you go by did you say?"

"Paul."

"Gotta last name?"

"Morrison."

"That's right, think I heard that when I gave you a lift after the fight."

"I don't remember any of that. The driving, I mean. I guess I don't remember much of the fight either."

"You didn't look none too good. Your buddy, the big kid with the curly blond hair, he was the only one who knew which was way up. I put you and that other boxer with the smashed nose in the back seat."

Marcy came to the back of the truck, getting a little too close while we were lifting heavy things. My mom did that in the barn, riling Dad when he had his arms full. "Excuse me, Mister—."

"Damn, girl, I ain't no mister. Maybe five years older, you figure?"

"Well, I—."

"Call me Louie."

"Louie, sir—."

"Just Louie. I ain't no sir either."

"Well, Louie, can I look at your car?" Marcy pointed to the black Chevy parked near the shack.

"How do you know it's mine?" He looked right at her. *Did he suspect something?* Then, "Go ahead and take a look. Don't be drivin' off with it."

I shot Louie a sideways glance but he acted like he didn't mean anything by that. Marcy ambled off while Louie and I finished loading. I wanted to go look at the car myself and wondered what Marcy was doing.

"Do you live up here?" I asked Louie.

"Do now. Over in Butte sometimes too. Long story."

"You go to high school?"

"Used to. Another long story."

"When did you come here?"

"Ace, you writin' my life history?"

"I wondered, that's all. You don't say much."

"What's your girlfriend want with my car?"

"Beats me."

"Fifty-five Chevy Bel Air with a V-eight that breathes fire if you wanna know. One of the best cars ever made. If she was a woman I'd marry her." Louie turned to admire his car or Marcy, I wasn't sure which. She looked great in shorts.

"It looks new," I told him.

"I take care of it."

"How did you get it?"

"Another long story."

Louie still scared me. Something about him felt like an older brother even if I didn't have a real one to compare. "You ever let anyone drive it?" I blurted out, regretting my carelessness.

"Never. Some damn punk stole it one time. Goin' to be lights out when I find him." Louie slammed the last timber into Dad's pickup for emphasis. "Worst thing any cat could do, rippin' off my car."

I wanted to climb into the cab and get away, but Marcy was ogling the Chevy, looking in the open driver's window. "Got something for you," Louie told me. He walked toward the car, his boots clunking on the hard clay where Hack Face dragged logs around. I followed, figuring he was going to pound me behind the shack. Worse yet, he'd beat me up in front of Marcy. No boy wanted to get pounded in front of his girlfriend. What would she tell the other girls at school? What would I tell my parents when I came home with another bloody face and my pair of new glasses smashed? Louie opened the door of the Chevy to let Marcy slip behind the wheel. She looked good. He even let her turn the key to fire it up. The motor rumbled just like the night of the dance. He let her rev it a few times. Such incredible power. Dad's pickup wheezed along but Louie's car was built for the open road. Then Louie reached into the Chevy to turn off the ignition. To my great relief Marcy slid out. I took her hand and hurried her back to the pickup, telling Louie my dad was waiting.

I hadn't even started the motor before he was beside me at the window. *Here it is, I reckon, the beating I knew would come. The fear that kept me awake at night. Is this why I came up here?*

Louie handed me a brown loafer, the one I had lost running from him the night of the dance. He leaned close, his eyes dark and full of daggers. "I know it was you, Ace."

# Kenny

*I popped the clutch* on Dad's pickup and beat it off that mountain as Marcy grabbed the dashboard to stay upright. Louie disappeared in the rearview mirror. I was pretty sure that now, finally, he would pound me and it would be over. I just wanted him to do it and then I wouldn't have to worry anymore. I wasn't a thief and well, I felt sorry for him. I can't tell you why. It was a feeling I got about people like when Max didn't get anything for Christmas one year. He didn't come right out and say so and I didn't need to ask. It was the first Christmas after his brother Kenny died in that car wreck. Mr. and Mrs. Jorgenson didn't put up a tree or decorations. Blue and I got transistor radios. Mine was red, with a big dial on top, and Blue got a black one in a leather case. We hid them from Max, feeling guilty, until we saved enough money to buy him a radio. It was just like Blue's. Max went around with that radio pressed to his ear but the sadness never left his face. I knew it wasn't as much about Christmas as about his brother. Louie looked like that right now. Something was hurting him more than losing his Chevy to a seventh grader on a Friday night.

/////

Just my luck that Dad walked around the corner of the warehouse, lighting a smoke, as I drove up with Marcy cuddling against me. Dad started to tell me that the lumber I had loaded in the pickup goes inside, which of course I knew, until he saw Marcy. Then his eyes moved to her bike parked in the grass. I won't belabor the scene that followed except to say that it was no less humiliating than what happened at Hack Face Heaven. Louie might have punched me or thrown me into the log saw or pulled down my pants in front of Marcy. She tried to joke around on the ride down the mountain by telling me it wasn't a bad deal to get pounded if I brought her along, a sudden newfound interest in the sawmill that I was beginning to regret, but Dad put an end to my driving privileges when he caught us in his pickup. I was careless, I admit. I should have let Marcy out a few blocks away. Honestly, I didn't care. I liked Marcy and liked to drive and Louie left my face alone. Life was good.

"What the hell?" was Dad's first reaction. He nearly dropped his cigarette. I cut the motor. Dad sauntered over, trying to look calm, but his stormy expression told me something different. I handed him the key chain with the rabbit's foot dangling from it. "Paul, did you take Marcy to the mill?" I nodded but he already knew the answer. "Marcy, you'd better head home. Tell your folks what you did this afternoon."

"Yes sir, Mr. Morrison." Marcy shot from the cab without a goodbye and pedaled off on her bike, leaving me to face the music. Dad didn't say much on the drive home that day. Of course he couldn't tell Mom that he let me drive. Instead he gave her a big story about how I was having trouble following directions at the lumberyard. He let me have it in the barn after work, yelling a lot and asking all kinds of dumb questions about why I took Marcy along. Then he grounded me for the rest of the weekend. I think he wanted to inflict more punishment but he had to admit that I came back with the lumber as he expected. I knew it was wrong to take Marcy. Being grounded meant not going to church on Sunday. That wasn't so bad. After everyone left the house I switched on the television in hopes of seeing the Twins play baseball. The only signal we got was from KXLF in Butte. Reception was fuzzy. I turned the vertical hold to stop the picture from bouncing but I didn't find the Twins and shut it off. When my parents and Sally got home I wandered out to the back yard to do nothing in particular. It was a hot day, filled with the promise of summer. I didn't want to stay inside. I'll bet I was the only boy in Deer Lodge grounded on a sun-drenched day with baseball starting at Jaycee Park in the morning. At least Dad didn't ruin that. Blue and Max rode their bikes past my house a couple of times with their baseball mitts looped over the handlebars, looking wistfully toward the backyard and hoping for a game of catch. I waved them away from the shade of our big cottonwood tree. Yes, I had done stupid things. Was that what it meant to grow up? If Dad's plan was to get me to thinking, it worked. I thought a lot about Dad and Louie while I sat out there, tossing my baseball. They could have done worse to me, both of them.

///////

I caught the score that night on the late news from Butte. The Twins whipped the Washington Senators 11-2 in Minneapolis with Dave Boswell on the mound. Twins slugger Harmon Killebrew was hurt but the team kept winning anyway. I missed spending summer evenings on my grandparents' screened porch in North Dakota where Grandpa and I would listen to the entire game on his electric radio. He wrote me in a letter that he thought the Twins might go all the way this year. We wouldn't be going to North Dakota, not this summer. Dad said that because the spring rain slowed down his business at the lumberyard we wouldn't take a vacation. I looked for box scores in the newspaper but it wasn't the same as hearing Herb Carneal's brisk play-by-play broadcasting from Metropolitan Stadium. I could see Tony Oliva at the plate, launching a home run into the cheap seats. Dad took me once to see the Twins play. It was a hot afternoon when the sun baked us red into ripe tomatoes. We sat a few dozen rows above third base. All the people in Deer Lodge would have fit in that stadium about four or five times over, Dad said. Our ball fields at Jaycee Park didn't have bleachers. Parents sat in their cars, honking their horns when someone hit the ball.

A thunderhead black with cold rain edged over Mount Powell when Blue and Max and I went to the outfield to catch fly balls at our first Babe Ruth practice. We wore our new caps. Blue decided to take a minute to pass judgment on the Little Leaguers practicing at the other end of the park. He dropped his glove long enough to imitate the younger boys swinging and missing. "Look at those little kids try to hit the ball. We weren't that puny—." A baseball whizzed past his head.

"Unless you guys want to join them over there you'd better pay attention," yelled Coach Harneke from home plate, his meaty hands swinging a bat like it was kindling wood.

"I don't think Coach tried to hit you," I assured Blue.

Max backed up, snagging a soaring baseball that fell into his mitt with a smack. "Then again, maybe he did," Max shouted. You can't tell about Blue. It took a lot to get him down. He felt a little sore about the coach but shook it off.

We played baseball all afternoon. I didn't think about Louie once, I swear. Being a boy felt good. So did playing baseball in the green grass without a care. Balls came screaming out of the sky again and again. When Coach Harneke tired of that he positioned us in the infield to practice catching ground balls. Blue got second and Max got third. Paul Wagner and I had to wait on the sidelines until somebody got tired. Sure enough, when Billy McGuire got smacked in the face with a baseball and cried like a baby, Coach sent me to cover first base. This was something new. Usually I was sent into the outfield where I couldn't do much damage. The clover grew ankle deep out there. It was easy to forget the ballgame while bumblebees flitted around my tennis shoes.

"Look sharp at first!" our coach bawled. He ripped a hot grounder my way. It came whipping like it had a mind of its own. I dropped to my knees and felt it slam into my bare hand. Coach laughed. "Try using your glove next time, Morrison!" At least I caught the ball but I wasn't so lucky with the next grounder. It jumped over my glove and hit me right between the legs. I fell. Blue stood over me, laughing, while I fought not to cry. "You're not allowed to stop the ball with your pecker either, buckaroo. It's the glove you're supposed to catch with."

Coach Harneke shooed the boys away. I think he understood how bad it hurt. Maybe it happened to him a few times when he was a kid. When he got me standing the sharp pain was gone but I felt sick. "If you gotta puke don't do it on the field, son." He helped me walk over to the faucet for a drink just as large raindrops fell. Coach tipped his blue cap and squinted toward the sky, now gray with swollen clouds. "Okay, boys, that's all for today. We've got rain and maybe lightning. Everybody head for home." With one side of his shirt hanging untucked from his trousers, he waved us toward our bicycles. We hadn't pedaled a block down the road toward home when the clouds let loose. We stood on our pedals to pump faster. "Better not slip," Blue advised. I turned to him, unsure what he meant. "If you think you were hurting before?" I got his drift and got off my bike. Blue and Max shot ahead into a silver curtain of rain. Going home soaked was one thing. Losing my manhood was another. I might need it someday.

### /////

When I parked my bike in the barn, out past the last house on the outskirts of town, there was Dad, counting coins at his workbench. It was early for him to leave the lumberyard. "Hello, son. What's the matter, get rained out?" My clothes stuck to my skin but Dad didn't say a word about that. A light bulb hanging on a cord swung lazily in the breeze from an open window beside him, casting a roving pool of light in the gloom.

"Why are you home so early, Dad?"

"Toby's got things under control down there. I figure, why not?" A neat stack of half dollars sat on the bench in front of him beside another stack of quarters. Dad ran his fingers through piles of dimes and nickels. "Know what I've got here, son?"

"Money?" I didn't mean to sound sarcastic. It's just that he was getting at something but I wasn't sure what.

"More than that, son. This here's a boat with a new Evinrude motor." He turned to me, still oblivious to the water dripping from clothes. "Now your mother doesn't know this, so it's a secret just between you and me, okay? I've been saving money for a long time to buy us this boat we can take up to Rock Creek Lake and maybe over to Georgetown Lake or up to Salmon Lake. Do a little fishing or water skiing or just go for rides, see? Now the thing is, this money's coming from the work I do right here in the barn. I fix a lawnmower engine, that's three or four bucks and the money goes in the coffee can. I build a shelf for somebody and that's a couple bucks more. You see what I'm doing?"

"Sure, you're saving up like I did when I wanted to buy a new camping packsack for Boy Scouts."

"Yeah, like that." Dad straightened on the old yellow stool. His eyes looked beyond me at something I couldn't see. "You see, son, I've always had this dream that I wanted my family to have a boat, a red and white one, with a windshield and lights and life jackets for everybody. We'd need a trailer, too."

"What's an Evinrude?"

"One of the best boat motors ever made, son. I know people who swear by them. We might go as big as a forty-horse. Now wouldn't that be a kick in the pants?" He sounded more like he was making a statement than asking a question. I didn't know much about horsepower but forty sounded big. Real big. Dad sighed. "We've got a ways to go, son. I'm thinking another year or two, tops."

"How much do you have?"

"Three, four hundred dollars, I reckon. I've been saving for a long time. A boat's gonna cost a lot more than that. I can tell you this, though." He stopped to light a cigarette, one of the handmade ones he rolled from a little red metal box on his workbench where he kept tobacco and papers. "Nobody ever saved a dime without saving a penny, saved a dollar without saving a quarter first, get my drift?"

"You mean if you save now you'll have more later?"

"Smart boy. There's good reason you got promoted to the eighth grade. No flunking kids in the Morrison family."

"Dad?"

He didn't answer right away, still dreaming. "Yeah?"

"Why don't you save some money from the lumberyard? Wouldn't that be faster?" I wanted to believe my father was a rich man. Our humble home told me otherwise. The old farmhouse leaked rain and it needed paint.

"Because that wouldn't be right." He sounded a bit like the gruffer man I knew at the lumberyard. "See, son, anything I earn goes to your mother to pay the bills, buy groceries, keep you and Sally in clothes. I've gotta pay Toby and Edna and sell lumber to pay for what I buy and hope we have extra money and some months we don't. It wouldn't be right to buy a boat with that money. But this money that I earn" — he waved his hand over the coins before him — "this money is extra, just like the boat."

"That's a lot of money, Dad."

He looked at me with a wide grin. "What you see here is part of a lot. I've got more coffee cans full in hiding places nobody will find. Someday we'll have empty cans and a new boat. Won't that be something?"

"And an Evinrude?"

I watched my father's face. For a moment, the haggard features were gone. He was a boy again, sharing his fondest dream. I hugged him.

When he felt my dripping clothes he pulled back for a full look. "How did you get so wet, Paul?"

///// 

After baseball practice on Friday, ending with Coach Harneke's feeble declaration that he considered us fit to play our first real game, Blue and his parents embarked for Billings to see his grandmother. Blue didn't mind the trip but he wasn't too hot about spending the weekend in a house full of doilies and knickknacks. Grandma Alice liked to keep her shades drawn during the day to deprive sunlight of its conspiracy to fade her furniture covers. "You don't know what you're missing," Blue told me once. "You walk around the house like a blind man, trying not to bump into teacups or slip on rugs she's got everywhere so the linoleum won't get dirty. She opens the shades for about an hour in the evening until the sun goes down and then closes them again before the Peeping Toms come around."

Blue got me to laughing about the time he confused a doily for a napkin after he ate a chocolate cupcake with extra frosting at Grandma Alice's house. I figured Blue did that on purpose given that he wasn't much for doilies draped over everything. "The thing about those shades is, if you saw the furniture in the daylight you'd want to pull the shades down yourself. She's got big old pink flowers on everything. It's a flower festival for old ladies in there." Blue's house wasn't like that at all. Mrs. Taylor said her mother was different from the rest of us and wasn't that way when she was younger. She used a word to describe her mother that we didn't understand. "Eccentric means, like I said, different," Mrs. Taylor said. That was that. Blue took to using the word all the time. The Taylors intended to drive clear to Billings and back in a single weekend. While Mr. Taylor loaded suitcases in the trunk, Blue flashed a smile and grabbed the bill of my cap and pulled it over my eyes. "Don't be eccentric while I'm gone."

Max had to work all weekend helping his dad clean out their garage. This I discovered when, after seeing Blue shove off for Billings, I found Max walking into his yard carrying a drive shaft wet with grease at either end. No wonder he'd skipped baseball practice that afternoon. Mr. Jorgenson had this wise idea to move everything out of the garage into the yard, sweep the garage floor, and move it all back again. I didn't see the point in that. Max said his parents had a big fight over the bill for his brother's funeral. It was sitting in a drawer, paid off, but his mother came across it and sat at the kitchen table and cried and yelled at his father. Max jumped on his bike and rode down to the creek. When he got home an hour later he found his father engaged in his ambitious plan to organize the garage, which involved moving car parts of every description. "Roll uppa yer sleeves, boy, we gotta work to do." Max didn't argue. The last thing he wanted to witness was his mother sobbing in Kenny's bedroom.

The room was just like always, Max said, with Kenny's felt pennants from the 1962 World's Fair in Seattle still pinned to the wall. It was the biggest trip the Jorgensons ever took because Kenny wanted to see the Space Needle and got them organized and on the road. That was Kenny, a born leader. Kenny's clothes, even his gold and white Wardens letter jacket, hung in the closet where he had left them. He had lettered in football, basketball and track since his freshman year. A shoe brush, still black with polish, lay on the dresser from the night of the crash. I crept into Kenny's bedroom once with Max. We looked around for a minute and left. The door creaked closed. It was creepy in there, smelling stale and dead.

With Blue gone to Billings and Max committed to helping his Dad grieve, I went home and moped. I thought about calling Marcy. She was probably in trouble anyway for going to the sawmill with me. I'd bet Marcy did just what my Dad told her to do. She went home and confessed. Maybe I didn't feel like calling her, or maybe I was afraid that Mr. Kersher would answer the phone and threaten to tear off my head. I couldn't decide which.

Sally went with Mom to a Girl Scouts meeting after dinner. It was a beautiful evening. Robins chirped and slants of golden light fell across our backyard. The screen door banged shut a couple of times after Sally came home and ran in and out of the house with her friends. Dad helped clear the table before heading out to his workbench to fix lawnmowers or count coins, I wasn't sure which. Sometimes he didn't say much. We all recognized when he wanted time alone. I went into my bedroom to play records. I had a small stack of forty-fives I'd bought with my allowance at the Safeway store. My favorite was a Beatles record. "Please Please Me" played on one side and "From Me to You" on the other. I popped it on my little record player and settled back on my bed to listen. After a while I realized I was looking at my three school shirts hanging in the closet and thought of Kenny, a big-boned boy who made all-conference tackle on the football team. Max and

Blue and I all loved Kenny. He had known everything about everything. I'll never forget the morning after Kenny died. Max came to our house, his eyes brimming with tears. My mother hugged him and cried while Dad bowed his head. I didn't know what to say. It didn't seem real. They don't teach you about death in school. *One of your two best friends and you don't know how to console him.*

When shadows washed over my bedroom walls I felt uneasy. The house was quiet. I saw Sally in the old farmyard. Her red pigtails bounced as she went back and forth like a pendulum on the swing set with her friends. Suddenly I felt like calling Marcy. After the operator connected my call, I fidgeted with the telephone cord. "Hello? Kersher residence," came Marcy's voice.

"Boy, I'm glad you answered. Are you grounded?"

"Paul! I thought you were locked up for good."

"That's what I figured happened to you. In jail maybe."

Marcy hesitated. "They don't know about it."

"What? But my dad —."

"I know he said to tell them. But it's not like we did anything bad or anything."

"Geez, Marcy. I figured you went home and blabbed all about it and your dad sent you down to the prison for a couple of years."

"You've got such an imagination, Paul. You're just such a — boy!"

"Maybe working on a chain gang."

"It's not like we did anything bad, Paul. My parents didn't tell me not to go. They just didn't know."

This didn't sound like Marcy at all. Not the same girl who was crying on the road to the sawmill. "So you want to go again?"

"Maybe." She sounded tentative. "Paul? I wouldn't be telling you this except that my parents went to the grocery store. I know sneaking around is wrong."

"But —."

"Paul? Let's go for a walk." Half an hour later we met on the grounds of the elementary school where she sat on the handlebars of the merry-go-round and I started it spinning. We got it going fast enough that everything was a blur except for Marcy's face. A trail of motion reflected from her deep green eyes as we went around.

"Paul, we're going together, right?"

"That's what I thought."

"Do you think we'll go steady when we're in high school? Cruise the drag so I can sit next to you like we did in your dad's pickup? Maybe I'll be a cheerleader and you'll be a basketball star."

"Like Toby." *Plowing points like nobody's business through the hoop in a hot noisy gymnasium. Snow outside so cold it squeaked.*

"Who's Toby?" I shook my head at her. Someday I'd tell Marcy about Toby's accomplishments in what the local sportswriter called the Cottonwood Palace, but not now. And then from her, "Well, will we?"

"Go steady? Sure. I mean, I hope so."

"You hope so? Aren't you sure?"

"Shouldn't I get a job so I can pay for our dates?"

"You already have a job at your father's lumberyard."

"I know, but a job that pays me money. Dad says that I'm working to help the family. He does give me a few dollars sometimes."

"Enough to take me to a movie, Paul?" Marcy's hair fluttered a bit, like a flag lifting and falling on a gentle breeze. She could see that she embarrassed me. "I didn't mean you had to."

"Sure, we can go. I save some of it."

"Then why don't you ask me to go?" It was a logical question. Here I was, so caught up with stealing cars and fighting bullies and being grounded that I'd forgotten to ask Marcy on a real date.

"We could hold hands," she added as a clincher.

"Sounds like you're asking me."

"I don't know what difference it makes, Paul. We wouldn't be sitting here talking about it if you hadn't asked me to dance over there that night." Marcy pointed to the gymnasium across the lawn, as if I needed reminding. As we spun around on the merry-go-round she chatted away and pointed everywhere at once, like drawing a pencil across the sky. I closed my eyes for a moment, picturing us together in the cool interior of the Rialto that smelled of hot buttered popcorn and musty maroon velvet curtains draped everywhere.

"And Paul? What about high school?"

"What about it?

"You've forgotten already? Will you go steady with me in high school or not?"

"Of course I will." Even if high school came after eighth grade, it was a distant journey from this summer evening on the playground. A year was eternity.

*/////*

Dad was scrubbing his hands at the kitchen sink when I got home. Flecks of black suds fell into the running water. "Call your sister home, will you?" He frowned, intent on working the last remnants of grease and sawdust from beneath his fingernails. I went outside and called for Sally. She came home regretfully, swinging her arms and taking all night about it. "Why do I have to come in, Paul?" She cast a longing glance at two girls and a boy sitting in the field across the road, talking about whatever little kids do. The boy, who looked about eight years old, tossed an orange and green beach ball into the air.

"Because Dad said. Besides, the sun's going down."

"But the other kids —."

"You're lucky Mom isn't home yet or you'd be in bed already. Now hurry up!" I sounded more impatient than I was but I didn't want Sally to get into trouble. She was a swell kid when she wasn't telling on me. We came inside to find Dad leaning against the counter, holding his glasses in one hand and, with the other, wiping his forehead with a dishtowel. The evening was cool but he was sweating.

"You know —." He paused like he was trying to think something through. "Paul, I've been thinking." He paused again to catch his breath. "I'd like to meet your friend Louie. Let's do it tomorrow."

# Dad

*We worked all Saturday morning* at the lumberyard. Dad had me busy stacking boards in the warehouse. I figured I'd have biceps like Charles Atlas. I saw him flexing his muscles in an advertisement in an old magazine. You could send away for some secret exercises guaranteed to make your muscles as coiled as dock rope for just a few dollars a month. When Toby came along I flexed my arms to show off the fruit of my labors, but he shook his head. "You've got to eat, boy. Put away more at the dinner table and you might see a bulge now and then." He smiled and walked away. "Maybe you ought to try boxing lessons instead," he yelled my way, laughing his head off. That Toby was a hoot.

When lunch hour came Dad and I sat in the office, eating roast beef sandwiches Mom had made. He drank coffee with his. I poured milk out of a thermos. The arrangement was that Edna went home for lunch while we ate. Toby watched over the warehouse. "So this Louie Moretti, you say he's up living with Hack Face?"

"That's what it looks like, Dad."

"And Hack Face is Louie's uncle?"

"That's what he said."

Dad's eyes narrowed. He did that when he tried to figure something out. "I don't recollect that Hack Face had family. Every time I've been up there he's been alone." He stopped to take a bite. Mom's cooking was the best ever. "Hell, I've been going for years."

"I saw him at the shack with the black Chevy."

With that, Dad perked up, then nodded his head. "Could be then. Old Hack Face isn't one to go around telling his life's history. Came over from Butte a long time ago, worked in the mines is all I know, likes his liquor. Treats me square. I do the same for him. Ain't no need to be nosy."

"Why do you want to see Louie then?" I couldn't understand Dad sometimes. Lately I didn't understand a lot of things.

Dad set his coffee mug down on the desk. "Well, son, he's a bit of a hell-raiser, I can see that. He did you a good turn when the tire on the pickup went flat. What about those damn Tuckers? He didn't drive right on by like most people. If he didn't come by when he did —." Dad's voice trailed off. "Someday you'll be old enough to understand what happened there. How it could have been bad, worse."

"So you want to tell Louie —."

"I want to meet him man to man, measure him up, tell him thanks. Soon as Toby finishes his lunch, you and me, we're going up there."

When Dad hung up his shop apron a bit after two o'clock that afternoon, Edna pretended she was flabbergasted and put on a teasing face. "Now Frank, don't you get into any trouble. These Saturday nights in Deer Lodge are bad enough without you kicking up your heels in the bars with those pretty cowgirls."

Dad smiled. "Edna, have you ever —."

"Paul, I'm just teasing your dad," she interrupted him. "I wouldn't want you to get the wrong idea."

"Yes, ma'am."

Edna shuffled some papers on the desk. I saw her glance with some disgust at the coffee stain Dad had left there. "Frank Morrison, I don't know that in fifteen years I ever saw you leave the yard on a Saturday afternoon much before five. But you know, honey, take a hint from old Edna. You're looking dog tired these days. Get yourself some rest."

Dad smiled again. He wouldn't take that advice from anyone else, not Toby and not even Mom, but Edna had logged enough mileage in her life that Dad respected her for it. He was fond of saying that you never turn your back on someone who is older than you because they've seen life inside out.

Dad jumped behind the wheel of the pickup without offering to let me drive. At first I thought he was still sore about my dalliance with Marcy. Then I could see that he had something on his mind. "Dad?" He turned his pale face to me as shoved the transmission in reverse. "Are you sick or mad or something?"

"Of course not, son. Just a little tired is all, like Edna said."

"You look tired a lot, Dad. You should go to the doctor."

"It's nothing, Paul." His tone of voice sounded final, so I dropped it. He pulled across the street to Red's Bar. "Wait here," he instructed. Men talked in loud voices through the open door. I could see four or five of them, their caps tipped back, sitting on tall stools. Dad came back with a case of beer under his arm. "Great Falls Select," it said on the carton. "For Hack Face," he explained. We bumped over the railroad tracks and up the sawmill road, which started in a grove of aspens near the river and then wound its way onto a treeless plateau. We chugged toward the great mountain while banks of cumulus clouds raced across the sky. After a few miles we were high above the valley. I thought of Marcy.

"Hear that?" Dad asked me. The sawmill was making a terrible racket like something was broken. It was good Hack Face did his work on the mountain. Any closer to Deer Lodge and we'd all be deaf. When we crested the hill I could see at first glance that the black Chevy was gone. "Just our luck," Dad complained, but he wasn't exactly mad about it. I think he felt good being away from work. He liked Hack Face, too. They were much different men. Dad was slim and balding, never prone to bragging and overstatement. Hack Face had the arms of a lumberjack and the demeanor to boot. I never heard Dad swear much, and never in the house, but Hack Face threw around coarse profanity that left me wondering about sex. Some of it had to do with women's bodies. Dad told me to pay no attention and if I ever heard a word I'd be uncomfortable saying in front of my parents, don't repeat it to anyone. Dad was full of advice like that.

Blue smoke pitched from the sawmill contraption. Hack Face, covered head to toe in grease, raged in the midst of it. He shut down the crashing drive engine when he saw us. "Damned sucking thing!" He kicked the strange contraption with his big boot. "Top of the afternoon to you, Frank! Brought the lad I see."

"Good to see you, Jimmy." I was stunned. That's the first time I knew that Hack Face O'Hanlon had a first name, I swear. "What's the smoke about?"

"She's got friction like a Butte whore's hind end on a Saturday night. I can't keep enough grease on it." Dad stepped out of the cab, wincing at the description but leaving me to think on it.

"You got a bearing out, Jimmy?"

"Could be, like metal to metal, no lube at all, burning like a miner's tool —."

"My boy, Jimmy."

"That kid of yours, hell, boy's got balls. Come up here with a cute little gal. I didn't see no kissy-face though." He sounded disappointed.

"I know about that," Dad told him in a tone intended to cut him off. "Say, Jimmy, you got a nephew by the name of Louie?" I was sitting in the pickup, listening to every word. I wanted to get out and look the place over, but I didn't want to miss hearing about Louie.

"Sure, damn punk kid but what do I know? Aw, he's not so bad. Just gets a wild hair now and then. Ever since he lost his parents he's been doing what he damn well pleases like a grown man. Can't complain," Hack Face concluded, his voice softening. "Kid's a worker, helps me out up here when he's not staying with his sister and her man in Butte."

"What happened to his parents?" I'm sure Dad knew he was prying but he wanted to know more and so did I. Hack Face suddenly was full of information.

"Terrible thing, Frank. Killed in a car accident when the boy was six. She was my sister, you know. Colleen. Colleen and Marco. He was one of those rich wops that ran around the Meaderville neighborhood before the Anaconda Company started diggin' that enormous pit up there. Damned if they're not tryin' to turn all of Butte into a big hole.

Anyway, picture Irish marrying Italian. Big sucking wedding in Meaderville back in the day when the wops ran the place. Marco was a damned good man. Don't get me wrong."

Dad toed the dirt, trying to digest this flood of information. "I came up here hoping to meet Louie. Thank him for what he did to help my boy."

"Heard about those fisticuffs down at the river. Wish I'd been there."

"Sounds like your nephew didn't need help. Put those boys down like nobody's business is what I hear."

Hack Face wiped an arm across his face, trailing a black streak on his scarred cheeks. "Hell, that kid's been a brawler since he was a pup in Butte. I seen him kick some sorry ass. Knocked hell outta a couple punk neighborhood kids who got their kicks shakin' down old ladies for whatever damn pocket change they could get. Louie broke one sad sack's nose and knocked some teeth clear out of the other kid. They ran off bawlin' and callin' for their momma whores over on Mercury Street. That damn kid Louie laughed and threw rocks at them as they hauled ass. I was sittin' on the porch enjoyin' the whole thing. I stopped worryin' about him after that." Hack Face reached for his tools. "Louie, he'll be along. Sent him for some grub."

Dad seemed satisfied with that. He and Hack Face bent over the contraption of belts and gears, intent on finding the source of the squealing. Hack Face towered over Dad, five-eleven in shoes. When they started banging around with wrenches I left the pickup and wandered through the grass, stepping over rotting tires, rusting fenders and a radiator sprouting an assortment of hoses. A mirror, still attached to a car door, winked in the afternoon sun. Hack Face had a fire going in the shack. Gray smoke wandered out of the broken chimney like a crooked finger pointing to the woods beyond the meadow. There, the mountain brimmed with timber to breathtaking heights. With the mill silenced, Rock Creek could be heard crashing through the trees and into a gully beyond the shack. Dad said if we followed the creek to where it started we'd be at the top of the world. I hoped we could do that someday, together.

Hack Face didn't seem to mind if I wandered around. He glanced at me once, throwing up his hand in greeting before turning his shaggy head back to the repair project that now deeply involved Dad. I heard a great amount of cussing, most of it from Hack Face, while Dad stood back to roll his sleeves past his elbows. That was always a signal, clearly understood in our family, that Dad was heading heels over eyebrows into a project that involved a combustible engine.

I walked over to get a look at the creek. It cascaded out of a high invisible place, spilling over granite boulders as big as the Chevy. The spray felt cool on my face. Water swirled in tight pools at my feet before hurrying down the foothills toward the Clark Fork in the valley. At that moment I was reminded that I never understood why people lived in flat places. Montana, to me, was heaven.

Up the creek a ways, I found the trail where Hack Face dragged logs to the saws. I'd watched him do it a few times. He cinched a heavy chain around a big log or two and hooked the chain to the hitch on his Jeep. The logs complained all the way down, flailing like a crabby duffer in a rocking chair, and when the clattering ended and the dust cloud drifted away, Hack Face rolled them to meet their fate at the saw. It looked like hard work to me. He lifted the logs onto the approach with ropes and pulleys, sometimes with his own sheer strength, sometimes with the Jeep's help. Dad said Hack Face knew a lot about leverage from working in the mines. Once positioned on the approach, the logs rolled one by one into the saw on a series of wheel rims taken off cars. Hack Face had devised a metal grip that pulled the logs through the saw, keeping them from snapping back. It operated from the same truck engine that powered the saw. He cut the round sides off before running the log through the saw again and again to pare it into dimensions. It looked to me like Hack Face was a genius at rigging machinery.

The forest shade felt cool to my skin. I dropped to the ground and leaned back against a Douglas fir to watch the work below me. Whatever Dad and Hack Face were doing with the saw appeared resolved because Dad retrieved the beer from the pickup. They stood around the mill, tipping bottles and pointing at the machinery. From my vantage point they looked miniature against the giant valley that opened below it like a gaping mouth. Far off, splotches of dark light streamed across the valley as clouds crossed the sun.

Dust boiled into view. Louie raced that black Chevy up the road, swerving to avoid rocks and potholes. Maybe he always drove fast. I watched him pull up beside the pickup and saunter over to Dad and Hack Face, a cigarette clenched in his lips. Louie walked like he was in no particular hurry. He was maybe too cool to move any faster. Cool, a word all the kids used in school. Maybe Louie was cool. I watched Dad stand. Hack Face pointed to Dad, then to Louie. Dad stuck out his hand. Louie reached out and shook it. I couldn't make out what they said but Dad looked serious while he talked.

Louie nodded his head. Then Louie talked while Dad nodded. They shook hands again. When that was over Dad evidently asked about the Chevy, because they turned to look at it. Dad handed Louie a beer. They walked over to pop the hood.

I rocketed down the hill to see for myself, hoping I didn't step on nails hidden in the grass. That happened once when I was chasing a fly ball in the tall grass beyond centerfield in Jaycee Park. The nail punctured the rubber sole on my tennis shoes and impaled my foot for an instant before my momentum pulled it out again. The tetanus shot wasn't so hot. I had to pull my pants down while a big old nurse with hair on her chin drove a needle about four inches into my butt cheeks. I made the mistake of telling Blue and Max about it and they rode me for weeks.

I arrived at the car hoping for some recognition from Louie but he ignored me. "Engine's stock," he was telling Dad. "Same as off the line in Detroit, except I pulled the pistons last year to do a ring job. Got the four-barrel carb on it and some real muscle in that V-eight. Glides pretty at more than a hundred miles an hour when the pedal's not even to the floor."

Dad whistled and leaned over the hot motor. "How many cubic inches?"

"In this model two sixty-five. Best Chevy ever made, the fifty-five Bel Air."

"Over a hundred, you say?" Dad sounded impressed. Mom's station wagon had some horsepower but if we hit sixty on the highway she got worried and told Dad to slow down. Mom and Dad weren't much for speed. They even talked about getting belts that clicked around our waists to hold us to the seat. I didn't know why people would strap themselves into their cars. It didn't make sense. Mom and Dad said they heard it would be all the rage someday.

"Yeah, this baby moves." Holding a beer bottle in one hand and a cigarette in the other, Louie stood back to admire his car from front to back, much as Blue and Max and I inspected girls at school.

"How much did this cost?" I blurted out. Dad turned, surprised that I was standing there. He stepped back from the car, as if to survey it more completely, and rocked on his heels with his hands in his pockets.

"Like the Chevy, do you son?" Dad smirked. Louie hung his head, looking at his boots. It struck me that they had talked about the night after the dance. Dad didn't seem too worried about it. Louie looked ashamed. It was hard to tell for sure. He just stared at his boots, pressing the cigarette to his lips to take a puff. I hoped that Louie would answer my question but he didn't. He was maybe four years older than me but he seemed more like a man, like Dad and Hack Face. Soon as Dad turned his back I would get a pounding. Either that or Louie would work me over right in front of everybody until I cried like a baby. Hack Face would pull Louie off me and laugh and pour down the whiskey until it ran off his chin. I would be crawling around in the dirt looking for my glasses while Louie smoked a cigarette.

Dad's voice brought me back. "Maybe Louie can tell you about our conversation someday," Dad said. He turned to Louie. "One sweet car, son. Stop by the house tomorrow. We'll see what we can do to fix that oil leak." Dad pointed to a shiny trickle below the valve cover.

Louie looked under the hood, surprised at Dad's discovery. "Damn gasket didn't hold. Just replaced it in March."

"Come by," Dad said again. "You know where?"

"Sure as hell do," Louie said, looking at me. Now he was smiling. I wasn't scared of Louie anymore. Dad's invitation made everything seem all right. We were a family of men up there on the mountain in that jumble of machinery, with Hack Face now napping in the shade and Dad and Louie popping another beer. I wasn't surprised that after Dad downed that one he decided I would drive the pickup back to town whenever we got around to leaving. "Just to the city limits," he warned. "We don't want to get pinched." Dad wasn't much of a drinker in the first place. It didn't help that after he and Louie polished off three or four bottles of beer, as Hack Face snored in the grass, that Louie ran to the shack for whiskey. He and Dad drank two shots apiece while I sat in the pickup, fiddling with the radio. I couldn't find a station on the mountain but in the end it didn't matter. Dad and Louie were singing.

//////

You might have guessed that Dad let me drive all the way home. He reasoned that it was better me than him if a cop stopped us. Dad was in a cheery mood but as drunk as I'd ever seen him, and that wasn't often. Mom wouldn't be happy. We crawled up alleys full of grass clippings and beat-up aluminum garbage cans, Dad content with me driving in low gear. Each time we crossed a street the pickup bucked as I braked to a stop and then tried to get a rhythm on the clutch. Dad didn't seem to mind except to rib me a few times about how I was a better driver with Marcy around. He sat with his red farm cap askew, looking more relaxed than I had seen him all spring. He turned the vent window inward to catch a breeze on his face. It was a futile gesture considering we weren't doing much more than ten miles an hour. Dad liked first gear, which he called compound. I never understood the meaning of that. He liked to drive in compound when we hunted deer along Spring Creek in the Deer Lodge Mountains east of town. He and Mom bought me a .22 single-shot rifle to carry along. It wasn't big enough to shoot deer, and I didn't have a license anyway, but when daylight began to fade Dad and I set up cans and bottles to shoot before we went home. Just the two of us, standing on dead Quaking Aspen leaves and a skiff of new snow on a late October afternoon, plugging away at tiny targets on tree stumps. Dad let me try his pump-action Remington. When I pulled the trigger the kick knocked me backwards on my butt.

"That Louie, he's got heart." Dad pulled his pipe out of his shirt pocket. Then, "Your mother doesn't need to know what went on this afternoon." I nodded. I knew what he meant. Dad told me during one of those hunting trips that there comes a time when a boy measures up to his father. I wondered if that moment had just happened.

"Dad, is Louie dangerous?"

He squinted at me for a moment. "Not dangerous, Paul, mixed up. Him losing both parents when he was a little boy and all —." Dad's voice trailed off. I thought he was finished on the topic but then he scratched a wooden match across the dashboard to light his pipe. The flame flared in the lenses of his glasses.

"It's like this, son. Some kids get to the point where they live like adults because of hard circumstances. Louie's one of those. He's both a man and a boy and doesn't know which one. Know what I mean?" He paused to blow a puff of blue smoke that smelled like cherries. "Thing is, I saw him for maybe two hours and I don't know if he's more man than boy either."

"You let him drink your beer."

"He's no stranger to alcohol, I reckon."

"Are you still mad at me for taking his car?"

"No more than him. If he's over it then so am I."

"But —."

"I told him right in front of Hack Face that chasing seventh graders with a car was a damn fool thing to do and never to pull a stunt like that again. If he'd hurt you —." Dad choked up for a moment. "Well, see, I thanked him for helping you those other times. I told him that's the mark of a good man. Maybe he'll learn from it."

We were closer to our old house. I saw the rust-brown barrel next to the barn where we burned newspapers and cereal boxes. "Did you get the machinery fixed?"

"Bearings were out. Metal against metal. Good thing Hack Face shut it down when he did. Might have burned up his contraption."

"Dad? How come you called him Jimmy?"

"That's his name. I've got a bad habit of calling him Hack Face like a lot of other people around town. To you he's Mr. O'Hanlon, never forget that." Then Dad smiled. "I'd be happy if you forgot some of that blue language you heard."

"Why is it blue?"

He laughed again. "You know damn well what I mean, son."

I parked behind the house. "Go inside and tell your mother I'll be along later, Paul." Evening shadows from our big cottonwood trees had begun to drift over the barn. I followed Dad inside, hoping he wanted to talk some more, but he switched on the light over his workbench and reached for a can of coins. I heard him pour them onto the bench as I left on my mission to stall her until Dad sobered up.

"It's about time," she greeted me from her station at the stove, but she didn't seem sore. "Where's your father?"

"Out in the barn. He had some work to do."

"Well, he's got time before supper." She had potatoes boiling and hamburgers on a slow sizzle. She wiped her hands on a green apron that was draped over her yellow pedal pushers. Mom always dressed up nice when she worked in the kitchen. She said it was important never to look dirty when working with food. She turned to me. "Paul, you look a mess. Go get scrubbed and set the table, will you dear?"

"What about —?"

"Sally went to Mary's birthday party, remember? And she swept the whole house for me today. Now be a dear and get to it because dinner will be ready soon."

After failing to pass inspection after the first scrubbing, I tried again. Mom finally declared me fit to handle silverware. I placed it just as she required, with the knife closest to the right side of the plate and the spoon next to the knife. The folded paper napkin went underneath. The fork went on the left side of the plate. I needed butter, catsup and salt and pepper. I set out milk for me and coffee cups for my parents.

Mom seemed happy. She hummed the theme to "Telstar" as she cooked. She played that record on her stereo all the time. When she flipped the hamburgers they sizzled in the bubbling grease and filled the house with a dinnertime aroma.

"Five minutes, tell your father."

I walked into the yard. A pair of robins skipped through the grass. A western meadowlark chirped from the fencepost near the barn. It was another beautiful evening in Deer Lodge.

Dad still sat at the bench, hunkered over those coins. "Mom says dinner is about ready," I called to him.

He turned halfway to face me. "Sounds good, son." He looked tired again, even worried. I don't know what it was but he didn't look right. I heard him dropping coins into the tin can when I stepped back into the yard. The meadowlark, much like a singer on stage, delivered a steady melody from the fencepost. Summer. *A boat for the family. An Evinrude. Maybe forty horse on that baby.*

I took my seat at the dinner table. We all had our places. Mom sat at one end near the phone on the wall. Dad's place was at the other, facing the back door and the barn beyond. I sat on one side by the windows with a clear view of the dishtowels and kitchen sink, Sally on the other where she could watch anyone passing on the road between us and our neighbors, the Benedicts. In the Morrison household habits were dictated by your view from the dinner table.

Mom loaded the table with food. Steam rose from the boiled potatoes, which we would mash with our forks and slather with butter. "Paul? Is your father coming?"

"He said yes," I told her. We sat for a minute, waiting. I figured Dad didn't want to come inside until the last possible second.

Mom glanced toward the back door. "Run out there and get him, will you? The food will be cold and Lord knows your father needs a hot dinner after putting in a long day at the lumberyard."

I tromped into the barn but didn't see him. "Dad, where are you?"

The first thing I saw was the lamp on its side. The beam shone on two neat stacks of quarters about five inches high. It was still daylight outside but the barn suddenly felt gloomy and strange. "Dad?" Then I saw him. He was on the floor, his right leg straddling the turned-over stool. When I leaned over him I saw his faraway face, his eyes stuck wide open. His glasses hung from one ear. I shook him but his pale empty face never changed.

I don't remember getting Mom. The house spun around me like I was on a carnival ride at the county fair. My ears fell deaf, silencing birds, even voices. Mrs. Benedict, who was pulling towels from her clothesline across the road, came sprinting in her blue dress, laundry bunched in her hands. Mom must have called to her because both women ran into the barn. I stood outside, unsure of whether I wanted to see Dad crumpled on the floor, until Mrs. Benedict emerged and took me by the hand. Tears splashed down her fat cheeks. I pulled away from her and crept inside. Mom held the black phone that Dad had installed over the winter. Now I could hear again.

"We need the ambulance right away. That's right, the Morrison place at the old Cottonwood farm on the east end of town. Please hurry, this is serious." When Mom hung up the phone she lifted Dad's head to stuff Mrs. Benedict's laundry underneath as a pillow. She worked fast, pulling the stool away and turning Dad so that his back was flat to the floor. Buttons clattered across the concrete as she tore open his gray work shirt. She pressed on his chest with one hand atop the other and then blew into his mouth. I didn't know what Mom was doing. She was a nurse before she married Dad. I stood watching her frantic efforts to save my father. She pushed on his chest in sharp motions. "Don't go, Frank, please God don't take him!" Her breath came in ragged gasps. Dad didn't move. Mom cried out in anguish.

The sirens startled me. They brought a blare of tragedy into the sanctity of our small-town life. First came the police, then an ambulance. Men charged into the barn with a stretcher. After they loaded Dad into the ambulance Mom climbed in beside him for the ride to St. Joe's. I saw the soiled knees of her yellow pants and the bottoms of Dad's boots before the door closed behind them. Someone screamed from Mrs. Benedict's yard. The ambulance sped off, wailing, disappearing into town. Neighbors watched from their porches. Old Mr. Nelson ran into the street holding a fork, a napkin tucked in his shirt. His wife stood beside him, tying a pink scarf under her chin. A block away, the old maid Butler sisters started walking toward me, May holding Eve by the arm. The birds had stopped singing.

I walked into our empty kitchen. Wasn't it minutes ago that Dad had said he was coming inside to eat? The boiled potatoes had quit steaming. Our food was cold.

# Susan

*Mom tried to comfort us* that night. "Dr. Klaus said your father died right away," she told us in measured tones, her voice shaking. We sat in our dark living room. Nobody felt inclined to turn on a light. Sally sobbed on the couch. I sat in Dad's favorite chair, felt awkward about it, and stood. "There's nothing we could have done. Your father was sick and we didn't know how bad it was. The arteries to his heart were plugged and the blood couldn't get through. ..." The deafening rush came to my ears again. I saw her lips move but she seemed far away, like a movie screen with the sound turned off. I went to my bedroom and pulled the window wide open to catch a breeze. The cottonwood trees rustled in the wind, mourning for Dad. Death haunted our house.

/////

Louie arrived Sunday afternoon. I didn't see him among all the people bringing their sympathies, but Uncle Don announced that someone who looked like Elvis Presley was nosing around the barn. I found Louie leaning on the hood of his Chevy, watching people bring pies and casseroles to the back door of our house. He seemed relieved to see me.

"You havin' a family reunion today, Ace? So many people. Your Dad said —."

"He can't help you with the oil leak." My words sounded like they came from someone else. Louie eased off the hood and looked around.

"Something wrong?"

"Dad died." It sounded too simple. *Dad lived, Dad died.* I felt ashamed that I couldn't muster a fuller explanation. I didn't even believe my own words.

"Say again?"

"It was last night after we got home. They told us it was a heart attack. I found him —." I started to sob. I hadn't cried at all. Now I couldn't stop. It was embarrassing, bawling right there in front of Louie. Seeing him reminded me of Dad's last hurrah with Hack Face and Louie. *His wisdom, his strength.*

Louie reached for me, pulling my face against his shirt. It smelled of sawdust and gasoline. "I know how it is. You'll hurt for a while."

We sat together, perched on the hood of the Chevy, while I talked about Dad. Louie listened, nodding and lighting a cigarette or two. He even offered me one. I was inclined to take it but Dad wouldn't approve. If Mom saw me she'd strap me good with the stick she kept in the pantry regardless of circumstances. The people coursing in and out of our house gave us a wide berth. I suppose Louie looked like trouble. When I got around to telling him how Dad saved money for a boat, I cried again. We went into the barn. Louie switched on a light and without a word knelt on the floor and scooped the spilled coins into a coffee can. I righted the overturned stool. When Louie filled the can he reached under the workbench. "You'll want this," he said quietly, handing me Dad's pipe, half filled with burned tobacco. He had sat there smoking his pipe as he spoke his last words to me. *Sounds good, son.*

"Those coins, Louie, they were his dream."

"Everyone oughta have one, Ace."

"I wish you had known him."

"Saw enough to know he was a good man. No way you coulda done better."

"Louie, why do people die?"

"Maybe bad luck, I don't know. Maybe makes the rest of us tougher."

"But —."

"C'mon, show you somethin'." We walked out to the Chevy. Louie popped open the glove box and eased a black and white photograph from a faded brown envelope. A tall granite-jawed man who resembled Louie and a lovely woman with long dark curly hair stood smiling in front of the Chevy, or a car that looked like it. It wasn't black but red and white. His arm was around her. They were dressed for winter. She held the collar of her coat tight against her throat. I knew I was looking at Louie's parents, but he didn't know what I had overheard Hack Face tell Dad. "Someday maybe I'll tell ya' the story," Louie said. He slid the photo back in the envelope before I could get a second look.

"They're your parents?"

"Still don't know why they hadda die." Louie pulled out his comb, looked at it, and put it back in his pocket. "Just wanted ya to know you ain't alone, that's all. It was a long time ago. No sense talkin' about it now. Someday, maybe."

I hung around with Louie until Reverend Bartlett drove up. When Mom came outside and motioned me to the house, Louie shook my hand and told me to make Dad proud. I was sure his lip quivered as he said it. I wanted to ask him more about his parents but he jumped into the Chevy and rumbled off in a cloud of dust. I went into the kitchen, crowded with people holding paper plates, where the minister had called everybody together for a prayer. He cleared his throat to signal for silence.

"We come in sorrow, Lord, for our loved one Frank Morrison. We ask that you welcome him into the Kingdom of Heaven, for he was a good, moral man, and a pillar of his church and this town. We ask that you bring comfort to his family and friends, who are assembled here today…." Reverend Bartlett went on and on. I was pretty sure this wasn't the real funeral but it felt like one. Mom stood behind me, bracing me with one arm and harboring Sally with the other. I'd heard Mom crying all night. She stayed in the living room, covered with an old pink blanket she had taken to our family picnics at Salmon Lake.

The house felt hot and confined. I searched the bent heads for Dad's kind face. It was hard to understand why he wasn't there. It was a hot sunny day in July, and like the clearing after a storm I hoped that Dad's death was a mistake and he would walk over from the hospital and show everyone in our kitchen that he was back with the living. It was a good bet he'd get everybody laughing about the near miss and maybe collect some coins for our boat. Uncle Don and Aunt Fran had driven from the High Line right after Mom called them with the news. My grandparents were riding the North Coast Limited passenger train from North Dakota, and Uncle Dale and Aunt Sophie and my cousins were on their way from northern Idaho. The girls were swell but the boy picked his nose a lot.

Uncle Don, my father's older brother, held a Bible while Reverend Bartlett prayed. Except for Uncle Don's bulging belly he looked a lot like Dad. We didn't see Don and Fran much because they farmed wheat somewhere north of Great Falls on the sea of prairie that ran clear to Canada. We drove to their farm for Thanksgiving once. Dad navigated forever on a patchwork of dirt roads, turning this way and that and stopping to read names on mailboxes.

People patted my head all afternoon, telling me that I should be proud of my father. I was relieved to see Max arrive with his parents in their familiar tow truck, the red paint faded to a dull orange. A hook and cable swung from the winch in the back. "I just heard," Max told me. I could see right away that he wanted to avoid the house, much like he couldn't stand to visit Kenny's bedroom. We went out back under the cottonwood trees while Mr. and Mrs. Jorgenson, looking hesitant, eased inside. She carried something in a dish under a yellow dishtowel. I couldn't tell whether they were on speaking terms again.

"Are you scared?" Max asked me.

"I feel like throwing up. I can't believe it happened."

We talked about death like boys do, never getting to the point, while the crowd in the house began to melt away. Max waved goodbye to his parents, who climbed back in the tow truck and left after they paid their respects. A couple of the men raised the hood on Reverend Bartlett's old Rambler because it wouldn't start. After the minister went back inside our house the men commented that his car needed a tune-up and the cracked fan belt would break anytime. Marcy showed up still dressed for church. She was Catholic and never missed a Sunday mass. Half of Deer Lodge was Catholic, I swear. She hugged me and whispered condolences and then sat in the grass, watching me like she was wondering what it would be like for a parent to die. I leaned against a tree, afraid I would fall if I didn't. *Legs of jelly. It hurts so bad.* Blue, fresh back from Billings, showed up on his bike. He flashed his trademark smile until he realized something was wrong. When Marcy told him, I cried again.

/////

The sun sank with a fury that evening, leaving a scalding pink hurricane of light over Mount Powell. Max and Blue and Marcy had gone home. Aunt Fran washed the dishes while Uncle Don swept Dad's shop. I guess he didn't know what else to do. Sally hung around the swing set with our cousins Dick and Barbara. Dick picked his nose like he always did. Susan, my other cousin, leaned on her dad's Pontiac station wagon, straining to hear faint rock music drifting from the radio. She was a sophomore. She had a habit of exhaling to blow waves of brown hair from her eyes. She wore a lot of pink lipstick, too. Uncle Don said she was crazy about some boy back in Idaho. I thought Susan was cute but I didn't feel much like talking to her. She didn't give me the time of day. I could care less. She was my cousin, after all. She saw me watching from the back steps where I sat punching my baseball glove.

"Take a picture, it'll last longer."

"What?" I thought that was a stupid thing to say with a funeral coming.

"Why are you staring at me?"

"I don't know why." I kept watching her.

"You're creeping me out, Paul."

"Sorry. You'd be better off finding the Butte station. That one from Omaha comes and goes until late at night."

"Like you'd know."

"I know a lot of stuff." She was cute, with white teeth and a dimple on her chin, but I hated her for talking to me like that. I walked over. "It's fourteen hundred on the dial, see? They play rock and roll until ten. KXLF in Butte."

"I've been trying to find Wooly Bully on the radio since we left Boise. Montana is such a hick place. Didn't anyone in this state ever hear of Sam the Sham and the Pharaohs?"

"What are you mad about? Did you come here for my dad?"

Susan dropped her eyes. "I thought Uncle Frank was swell. Is it bad?"

"Worst ever. I don't understand what happened. He took me hunting and fishing and bought this baseball glove for me down at Gamble's. I thought he'd live forever."

"Sit with me." She crawled behind the wheel of the Pontiac. I opened the passenger door and slid onto the front seat. Susan smiled at me. "Do you kiss girls?"

"I have a girlfriend."

"Well, do you?"

"Yes, sometimes."

"Get a feel ever?"

I shot a look at Susan's generous chest but she didn't notice. She was watching two high school boys, their shirttails hanging out, walk past on the gravel road.

"Well, did you, Paul? You don't say much."

"Not yet."

"Maybe it's about time. How old are you anyway?"

"Thirteen, if it's any of your business."

Susan reached for her mother's pack of Winstons on the dashboard and with long brown fingers pulled out two cigarettes.

"Ever smoked?"

"My mother would kill me."

"What Aunt Martha doesn't know won't hurt you."

"What do you mean?"

"I dare you."

"Right here?"

"No, not right here. Dick and Barbara would run tell. They're such babies about everything."

"I have a place." I looked at Susan in a new light, suddenly consumed with the conspiracy to smoke. "In the loft of the barn."

Susan extracted two more cigarettes from the Winston pack. She saw my concern. "She'll never know, trust me. Got matches?"

"On the shelf over Dad's workbench." Our siblings paid no attention when we walked past them into the barn, freshly swept. I slipped a matchbook into my pocket and stood a ladder to the loft. I went up first to find the light switch. Dad thought of everything. We sat in the yellow glow, the loft stinking from the mixed aroma of sun-baked wood and pigeon droppings. If Susan noticed, she didn't show it. She held a match to a cigarette and puffed until the end glowed red. She handed it to me, then lit another. "Like this, see." Her eyes narrowed as she sucked on the cigarette before exhaling a blue cloud of smoke.

I did the same. The smoke burned in my lungs. I coughed, nearly tumbling off the cardboard box full of old curtains that I was using as a stool.

"Paul, you idiot, you're not supposed to breathe it all the way in, just hold it in your mouth."

"You didn't tell me that."

"Watch me." Susan took a long drag. She pulled the cigarette away to let the smoke drift out of her mouth. "See what I mean? Now you try."

The next puff wasn't so bad for me. We sat there, sharing our secret. I felt a little in awe of Susan because I'd never been around a high school girl. She was cute for sure. She sat there watching me with riveting brown eyes. "You know what Paul? If you weren't my cousin I might let you try something."

///// 

Something about Dad's glasses set me off. Mom left them on the kitchen counter, just as he did when he washed up after coming home from work.

"Why are you doing this?" I demanded of her. It was Wednesday, the morning of the funeral. I admit I was feeling sore about Dad going away and angry with Mom for leaving a careless reminder right in plain view.

"Doing what?" She watched me while she snapped on silver earrings. She wore the same black dress I remembered from my Grandpa Henry's funeral when I was in kindergarten. I couldn't recall much about him except that he had a happy face and gave me oranges. He liked crab apples too and cut them into slices with his pocketknife.

"You know what — putting Dad's glasses out like he was here and going with us."

"Now Paul —."

"Mom, why did he need to die? I mean, are you getting old when you're forty-one?"

"When somebody's sick, son, age sometimes has nothing to do with how long they live."

"Why didn't he go to the doctor?"

She looked at me like I should know better. "I told him, Paul. We argued about it. You know how he was."

We climbed into the station wagon, our dwindling family, and headed to the Presbyterian Church. Uncle Don drove our grandparents from the Downtowner Motel. They like to stay there because the sheets were clean and they could walk to the bakery on the corner in the mornings. All of us congregated in Reverend Bartlett's office while he said another prayer. The man sure liked to pray. Then we trooped into the church to look at Dad in the casket. He was the first dead person I'd seen. The body before me didn't look like Dad at all. He looked waxy and shrunken, dressed in his blue Sunday church suit. What reposed before me was an unfamiliar version of Dad. I suppose at that moment I began to see the value of religion because I was pretty sure I wasn't looking at Dad at all but only his body, still and pale, and the real Dad was gone somewhere. I felt like throwing up.

Louie came to the funeral. So did Hack Face. They wore fresh shirts that buttoned up the front. Hack Face had combed his hair. Toby and Edna were there, too. People came from all over the Deer Lodge valley. I doubt there wasn't a board sawed that week that didn't remind people of Dad. Toby locked the lumberyard that morning with a sign, "Closed today in memory of Frank Morrison." The funeral, full of crying people, passed in a blur. Six men in dark suits carried Dad outside to the hearse for the burial at Hillcrest Cemetery.

I don't remember much of what was said at the gravesite. Angry clouds filled the sky when they lowered him into a dark hole where I would never see him again. The fresh earth smelled like Mom's flowerbed. I would never again use a shovel without thinking of Dad. *Someday we'll have empty cans and a new boat. Won't that be something?"*

///// 

After the church ladies fed us lunch, Susan and her family loaded into the Pontiac to drive back to Boise. Their departure came in the nick of time because Susan was throwing herself at Louie. He was warming to her suggestions that they go for a ride in the Chevy when Aunt Sophie, getting the drift, marched Susan outside with Dick and Barbara and pushed them all into the back seat. Susan glowered while her parents said their goodbyes. When they rumbled away, the Pontiac drooping at the back bumper from the weight of overstuffed suitcases, Susan managed a feeble wave as they rounded the corner.

"Know her, Ace?" I realized, at seeing Louie standing beside me, Susan's wave was for him. "I mean, she's a good-lookin' doll."

"She's my cousin."

"Think she puts out?"

"Probably."

"Won't never know, will we Ace?" Louie smiled and turned toward the church. Strands of branches from a weeping willow hung around him. "Where's my uncle? First time he come off that there mountain since who knows when. Says your dad was one of the best men he ever knew. Why was that do ya think?"

"Because he did good by Mr. O'Hanlon?"

"That's right, Ace. My uncle might be a crazy old bastard but he can judge a good man. You oughta be proud for what your old man was." Louie didn't wait for an answer. "Where are them boxin' buddies of yours?"

"Blue and Max? Over there." They stood in the shade by the church, watching us. I figured they didn't want to get too close.

"Blue? What hell kinda name is that?"

"That's his nickname. His real name is Bobby but nobody calls him that."

"I gotta get the old man back up the mountain before he gets up a thirst at the Corner Bar. Ride along and then we'll go cruisin'. Hit the highway and see what that chariot can do." He motioned toward the black Chevy, parked in a row of family sedans. "Ever really hauled ass down the highway with the windows down, Ace? Sweet smell of sagebrush blastin' you in the face and a rumble in your ears? Nothin' like it."

"I'll ask."

"And bring that sweet doll you play kissy face with. Just don't get me in no trouble for doin' it."

A few minutes later five of us piled into the Chevy. Marcy shook her head and walked away after a heated conversation with her parents. The rest of us got to go because Louie had saved us from the Tucker brothers. With Blue and Max and me in the back and Hack Face riding shotgun, we raced down Milwaukee Avenue and across the river. It was the same route we had taken to the cemetery except that the road to the mill branched to the north. Louie watched me in the rearview mirror as if to assure me he wouldn't take a wrong turn.

"Hell, a man needs a drink after that," Hack Face boomed. He turned to me. "Sorry, kid, sorry as can be. Can't get over your old man being gone. Reckon you can't either. Damn sorry mess." He never said another word but laid a match to a fat brown cigar. We gagged at the foul stench wafting through the back seat. Hack Face stared straight ahead, brooding. Louie put the pedal to the metal on the flat stretches, leaving a trail of thick dust. He slowed for dips and rocks before gunning the Chevy again. "Damn fine machine!" Max exclaimed in admiration.

After Hack Face climbed out and disappeared into the shack on a mission of finding hard liquor, I took his place in the front seat. Louie popped the Chevy in reverse, spun around in the field grass, and just as quickly lurched it forward. We roared down the mountain, Blue and Max whooping from the back seat when the Chevy launched over the rises, leaving our stomachs on the road. I turned the vent window inward to catch the wind. It poured across my face like clean water, bathing me with unfamiliar freedom.

Louie rolled onto Main Street and then shot the Chevy south on the highway toward Butte. Within minutes the telephone poles whipped past. "Look at that, baby!" Max whistled from the back seat. "Louie's got the needle buried!" I stole a look at Blue, who didn't appear as enthusiastic. We were humping at well past a hundred.

"Still room to spare, you hepcats!" Louie yelled over the roar of the engine. He gripped the wheel with both hands. "Ain't got the pedal to the floor yet! Ace! Wanna hit one-ten?" I nodded and watched Louie lower his black boot on the gas pedal. The Chevy surged. Trees flew past like props on a movie set. White dashes painted down the center of the highway became a streaming ribbon. The Chevy hit a dip in the pavement and felt like it was taking flight. "Hell O'Mighty!" Blue screamed from the back seat. We thumped down again, leaving a trail of sparks. I thought about rolling the window up but the wind was too exhilarating. We were sitting in a tornado.

I shouted to Louie over the roar of wind and motor. "Can you get in trouble for going fast?"

"Hell, Ace, ain't no speed limit in Montana," he yelled back. The wind barely stirred his hair. He leaned over the steering wheel as if he was urging the Chevy to go faster.

Blue and Max hugged the front seat, their eyes fixed on the speedometer. When Louie hit one-ten, he eased off on the gas and slowed to sixty. "Can't push it too hard too long. Blew a head gasket drivin' like this back last year."

Blue spoke from the back seat. "What's a head gasket?" That set off a painfully detailed explanation from Max who had helped his father tear down engines in the garage. Louie nodded his head to show his agreement with the description. We pulled off the highway into a wayside rest where water trickled from a pipe. A few cars passed on Highway 10, some with luggage racks strapped to the roofs and bug screens mounted over the grills. "Vacationers," Blue observed to no one in particular.

Louie popped the hood. We pressed close for a look but the motor's heat drove us back. "Something you'll learn," Louie said. "When you're pushin' a car to get all hot and bothered you've gotta let her cool off once and awhile, like when you got a chick goin' ass over eyebrows for you at the drive-in." He laughed at us. "Not that you junior high punks would know nothin' about that."

Blue straightened up. "I know a thing or two about girls."

"Yeah, what, Kemosabe?"

"Well, that you can get them going."

"Is that right? So you're tellin' us you got laid?" Louie walked over to Blue and put his hands on Blue's shoulders. I didn't realize until that moment how much they resembled each other with their black hair and blazing good looks. Louie was bigger and stouter but in many ways Blue was a younger version of him, right down to the penetrating blue eyes.

"No, I didn't ... say that," Blue stammered. It looked to me that Blue, for all of his bravado, was afraid of Louie. I didn't blame him. There was something in the muscled older boy we didn't understand, maybe even feared, and it was in that dark corner where the unpredictable Louie hid. Hack Face had called Louie a rebel. The only rebels I knew were the ones wearing gray uniforms in the Civil War books. I thought more and more of Louie as Chad Buford, not a rebel but a Union soldier fighting to preserve honor and dignity. Didn't that explain why Louie charged into the Tucker boys that day on the river? He was Chad and they were the Dillon brothers in the backwoods of Kentucky? Scrapping for what was right and he won? Like Chad in "Little Shepherd from Kingdom Come," Louie seemed a creature of two worlds, both a lost boy and a tough survivor. I saw two sides to Louie and was pretty sure Blue and Max did too.

"But you like the ladies?" For a moment I thought Louie was riding Blue. Then Louie relaxed his grip and stepped back, smiling. "Wanna see a real woman?"

Blue looked at him with some surprise. Even Max, who was inspecting the Chevy's motor, lifted his head to see what was coming.

"Got a girlfriend over in Anaconda, see? Now don't get any big ideas. She's too much for you punks to handle. But since you showed some brass fightin' them hillbillies I'll show you whatta shoot for." We sat around the wayside rest talking while the motor on the Chevy cooled. A great cloud fell over the valley, threatening rain. For a moment I had a fleeting picture of Dad, wondering if he'd stay dry under six feet of gravel and clay.

"Ace, you with us here?" Louie leaned against a boulder, drawing a comb through his hair. "You remember Faye, right? That night you stole my car?"

"That night you tried to run us down?" I was scared for having said that, but Louie shook it off and smiled again. He was cutting me some slack because of Dad's funeral.

Max spoke up. "How come if you're from Butte you're dating a girl from Anaconda?" That started an intense conversation of the merits of Butte vs. Anaconda, and when Max informed Louie of his own Butte roots, they shook hands and started comparing neighborhood stories. Blue and I didn't think much of Butte, or Anaconda either for that matter, but we didn't say anything. Butte to me was a dirty brawling place full of characters, like the man who didn't have a body from the waist down and rolled around uptown on a round board with little wheels, propelling himself along the sidewalks with filthy hands. Mom drove us to Butte when she wanted to shop at Hennessy's. While she looked at women's clothing Sally and I rode the escalator between floors in the big department store. I had never seen an escalator until then. We had a couple of two-story buildings in Deer Lodge. One had a real elevator. In the rest, like the Elks and Moose clubs, it was a steep climb on creaking wooden stairs. Anaconda was a smaller city than Butte but the smelter smokestack ruled over mountains of black slag that glistened in the sun. I never figured out the rivalry because Anaconda smelted the ore that Butte dug out of the ground. One city depended on the other. Both had company houses built a foot apart. We always wondered how anybody got between them to nail siding to the walls. I preferred Deer Lodge with its shady boulevards and wide, if potholed, streets. About the only real excitement we saw was the Tri-County Fair when the country folk came to town in August and a carnival with four or five rides showed up.

Blue and I listened to the Butte talk. Max was talking big, dressing up his accomplishments for Louie, but Louie didn't seem much impressed. I got to thinking about my father and all that had changed since the school dance. It was too much. I waded into the tall weeds behind the wayside rest and cried. Blue followed.

"Hurts bad, huh?"

"You know it does."

"I'm sorry, Paul, real sorry. Your dad was a great guy."

I wiped my tears with the back of my hand. "Know what, Blue? I thought my dad would live forever. It doesn't seem real that he's gone."

"I get it." Who knows where I would be without Blue. He was my best friend ever since that day on the fire escape in second grade. I almost laughed thinking about the blue chalk dust all over his face. I hadn't called him Bobby, ever.

"Now I'm worried about my mother."

"She's fine, Paul. You know that."

"I thought Dad was too."

We walked back to the Chevy. I was feeling as low as ever. Louie read my mood right away. "Know what, girls? We're gonna see Faye another day."

"When?" Blue insisted. He wouldn't be denied when girls were involved.

Louie slammed the hood on the Chevy. "I'm thinkin' Saturday. Right now we're drivin' back to Deer Lodge." He flipped the keys to me. "Don't hit anything, Ace." Max stared at me with eyes as big as saucers. Blue, looking scared, backed off from getting in the car.

"I'm not old enough."

Louie laughed. "Didn't stop you before."

Sitting behind the wheel of the Chevy scared me a little. Louie rode shotgun. Blue and Max popped into the backseat, intent on watching this unexpected development. "Now here's the deal, Ace. You hit sixty-five, that's tops. Pull into that wrecking yard before we get into town. I'll take over then."

I turned the key and the motor came to life. This wasn't like driving Dad's old truck. The Chevy had power. I buried the clutch and pulled the column shift toward me and down. "Watch for cars," Louie warned, sounding in a strange way like Dad. I turned the Chevy around in the wayside rest and when the highway was clear Louie leaned toward me.

"Floor it!" he yelled. I hit the gas. We threw gravel for a good twenty yards as I roared out of first, shifted into second and hit the pavement with a squeal and a bounce. Even in third we kept burning rubber toward Deer Lodge. "Whoooeee! Like that, Ace?" Louie pounded the dashboard, drinking up the speed. With Blue and Max yelling encouragement we pounded down the road in the dark afternoon. I felt a little bit ashamed for having fun on the day we buried my father. Maybe this was Louie's way of showing me that life goes on.

Louie dropped me off at the house. I found Mom in Sally's bedroom, making up a cot for herself. Grandpa and Grandma had moved from the motel and decided to stay a few weeks in my parents' bedroom at the front of the house. They sat in the living room, watching the news on TV and looking glum. Mom, still in her black dress, wasn't inclined to talk. She touched a tissue to her eyes as she straightened the sheets. It was nearly time for dinner but nothing was cooking. Dad's glasses were missing from the counter.

# Faye

*I can't say my life* was much like Chad Buford's. He carried a sword, fought the Rebels and helped the Yankees win the Civil War to save the Union. He had a fine horse named, paradoxically, Dixie. I'd never seen a real sword. The only Rebel in my life was Nick Adams who played Johnny Yuma on television. I didn't know any Yankees, either, except for the boys on my Little League team the summer before sixth grade, and Maris and Mantle and Ford and the other heroes in New York.

Blue took me out to ride old Betsy a time or two, but after he got bucked off and broke his arm I didn't see any sense in winding up like him. Mostly we sat on the fence, pretending we were cowboys. We talked big about taking Betsy to rodeos. She grazed with one ornery eye fixed on us. I was a little ashamed to think of Chad Buford dashing into the enemy lines on his fleeting horse, his blue uniform a brilliant target for dead-eye Rebs. I'd probably fall off before we got started. Chad Buford had two girlfriends. I still had Marcy, although after Dad died the girl stuff didn't seem important anymore. She brought a sympathy card to the house and I called her a few times but we drifted apart as summer ripened into August. I never thought of Marcy as Chad's

Melissa in her homespun mountain clothes or Margaret in her plantation finery until I saw less and less of her. Then I began to miss her. I knew how Chad yearned for the young women in his life but the war got in the way. I yearned for Marcy, for slow walks from her house up California Avenue to the park, but Dad's death got in the way. I didn't feel like being in love, not now. It didn't seem right. Lost love hurts even young boys.

Like Chad, who discovered a series of torments and conflicts with the people he loved, I was beginning to think I didn't fit with anyone. Some days I was still a kid, other days feeling grown up and confused. I was feeling grief, Mom assured me, but I sensed that wasn't the entire story. I was changing.

After Dad's death the excitement of becoming a teenager faded as fast as dew after dawn. I played in a few baseball games but it wasn't the same without him yelling encouragement whenever my team got a hit. Coach started me in every game, even when other kids had to take turns, and moved me to third base where I could be closer to the action. I knew what he was doing. Mom wouldn't let me quit so I worked hard to learn the game. I was on a mission to show her and Coach and the world that Dad would be proud of me. I learned to catch hot grounders and in the third game after we buried Dad, I hit a triple with two runners aboard. Horns honked on all the family sedans and farm trucks while I scooted over the bags, pounding a cloud of dust to third base. Toby became a regular visitor at my games. He parked his tall frame against our dugout while old men stopped to marvel about his glory days on the high school basketball team. They always reached to pat his shoulders before walking away. Old heroes never grew old in Deer Lodge.

Grandpa and Grandma took Sally back to North Dakota on the train until Labor Day. Mom didn't say much around the house. Sometimes she talked for hours with Mrs. Benedict across the road as the two of them swayed on the porch swing. Mrs. Benedict was a widow too, raising two young sons after Mr. Benedict died in a mine accident. I'd bet they talked about lost husbands because first Mom cried and then Mrs. Benedict. When Mom wasn't doing that she fussed with her marigolds and petunias in her little garden behind the house. Some evenings, in the twilight, she drove alone to the cemetery. I think she was talking to Dad.

Toby bought the lumberyard. Mom said he offered her a handsome price for it, more than she asked, on account of its good reputation. Dad had life insurance but it couldn't have been worth much because Mom talked about needing to find a job. One day she put on a new blue dress and went for an interview at the clinic down on Main Street. She came home an hour later. "They want me to start next Monday," she told me without enthusiasm, in the same resigned tone of voice she used to remind me to turn off lights in empty rooms. "I have to call over to Helena to get my nursing license renewed. I've got to buy a new uniform and school clothes for you kids and shop for groceries and figure out how to pay the bills and —." She sat at the kitchen table and cried for an hour. Mom spilled enough tears for both of us.

/////

Louie managed to pull off a trip to Anaconda to introduce us to the lovely Faye. He came to the house on a Saturday morning wearing a new button-up black cotton shirt with the collar turned up. Instead of boots he wore penny loafers. They were buffed to a black shine. He greased the sides of his hair back except for a single black curl that hung down the center of his forehead. Everything about Louie seemed black except for his smile. I'd never seen a movie star in person. Louie looked like one.

"Ready to roll, Ace? Faye don't wait for no man, especially the little ones." Louie had a way of getting a dig in now and then. He smiled and struck a match off the bark of our willow tree to light his cigarette before nodding his head toward the house. "Tell Mama I won't let you do nothin' stupid, okay, hepcat?" Mom was in one of her funks. When I asked her if I could go she at first shook her head vigorously in disapproval, but being that I was thirteen years old I whined again and again until she nodded in defeat and waved me toward the door. On another day she would have put up a fight. She stood there looking sad or distracted, I wasn't sure. "I'm going to see your father anyway so go right along. I can't imagine what there is to do in Anaconda when you're thirteen years old." Louie leaned against the Chevy with one loafer crossed over the other. He flashed a victory grin. "Won, didya Ace?" He looked pleased at my conquest.

We rolled off to find Blue, whose parents begrudgingly let him go. Of course, they didn't know we were going to see a girl. Blue didn't exactly lie, and Louie didn't offer any real explanation, and I think his parents were relieved to see Louie leave their house. Mr. Taylor wore white shirts and black ties at his job in a bank downtown. He looked to me like he wasn't comfortable around tough guys like Louie. It was a different story with Mr. Jorgenson, who was working with

Max to drop a transmission when we drove up. They spent a good half hour examining the Chevy's mechanical parts. Louie acted like we had all day. He and Mr. Jorgenson started trading stories about strokes and bores and the importance of grinding valves every so often. They lost me there. Blue and I sat on some barrels in the shade and watched Max bend over the motor and slide under the car. He wore a green t-shirt with the sleeves ripped off at the shoulders. Grease covered his hands and arms to the elbows. Max looked bigger every day. He went out for football on the eighth grade Griffins team. I'd hate for Max to tackle me. He outweighed me by at least thirty pounds. He grew bigger and bigger while I stayed about the same, thin as a broomstick.

Max changed, but his mother's sorrow didn't. She came outside in a flapping yellow housecoat, waving him away from the Chevy right after Mr. Jorgenson told Max he could go with us. A scarf tied over her head barely hid curlers as big as orange juice cans. I could see that Mrs. Jorgenson was having a difficult time and so did Max. He shrugged and waved and turned back to the garage. She stood in the yard to make sure Max didn't go with us.

We were halfway to Anaconda before Louie asked about her. "What's with the crazy old lady? Doesn't seem she's put together right." I told him how she'd been strange ever since Kenny died in an auto wreck, throwing in a description of the smashed car for good measure. Louie fell quiet. I could see that his mind was somewhere else. I looked at Blue, who was sitting in the back seat. We both felt uncomfortable. Maybe in that exchanged glance we admitted we didn't know much about Louie. I hadn't told Blue about the photo of Louie's parents in the glove box. I was pretty sure Louie was thinking about them. I felt ashamed for embellishing Kenny's death and the Jorgensons' private business. Now that I knew real grief, the kind that stabs you in the heart and leaves you shaking in the night, I wondered what it was like for Louie to lose both parents at once. I pondered this until Louie came back from wherever he was. He looked me straight in the eye. "I shoulda hugged her, Ace."

Going to Anaconda got Blue talking about Wayne Estes, the basketball star electrocuted at the scene of a car accident. It happened that winter, in Utah, two hours after he had scored forty-eight points in a college game. "He's the greatest basketball player Montana ever produced," Blue said, repeating a common praise heard since the early 1965 tragedy. "He was just tall enough that his head bumped into that fallen power line and zap! He was going to play for the Lakers and then that stupid thing happened." We all knew the story. Everyone knew it. Wayne and two teammates had gone for pizza when they came across the accident. They tried to help. The two shorter men cleared the power line but Wayne walked right into it. The most famous basketball player in Montana history was gone, just like that. Five thousand people came to his funeral in Anaconda. "Why do good people die?" Blue asked, but there was nothing more to say.

/////

Louie drove in silence the rest of the way. When I asked if I could play the radio, he nodded, still deep in thought. The Butte station had polka. I turned the dial, watching the red band scroll across the stations, until I found Donny Vu on KANA. They said Donny was blind but he sure played good country and western. I wondered how he could tell one record from another before he played them on the turntable. This wasn't my favorite music but it was all you could get on a Saturday morning in the Deer Lodge Valley. Blue hated it but Louie didn't seem to mind.

We rumbled into Anaconda in time for lunch. Louie pulled into a drive-in where a carhop hooked a metal tray on the side window next to him. She wore a paper hat that almost fell off when she leaned down to get a good look at Louie. He paid for our hamburgers and milk shakes with four silver dollars. I had no idea where he got his money or how he could afford the Chevy but he acted like he knew what he was doing. He was in charge, always, and we knew it.

"Four bucks!" he complained to us. "Over in Butte you can get the same for three-fifty and the girls are better lookin'." Just then he laid on the horn as two girls big as heifers ambled past the Chevy. They jumped and screamed and one stuck up her middle finger. Louie laughed so hard that strawberry milk shake squirted from his nose. Blue gulped and nearly spit up and laughed too. So did I. The oversized girls stuffed themselves into a croaking Rambler and idled away, one finger still waving to us as they disappeared down the street. "Now that's what I'm talkin' about," Louie reminded us after he wiped milk shake from his chin.

"What's that?" Blue inquired from the back seat.

Louie continued with his tutorial on women. "Good-lookin' girls are flattered by attention. Never forget that. You gotta show 'em you're interested and they don't walk away flippin' you the finger like those two did. Ugly fat ones live by another code. Don't know what that is and who the hell cares?" He got us laughing again.

Then I got curious. "Who is Faye anyway?"

Louie took another bite of his hamburger, pickles but no onions, lots of catsup. "Somebody who understands," he mumbled with a mouthful.

"Understands what, Louie?"

"Me, Ace. She understands me."

Blue leaned forward from the back seat. "And I'll bet because she's a hot chick?"

Louie lifted his eyes to find Blue in the rearview mirror. "Righty-o, baby. I ain't gonna explain the particulars to you junior high punks but I'll tell you this, Faye don't send me home disappointed." Blue eased back, his grin a mile wide and his mind no doubt full of imagery, while I tried to decide just what Louie meant. Did they kiss a lot? Did she let him feel her up? I found myself thinking about Marcy again. Maybe I could take her down to Jaycee Park in the dark and make out for a couple of hours.

"Time to rumble," Louie decided. When he fired up the Chevy the girl in the funny hat took away our tray but not before launching a look of regret in Louie's direction. We roared away from the drive-in, leaving dust swirling around her. She was pretty cute.

Faye lived up a rutted dirt road on the hill above Anaconda. The sunlight fell in blinding slashes between matchbox houses, some of them no more than shacks. A few of the nicer ones were made of stucco. Others looked like the painter died because flakes curled from the weather-beaten wood in great waves. Louie braked to a stop in front of a tipsy house with blankets for curtains. A car with no tires and no windows rusted in the weeds. A dog mean as sin snarled from the yard, straining at a feeble chain that tethered him to a metal stake. Louie paid no attention. He walked straight to the front door and pounded. Blue surveyed the scene from the back seat. "Let's hope Faye's better looking than this house. I mean, look at the place."

I turned to him to instill some confidence. "I saw her, remember?"

Blue got that smile on. It was the envy, I tell you, of every girl at Deer Lodge Junior High School. "Only at night, cowboy. And during a car theft, wasn't it? You were in love then but you're about to be surprised. I'll bet she's as ugly as that mutt over there." Blue had me worried. Someone at the house opened the door. Louie went inside. Blue continued his rant. "We came over here thinking Louie was going to find us some action. All we're going to get over here is the clap." The clap had something to do with sex, I was pretty sure, but I wasn't going to ask Blue for details. He'd blab all over school and the other kids would show me no mercy.

"So Paul, remember Miss O'Leary back at Central School?"

"How could I forget seeing you face down on the prettiest teacher in school?"

"When I get a car I'm going to drive to Missoula and see if she'll go out with me."

"She's an old lady by now, for chrissakes."

"Old enough to know a thing or two, that's all I care about. She's a teacher and I'm a willing student. How hard can it be?"

"Geez, Blue. She's probably married and has kids. Maybe she uses a cane."

"You were never good at math. She can't be more than fifteen, sixteen years older than us."

"That makes her ancient by now."

My skepticism didn't faze Blue at all. "Besides, she felt good that day when I fell out of the fire escape and knocked her on the ground. I'll bet she thinks about me all the time."

"Did you feel her up?"

"Damn near."

"Missoula's a big city."

"I'll find her."

Louie emerged from the house with Faye behind him. Blue exhaled a low whistle of admiration. A pink sleeveless blouse barely contained her abundant chest. Jeans cutoffs rode high on freckled legs as shapely as any I'd seen. Somewhere under her makeup was a gorgeous face. Faye sure laid it on thick around the eyes. Louie jerked open the driver door. "In the back, Ace." I popped the front seat forward and climbed in beside Blue, while Faye slid behind the steering wheel and to the center of the front seat. She put her arm around Louie as soon as he revved up the Chevy. "Ace, Blue, this is Faye."

She turned to look us over. "You teaching nursery school again, Louie?" I didn't even mind the insult. She was stunning, even more beautiful than I remembered her. "So which baby is which?" she asked Louie.

"Four eyes there with the maroon baseball cap is Ace. He's the cat who ripped off my car."

Faye turned again and fixed me with the hard eye but I detected kindness flickering in her face. "Lucky you lived. You mess with Louie's car, you mess with death." Her face softened. "Louie told me your father died. I'm sorry." I was in love, just like that.

"And the other one is Blue? What kind of name is that?"

"Short for Bobby," Blue confessed, as entranced as me.

Louie dropped the Chevy in reverse to pull away from the house. Just then an old man in a stained undershirt burst outside, sloshing brown liquid from a tin cup. "Dammit girl, you be back in time to make dinner before I go on shift! A working man deserves a hot meal!"

Louie sped away, leaving Faye's father ranting to himself. "Crazy old fool," he said. Faye seemed unconcerned. She pulled a long comb from her purse to feather her brown bangs. "What are we doing with these juveniles, anyway, big boy? I ask for a date and you bring along two pups who wouldn't know a hard-on from a stick shift." Louie didn't answer. Faye reached up to adjust the rearview mirror. She was looking straight into my eyes. "You boys been laid, ever?"

I shook my head, embarrassed. I wasn't stupid enough to think she was offering. "Maybe," Blue told her, to which Faye shook with a deep laugh. "I mean, I've got prospects."

She shifted her eyes to find his face in the mirror. "You got prospects? What the hell does that mean?"

Blue was tongue-tied for once. He was no match for the lovely Faye and we both knew it. I came to his rescue. "Girls think he's cool."

That seemed to appease Faye. She leaned her head on Louie's shoulder while he charged the Chevy back down the hill toward downtown to cruise the main drag a few times. Anaconda looked busy. Women emerged from stores with packages. Old men sat on benches watching traffic. Parents led little kids up and down the cracked sidewalks. This was a much bigger place than Deer Lodge. Louie eased back on the gas and turned into a parking stall in front of a bar. It was early afternoon but the neon sign above the door flickered with the words, "Sam's Smelter Saloon." The big window in front was smashed out. A relic of a man in sagging brown trousers held afloat with red suspenders leaned into the bar from the sidewalk to inspect the damage. Louie laughed. "Look there, some sorry ass took a dive through the window. Bet that hurt." Faye got a big kick out of that. It didn't seem too funny to me, somebody being shoved through a window, but this was Anaconda. After Louie disappeared into the bar, Blue and I scooted forward on the seat on the excuse that we wanted to talk to Faye, but we both knew it was to look at her legs. Faye had the best legs I'd ever seen. They were creamy and perfect like the women we saw in cigarette ads on the billboards.

We didn't get to look long because Louie hurried back with two six-packs of beer under his arm. "Great Falls Select, Ace, as I recollect your dad's brand." He had me there. I never saw Dad drink much except for the day he died. Blue looked a little excited when he saw the beer. "You old enough to buy that?" he asked Louie with some concern.

"Old enough. How old you gotta be?"

"Twenty-one I thought."

"Close enough."

"How old are you?"

"Seventeen."

Louie backed the Chevy away and crept through Anaconda like a Sunday gentleman, paying more attention to Faye than to where he was going. I recognized the Lost Creek

Road outside town because Dad used to take us there for picnics. Louie followed it several miles into a crease in the Flint Range and parked in a canopy of shade. We could hear the creek thrashing after he cut the motor. It was a beautiful Montana afternoon with a blissful blue sky. The air felt warm and dry. A yellow butterfly landed on the windshield before flitting away. Louie rustled his hand under the front seat until he found a can opener. He punched a triangle-sized hole on one side of a beer can, then another on the other. "One's for drinking, the other is the air hole," he explained to us. Blue and I leaned against the front seat, watching. I almost forgot about Faye's legs. Louie handed the first can to Faye, then one to me and one to Blue. The can felt cold in my hand. White foam oozed from the holes that Louie made.

"Now here's the deal." I heard a snap as Louie popped a beer for himself. "You spill beer on the seats back there, I drag your sorry asses behind the car all the way back to Deer Lodge. Savvy?"

Blue and I nodded in grateful appreciation and took our first tentative sips. The beer tasted bitter to my tongue and not at all sweet like a bottle of Coca-Cola from the red machine in front of the gas station. I didn't want Blue to think I was a wimp. He took a big gulp so I did too. I knew my mother would kill me but the beer wasn't so bad after the first few sips. I took another swallow while Louie and Faye made out right in front of us. It was a little like being at a beach party movie at the drive-in theater. After a few minutes they went to sit on the edge of the creek, leaving a six-pack on the front seat. Louie left the opener, too. I was feeling a buzz. "What the hell you two doing?" I yelled to them through the open window. If the Tuckers showed up this time I'd take them all on. I popped open two more cans of beer, handing one to Blue.

"I don't want to scare you, Paul, but my guess is he didn't want us to have these."

"So what?" We drank those down, in the meantime making lewd observations about girls we knew from school. Except for Marcy, of course. Blue knew she was forbidden territory. Every girl I named drew the same predictable retort from Blue. "Think she puts out?" he hollered, before we clanked our beer cans together and took another swallow. When that was gone I reached for the remaining four beers. Blue didn't feel inclined to argue. I heard myself talking.

"Louie bought some strong stuff. Tastes damn good. Says right here on the can it's brewed with extra care. That means teenagers won't get sick on it and puke." I waved my beer at Blue. Some sloshed out of the holes onto the red vinyl seat. Blue looked scared and wiped the beer away with the bottom of his t-shirt.

"Paul, you trying to get us clobbered? You're getting sloppy and talking like an idiot."

"So are you, buddy."

"Are we drunk?"

"I feel all loose and funny."

"You look funny too."

Louie and Faye crossed the creek and disappeared into the woods. Blue spoke aloud for both of us as we watched Faye's hind end slide into the underbrush behind Louie. "Damn, she's fine. Bet Louie's getting some back there. Maybe he can get us some girls. Too bad we don't have rubbers —."

"What's a rubber?"

"You serious, Paul? You buy rubbers down at the drug store so you don't get girls pregnant."

"Is that what you do?"

Blue rolled his eyes. "They can't sell rubbers to kids. Ole Mister Sampson would tell. He won't sell dirty magazines to kids either. You gotta get somebody like Louie to buy it." Blue shook his head. "Should have left you to help Mr. Jorgenson overhaul motors and brought Max instead." He pitched an empty can into the meadow. "All out. What we gonna do now?" I peered over the front seat looking for more. I felt dizzy and had to pee bad.

"We's out of beer," I told Blue, who already stood in the meadow shooting a stream of glistening water that arced like a rainbow. I stood beside him, taking aim at a boulder. I won the peeing contest by two feet at least.

"You saved up, Paul. I was just about done. You come over here bursting like a rain barrel when all I got left is a trickle." Blue zipped up and looked toward the car. "Where we gonna get more beer then?" He tripped on a tree root, falling to his knees. His cap fell off in the tall grass.

"Bluesey, you looking drunk."

"So you, Paul." He watched me stumble around, searching for the zipper on my overalls. "Nothing there ole Faye could find with a magnifying glass," Blue managed to spit out. I went over and helped him out of the grass. "Gonna puke, Paul." I steadied him while he bent over and heaved beer, milkshake and identifiable nuggets of hamburger and pickles. It wasn't Blue's proudest moment, I'll tell you that.

"Bluesy, that's gross. House much beer did you drink?" My lips and tongue felt numb like when I went to the dentist and he stuck me in the gums with a needle and lied that it wouldn't hurt. I wasn't feeling so good myself. I dragged Blue over to the Chevy. We sat in the grass, leaning against the fender. Butterflies and bees flitted through the meadow. The aroma of sagebrush and mustard weed and Blue's vomit engulfed us.

"Paul, I's really sorry about your old man," Blue said out of nowhere. "I shoulda been there to help. You are my best friend. I didn't know what to say to you. I didn't know what it's like —."

Blue went on and on about his remorse. I wished he would stop because he was making me sad. We both were in tears when Louie and Faye showed up looking flushed. Leaves stuck to the back of her blouse. "What the hell?" I heard Louie say. He grabbed my collar, lifting me off the ground. "Take Paul's glasses," Louie ordered Faye. I stood there crying and drunk. Louie was going to pound us both and leave us for dead. It was clear to me now. He got me to pal around with him until he found a place to dump our bodies. We drank his beer to remove any doubt of our fate.

I wanted to run but my legs felt weak. Blue was heavier than me, and taller, but Louie, with a tight curl of his arm, lifted him with no effort at all. When Faye pulled my glasses away the meadow dissolved in a blur. Blue could see what was coming. Louie half-dragged us through the grass to the creek. So this is it. He's going to drown us. With one mighty push he dropped us to our knees on the bank, forcing our heads into a pool of numbing mountain water from some distant snow pack. I counted five times he dunked us, holding our heads above the water long enough that we could gulp for air. He stopped before we were dead. "No way I'm takin' you two home cryin' like babies and smellin' like a barroom floor." He acted angry but I heard him laughing with Faye over by the Chevy while we rolled around in the grass, wheezing for air.

"Know what Blue?"

"What, Paul?"

"I not drunk anymore."

"You sound like it, buddy."

"Sose you."

Faye laid it on thick when she saw us staggering back to the Chevy. "The Ace kid must be as blind as a bat. Look here, Louie, how thick these lenses are." She handed them back to me after holding them to her face five or six times, making fun of me. She made us sit in the sun to dry off while she and Louie took a walk up the road. My head quit buzzing. Blue and I got to talking about his comic book collection. That was better than beer and people dying. When Louie and Faye finally came back he tossed me the keys to the Chevy. "You and your drinking buddy up front, Ace. Don't hit nothin'. Me and the little woman gonna play some back-seat bingo and enjoy the ride."

"You mean you want me to drive?" My voice sounded normal. I didn't feel drunk anymore. I couldn't figure Louie out, one moment drowning me in the creek, next moment letting me drive the Chevy.

"Whaddya think, I want you to open the trunk with those?" He pointed to the keys. "No haulin' ass. Back down the mountain. I'll tell you when to stop."

I got the Chevy rolling. Blue looked at me like I was a big shot. I caught a few glimpses of Louie and Faye mashing down in the back seat but after the dunking we took down at the creek I figured it would be wise to keep my eyes on the road. Mountain air rushing through the open windows helped clear my head. Louie wouldn't be so forgiving if I creamed the Chevy. Blue and I folded our arms over the doors like our parents did. Louie or Faye struck a match. The car filled with the odor of burning tobacco. A hand offered a smoldering cigarette over the seat. I reached for it, taking a puff before I passed it to Blue. He pushed it away. Blue wasn't looking so good. I pulled over while he stumbled into the ditch to puke again. Even over the rumbling of the motor we heard his retching.

"Amateur!" Louie yelled at Blue.

I had an inspiration. "Louie? Can Blue drive?"

"Damn better stay on the road."

Off we went again, Blue looking like he might survive after heaving all the beer but driving like an old woman, bent over with a death grip on the steering wheel. I'd seen him do the same thing the first time he rode Betsy after she broke his arm. He held the reins for dear life while she shuffled in circles, her eyes wide open and her feet dancing, but she didn't throw him again. Blue wasn't much of a driver. For all I knew it was the first time he'd tried. He never shifted out of first gear. It seemed like he took an hour to cover a mile. We tried to ignore the rustling from the back seat. I had no idea why Louie brought us along when he wanted to get in Faye's pants. We rolled off the mountain, Blue nursing the brake every five feet, onto a gravel road in the direction of Anaconda. He swung wide on a sharp turn, forcing an oncoming farm truck into the ditch. Blue was so shook up we just sat there idling in the road while the farmer charged out of his truck. He was a slender man in coveralls but his mouth talked big. "You jackass! Where'd you learn to drive?"

Tobacco juice dribbled from the corners of his mouth. "I oughta whip you good right now, step out here, boy." He looked plenty mad. If it dawned on him that Blue was just thirteen, he didn't show it. Then the farmer kicked the Chevy. Louie opened the back door. I saw the farmer step back and spit a brown stream and put up his fists. "Looky here, we got Elvis Presley out here driving around?"

Louie didn't reply. He stooped to inspect the door. I turned to see Faye watching with some amusement. Louie looked at the farmer, who struck a ridiculous pose like a boxer in the middle of nowhere. Louie's voice sounded measured and quiet. "We forced you in the ditch, you kicked my door. We're even." Louie stared at him. The farmer looked uncertain. I think he recognized the danger in Louie, the strength that rippled through his arms, the will to attack. The farmer turned without responding and walked to his truck. He goosed it out of the ditch and drove off.

"Should have clobbered him," I told Louie.

"No reason. He left a footprint on the door. That's all."

"But he was going to fight you."

"I got no beef with him. He's just a man goin' about his business." Louie waved Blue and I out of the front seat. Faye emerged from the back, her blouse unbuttoned halfway down. She turned away from us to close it up. Louie drove back into Anaconda to deposit the lovely Faye at her house. The old man, her father I presumed, came outside to yell some more but she waved him away while she kissed Louie outside the car. She gave him the tongue, I was sure of it. Then she turned to Blue and me.

"You pups come here." She mashed my face into her breasts. Then she pushed me back and leaned down and pecked me right on the lips. I nearly fainted. She did the same to Blue, ignoring the puke. I walked back to the car on shaky legs, riding shotgun, while Blue fell over in exaggerated fashion in the back seat.

"That girl's a dream! I'm in love!" he hollered. He even got a smile from Louie with that crack. In the good half hour drive back to Deer Lodge, windows wide open to air out our clothes, Louie tutored us in the art of avoiding detection after drinking beer. "Remember, losers, when you get home avoid direct contact with the old tigers if you can, brush your teeth, drink lots of water and don't say nothin' about going to a bar or kissin' a girl. Don't be dumb. Tell 'em we went to Washoe Park to see the ducks." We dropped off Blue, who seemed his normal self again, before Louie drove me home. I didn't want him to go. I sensed a quiet resolve in him, even when he did crazy things.

It was near dinnertime but my mother's station wagon was gone. "You're in luck, Ace. Run inside and slam down some water. She won't be happy about beer breath."

I had to know. "Louie?"

He suddenly looked impatient. "Make it fast, Ace."

"Why did you take us to Anaconda? I mean, I had fun and everything but you didn't need a couple of junior high kids tagging along."

"Maybe I did, Ace. I'll explain it to you sometime." I stepped out of the Chevy and he was gone, just like that. I really didn't know much about Louie Moretti, nor did I know his dark secret.

# Danny

*Mom breezed into my bedroom* the next morning swinging a frying pan. I pulled the covers over my face, thinking she was going to gong me with it.

"What time is it?" My head pounded and I had a pretty good idea why. It was my first hangover.

"Almost nine o'clock, Paul. Your father would never approve of you sleeping this late on a Sunday morning. Now roll out and let's get going. Church at eleven."

"Ah, Mom, jeez—."

"Hurry up. Bacon and eggs for you. I might even cook up some pancakes." With that she stepped back in the kitchen to rattle and bang her pots and pans. I thought she might suspect my brazen drinking spree until I heard her humming. I dressed and noticed in the mirror that I needed a haircut. She'd be sending me downtown to the barbershop soon.

"Paul? How many eggs?"

"Uh, three. And lots of bacon." I couldn't believe my good fortune. Mom never cooked before church. We ate Wheaties and Cheerios.

"Then get washed. I've got something to tell you." She stood at the stove, teasing the crackling bacon with a fork. She hadn't cooked since Dad died. I ate a lot of peanut butter and jelly sandwiches. Sometimes I ate a whole can of green peas for lunch. Nothing around our house was the same anymore. It was like Dad took our routine with him when he died. Sally had been gone a month with our grandparents.

I scrubbed with Lava at the kitchen sink, dabbing water and soap around my face to look sincere. Mom paid no attention. She just kept humming at the stove. It was a song from church but I didn't know the words. I never paid attention. None of the boys did. I wished that Sally was sitting with me because Mom was acting strange. I guess I was used to seeing her cry all the time. At least she didn't ask dumb questions about my trip to Anaconda with Louie. She'd probably flip if she knew I drank beer, drove a car and kissed a high school girl. I couldn't figure out why she wasn't giving me the third degree. I could hear her say it: "What possibly would an eighth grade boy be doing in Anaconda if he wasn't there for his mother to buy him school clothes?" When Mom was mad she spoke like that. Strange as it was, it kind of took the heat off me.

"Why don't you sit in your father's place?" She bowled me over with that one. Nobody sat in Dad's chair since he died. I mean nobody, not even Uncle Don. It felt a little creepy that Mom was even suggesting it, but I sat down. I somehow felt closer to Dad.

Mom brought me a steaming plate of eggs over easy with five strips of bacon, still sizzling. Then she handed me a separate plate piled with pancakes. As I tucked into all that, she slid a tall glass of orange juice in front of me.

"Mom —."

"Eat up, Paul, you're the man of the house now."

"No, I'm not, I'm thirteen."

"Almost fourteen, and yes you are." My birthday came in October, right before Halloween. She sat down beside me, in Sally's place, with a smaller portion of bacon and eggs. Steam rolled off hot coffee, which she'd poured into Dad's favorite mug. The aroma of it made me think of Saturday mornings at the lumberyard. It didn't seem right, chowing down like this with Dad gone and Mom suddenly acting like she wasn't sad anymore. He'd been gone, what, five weeks? It seemed like yesterday, or like eternity. It was all the same to me.

"Mom, what's going on? This breakfast and all —."

She looked at me like she had something on her mind. Mom was quite pretty with her hazy green eyes and perfect white teeth. She was a killer in high school. I'd seen her annuals. Prom queen. Cheerleader. Voted most popular girl in senior class. She made a name in Poetry Club, too, and got an A in almost every subject. I don't know why she occasionally ranted and raved at me like on the night of the school dance. Perhaps the stress of raising kids was too much. I don't know. I couldn't understand her sometimes.

"So Paul?" She held the coffee cup halfway to her lips, then put it down and fidgeted with her silverware. "When I went to the cemetery yesterday —."

"What?"

" — I saw your father."

I nearly spit out a mouthful of bacon. A chill raced up my back. Mom saw my stricken look.

"I know it sounds frightening, Paul, but it wasn't. I saw your father. I know he's all right. And he made me understand that everything's okay."

I felt like running. "You saw … Dad's ghost?"

Mom smiled. "Something like that. I want to tell you about seeing your father because you should know that he appeared to me at the cemetery. You're thinking I was scared but I wasn't. Now what I'm going to tell you, don't repeat to Sally when Grandpa and Grandma bring her home next week. She wouldn't understand and it would alarm her, get it?"

"This is too creepy, Mom." I was thankful she was telling me this in broad daylight. In seventh grade book club I'd ordered a ghost story. It was all about doors slamming shut by themselves and lights bobbing in dark rooms that were empty. Or the girl killed in a car wreck who was seen by her roommate a couple of hours afterwards calmly packing a suitcase beside her bed. That kind of terrifying stuff. *Maybe Dad knows I got drunk and kissed Faye.*

"You're old enough to know. I didn't feel scared at all. Now eat and I'll tell you about it."

I had to admit those eggs tasted darn fine and the bacon too. I finally understood why Mom cooked the big breakfast. I wasn't going anywhere until she was done talking.

"So there I was, kneeling in front of your father's headstone, talking to him like I do when I'm out there."

"What do you tell him?"

"What I'm feeling. How sad I am that he's gone. And I tell him about you and your sister and catch him up on the news around town and what Toby hears at the lumberyard."

"And your job?"

"Yes, I tell him that I'm a nurse at the clinic now and how hard it is making ends meet. I don't know what I'm going to do when Sally gets home." She stopped to wipe a tear. Then she forced a smile. "I do worry."

"Mom? What happened?"

"I'm kneeling at your father's grave, feeling sorry for myself. It's one of those gorgeous Montana afternoons where everything seems exactly right if I wasn't mourning in the cemetery. I mean, nobody's around except for some boys setting sprinklers over in the next section, and I'm sitting there feeling sorry for myself."

Mom had me feeling bad now. While she was draped over Dad's grave I was getting drunk with Blue. It didn't seem right.

"I'm looking at the headstone, right at the name "Frank Scott Morrison" chiseled into it, and somebody's standing behind it just like that. I mean, all of a sudden I see a pair of overalls. And I look up and there's your father, smiling at me. Except he doesn't look like he did when he died. I see a much younger man, about the age when we got married."

"How did you know it was him?"

"Because I remembered. And you know what else? He wore a sweater I'd knitted for him after we met. A blue sweater with the initials 'FM' over his heart. It's still in his dresser, the very same one. There he was, on a hot summer day, wearing that sweater. He didn't seem uncomfortable at all."

"Did he talk to you?" Hearing this was creeping me out but I kept eating. I squeezed more syrup on my pancakes. *He knows for sure.*

"Not like we're talking now. I could hear his voice but his lips weren't moving. He was talking inside my head somehow. And you know what he said, Paul? He said that he's in a beautiful place and not to grieve. He said that he's never far away from us. And he said don't be sad, but happy, because Heaven really does exist. He smiled at me and then he was gone. But there was something more, Paul. I've never felt such peace. He did something to me. I just don't know what, but it was like he filled me with his happiness and wants the same for you and Sally."

"I haven't seen Dad. I'm not sure I want to. But I'm glad you did. I mean, Mom, you're so different today."

"I love your father, Paul. You know something? He hardly ever told me that he loved me and yet I never doubted that he did. Your father wasn't much for sentimentalities. Now that I saw him at the cemetery, well, it's different. I felt instant love from him. Does this make sense to you?"

"It does, Mom." Her story was beginning to sound like a private matter and I didn't want to hear more of it. I carved up my pancakes and kept my eyes low. She squeezed my shoulder and went back to eating. "He loves me," she said once, as her utensils clinked on her plate.

##### /////

It was on the Friday night that Louie took me to the Rustic Drive-In that Marcy and I got back together. The worst part was that I started off mad after seeing her holding hands with Danny Mulligan that morning. They were strolling down Main Street as bold as you please. I was riding with Mom in the station wagon with sacks of groceries in the back seat. She could see that I was boiling mad but didn't say anything. It was bad enough riding around with your mother when your girlfriend was hanging out with another guy. That was all it took to get me interested in Marcy again. I suppose she was sore that I wasn't calling her on the phone. Some evenings when I felt like it Mom was sitting around and I knew she would listen to every word.

Louie stopped by the house that afternoon to ask Mom if he could use the barn to work on the Chevy. He could see I was teed off.

"Problem, Ace?"

"Yeah, this kid Danny is moving in on Marcy. I saw them. I want to pound his ugly face in."

Louie leaned beside the Chevy, studying himself in the rearview mirror. "Well, I reckon you could after the thrashin' you gave them Tucker boys." Louie smiled. "Or, you could use your head for something other than a damn punchin' bag."

"What do you mean?"

"I mean if you go pound this kid's brains out, you rile Marcy's sympathy. For him, see?"

"What would you do if some guy tried to hustle Faye?"

"Pound his brains out."

"So why—."

"You ask too many questions, Ace. What's the real problem here?"

"Maybe she doesn't like me anymore."

"What the hell? Don't be a dumb junior high kid, Ace. If you want a girl you go and get her. You don't stand around worryin' about what she's doin' if she could be doin' it with you, get it?" Louie sounded like he knew his business, I'll give him that.

"I need to call her up."

"You do that, Ace. Don't take no for an answer." While I was pondering that, Mom came outside. She didn't seem to know what to do with Louie. She waved him toward the barn and went back in the house.

"Louie, my mother acts like she doesn't want us to go into the barn. I don't get it."

"You know why, don't ya Ace? It's your old man's place, right? That's why we're gonna take good care of it." Dad's shop, brimming with tools, was at one end. In part of the other end, Dad had built a bedroom. Blue and Max got a kick out of us having a bedroom in the barn. Nobody wanted to stay there because mice had taken over. My parents had taken to using the room for storage.

Louie eased Dad's old Ford pickup into a corner of the barn, taking care not to scratch the fenders, and then nosed the Chevy inside. I saw the brake lights blink before he cut the motor. I followed him inside. Louie saw me staring at Dad's workbench where he died. I had avoided the barn most of the summer.

"Where are those coins, Ace?" I pointed to a row of Folgers coffee cans on the shelf above the bench. Louie lifted one down but put it back when he saw it was full to the top. Then second and third cans were full too, but the fourth had room. Louie set it on the workbench. Then he walked around to the back of the Chevy where he popped the trunk and rustled around awhile. He carried a wrinkled paper sack to the bench and poured a clinking stream of coins into Dad's old coffee can.

"Louie?"

"Can't have no boat if you don't save for it, Ace." He lifted the can back onto the shelf. "Your old man musta saved three hundred dollars in these cans. Look here at all the silver dollars." Louie rummaged through the can, pulling out fistfuls of coins to show me.

"How much does a boat cost, do you think?"

Louie scratched his head. "Maybe seven hundred big ones. The motor costs more."

I had to ask. "Louie? What happened to your parents? You showed me that picture —." Pain flashed in his face, something deep and terrible, and for an instant I saw a boy much younger than Louie the teenager. I dared not to say more. He straightened and turned to me.

"Not much to tell. I was a kid, even younger than you. We lived in Butte. I go to school that morning, see? When I get home they were dead." He spit out the last word. "And you wanna know how. They had a car, Ace, an old Plymouth that died on the tracks just when the ore train was comin' down the hill and —." He stopped just like that and lifted the hood on the Chevy.

"How did—."

"Maybe some other time, Ace, not now." Then, "Find me a socket wrench, will ya? We've gotta pull these plugs and check for carbon deposits."

"What's that?"

"Gunk that closes the gap where the spark should be. Here." He reached for the socket, and after half a dozen quick twists, pulled a spark plug out of the engine block. "See here, not much to worry about on this one, but if you let it go the plug don't fire right and you lose power." Louie scraped the spark plug with a little wire brush. Bits of carbon fell to the floor like spilled pepper. He held the gleaming plug against a stream of sunlight trying to penetrate a window caked with sawdust. "Watch close, Ace, you brush it good and clean like this."

"How come you never call me Paul?"

"Cause you're Ace to me, no other reason. Now look, be careful when you screw the plug back in 'cause no way you wanna strip the threads. Turn it with your fingers first. After you feel it turn real smooth tighten it with the socket just enough to make it snug. Go too tight and you'll break the plug. Hell, we'll have problems then."

Louie handed me the wrench. "What, you—?"

"You got seven more, Ace, get busy. Three more on this side of the engine, four on the other. I gotta a tailpipe threatenin' to come apart back here. Rocky road up to Uncle Jimmy's place. Damn, Ace, where'd your old man find all these tools? And what's with the green paint?"

"Dad got tired of people borrowing his tools and not bringing them back. He sprayed paint all over them so nobody would forget they belonged to him, I guess." Louie grabbed a trouble light off the wall, plugged it in, and slid a canvas under the Chevy. Next thing I knew I was looking at his boots.

"So Louie?"

"Yeah?" he spoke from somewhere underneath, punctuated with plenty of profanity and the banging of tools on metal.

"Why do you trust me to work on your car? I mean, Dad never let me mess with stuff like this."

"Somethin' you gotta learn, Ace." Louie banged and swore some more. The Chevy shook. "Damn bolts!" He let up for a second to catch his breath. "Look here. Your dad's gone and you can't be a kid no more, Ace."

"I'm only thirteen."

"Ain't too young. I was in the first grade."

"After your parents died? Where did you live?"

"With Uncle Jimmy sometimes when he wasn't bitchin' drunk. Later with my sister in Walkerville. She's older but I wouldn't give a rat's ass for that wimp of a no-account husband. He ain't got shit for brains." Louie banged around again. "So my point is, you and me, we gotta figure out things for ourselves. You got a mom but she can't teach you how to keep a car runnin', how to get laid, that kind of thing."

"You mean you're going to help me get laid?"

"Depends. I'll ask Faye who she knows over in Anaconda. Or there's that girlfriend you've been cryin' over. You oughta ask her."

"Marcy? She'd never do that."

"You'd better hope not, Ace, since you're not doin' a damn thing to make sure she's not doin' it with someone else."

The meaning of that hit me like a hammer. I was halfway to the black phone that hung on the wall of the shop before he stopped me.

"Get back over to this car and start pullin' plugs. If you wanna drive the Chevy, you keep it runnin'."

I reached along the second plug wire until I found the nipple, pulling it off the plug with a plop. I slid the socket wrench over the plug and cracked it loose. Louie slid under the car until I could see his face in the tungsten glow from the trouble light.

"Get those plugs right and then go call your girl, Ace. That sweet doll's waited long enough."

/////

The Rustic Drive-In was three miles south of Deer Lodge. The giant screen faced away from the state highway as if turning a cold shoulder to nonpaying motorists. I had gone to the outdoor theater with my parents when I was young enough to dress in pajamas and fall asleep with blankets and pillows in the back seat of the station wagon. Now, the back seat was taking on new meaning.

After I finished with the spark plugs, I called Marcy from the phone in the barn. I didn't care if Louie heard what I said. He kept working under the car.

"Hello?" It was Marcy, answering the phone.

"Marcy, it's me, Paul."

"Yes?" She sounded cheesed off at first. I guess she was mad that I didn't call her. She warmed up after we got to talking. "Don't you want to take me out, Paul?"

"How about tonight, to the Rialto?" If Danny Mulligan thought he had dibs on Marcy, I wanted to make him suffer while Marcy and I held hands and kissed in the dark. "There's a new movie about men and their flying machines. I saw it on the show bill outside the theater."

"I'm going to see a movie, Paul, but not that one. My parents are taking us to the drive-in. My father won't let me stay home. He's on this kick lately about our family spending time together. Will I see you there?"

That's how I came to talk Louie into taking me to the drive-in. He acted like it wasn't any big deal taking a junior high kid but I knew Mom would never go for it. I fibbed and told her I was going to see Blue and wouldn't be home until late. I felt terrible for lying to her but I was a man now. Louie had said so. I needed to make my own decisions.

"Your old lady catches you, I'm out of it," Louie told me as we cruised to Anaconda to get Faye. I was hoping he'd let me drive but he didn't bring it up. He lit a cigarette and pushed the Chevy to eighty. Telephone poles flew past.

"When I get to the drive-in do you mind if Marcy hangs out with us in the Chevy?"

"That's the idea, Ace. You mess around and get her pregnant, that's your problem."

"How come everything's my problem, Louie?"

"That's the way the world turns, Ace. You oughta know sooner than later."

We loaded up Faye and got the Chevy rolling as her drunken father swore in our dust. "He's laid off again," Faye explained. "Showed up soaked for swing shift at the Smelter and they'll only tolerate that a few times, you know. So the old boy's been on a bender blaming me and every other damn person he knows. I don't know how in hell he expects to buy groceries. I should have got a job in California this summer."

That got me to wondering. "Do you go to school?" Faye, squeezed between Louie and I on the front seat, shot me a look that could kill through makeup-caked eyes. "Wise guy, huh? Hell yes I go to school. Going to be a junior this year at Anaconda High School. Ever hear of the Copperheads?" She hissed and snapped her forearm at me with her fingers extended, like a striking snake. I just about jumped out the window. "Louie, where'd you get this kid? Get him laid, will ya?"

"Tryin', Faye, old Ace over there has a lot to learn."

"Louie, where do you go to school?"

"What, Ace, you keep a diary?"

"Just wondering, that's all." It occurred to me that I didn't know much about Louie at all. He didn't show much of himself. Dad once told me that some people don't say much because it's nobody's business. Others, he said, are running from something.

Louie turned up volume on the radio and motioned for me to hush up. "Hottest song on the charts!" he yelled over a guitar solo that had him bouncing on the seat. That was the first time I heard the Rolling Stones play "I Can't Get No Satisfaction," and I doubted I would ever forget. Louie and Faye shouted out the chorus over and over. They would have pushed Mick Jagger off stage and taken over his band that very moment, I swear. When the song finished, Louie switched off the radio and turned to me. "So you want my life's history, Ace? Last year I went to Butte High. Got tired of bunkin' at my sister's place. So I come over here to Deer Lodge with Uncle Jimmy. The old sot thinks I oughta go to Deer Lodge High School this year."

"Powell County High School," I corrected him.

"I told Uncle Jimmy, well, I'll be eighteen and can make my own way. Don't know why I need to go another year anyway. I already did eleven, most of the time."

That got Faye to laughing. "Don't you want to become an astronaut? Maybe you could fly to the moon someday."

"Bunch of crap," Louie said. "Ain't nobody ever goin' to do that."

I felt like reminding Louie and Faye of the disappearing summer. "Well, school starts Monday, you know." It was depressing to think of it. I was sorry I brought it up and so were they. Summers in Montana came and went too fast. Then, "Louie, are we bringing beer to the drive-in?"

"Hell, yes, Ace. You never go to the drive-in dry." He pulled off the highway at a collection of buildings with a solitary gas pump in front. A row of pickup trucks with gun racks in their back windows were parked nose-in to a bar equipped with a front door that looked like a log on hinges. "They don't card in here. Eighteen years old, fifty, a voice from the graveyard, they don't give a rip." He came out a few minutes later with armfuls of six packs that he stashed in the trunk.

"How many cans, Louie?" He slipped behind the wheel and fired up the motor.

"Afraid you ain't going to get enough, Ace? Twenty four. Save some for Faye." She flipped her hair and shot me a smirk. I was in love with Faye but I knew better than to mess with Louie's girl. She was out of my league anyway, but Faye had some uncommon beauty about her. I could see why she liked hanging around with Louie. She was just like him. They both seemed lost with no good family life. They were better looking than everybody else, too. I knew hardly anything about Faye except that her father shouting from the porch told me a lot. I didn't know if she had a mother. I'd have to ask her sometime.

Louie pulled the Chevy into a grove of trees about a mile from the Rustic to lock me in the trunk. "Nobody sees you, we save paying for a ticket, Ace." The trunk was dark and musty and smelled of tire rubber and gasoline. We stopped at the little ticket booth before I felt the car rise and fall over the mounds until Louie found a good place to park. The beer felt cold against my face. Too bad Blue and Max would miss out. I wondered what they were doing. Blue found this new girl named Rosie who had just moved from Missoula. Her dad worked down at the Milwaukee Road roundhouse fixing locomotives. Blue and Rosie went to the Keystone Drug for milk shakes a few times. He said it was serious. I hadn't seen much of Max, whose parents all of a sudden acted like he had too many responsibilities at home to go anywhere. They did let him hang around with Peg on Saturday nights when her parents drove into town from their farm near Galen. I think Dad's heart attack somehow brought all the pain of Kenny's death back to them. It couldn't be easy, the way Kenny's face was driven through the windshield. Max told me they kept the casket closed.

I figured Louie might mess around and leave me in the trunk but he popped the lid right away, probably for the beer. The sun, glowing like a giant red basketball, fell behind Mount Powell. My arms felt a little cold. I wished I'd brought a jacket. Louie opened a beer for Faye with his church key. Then he reached out the window for the speaker. It was a clunky brown thing that clipped over the side window. Putting sound to images of Coca Cola and buttered popcorn on the movie screen, it crackled with appeals to spend money at the snack bar.

"Hell with that," Louie said. "Let's drink beer." He opened a Rainier for me, wiping the foam away with his hand. He turned to Faye. "Ace here helped me tune up the Chevy. Kid's showing progress."

Faye turned to me and sniffed. "He still looks like a pup to me, wet around the ears and no place to go." That Faye, always trying to make me feel good. Her white shorts slid high on her freckled legs. It was hard not to look.

Louie caught on. "Look, Ace, why don't you drink up and go look for that chick you've got the hots for? You come back with her, sit up front, got it? Faye likes the back seat." They laughed at that. It was hard being too young to understand. I admired Louie. The beer burned my throat a bit and by the time I finished the sky was dark. I started on my quest to find Marcy while previews flashed on the big movie screen. On a patch of grass in front of all the cars full of people, little kids played on swing sets in the light from the screen above them. The wind eased through, as if looking for a parking place. It felt sweet and wet like the first breath of rain. Mom would be home alone thinking I was visiting Blue. To tell you the truth I felt a little bit guilty. I hoped she understood that things were different now. Like Louie said, I had to figure things out for myself. I didn't have a dad. I would be a man soon. I felt a tingle from the beer.

After the movie featuring Jimmy Stewart started, I saw Marcy tossing her ponytail and walking toward the snack bar. I jumped out of the Chevy and hurried to catch her but Danny Mulligan showed up first. I never had much use for Danny. His mouth never stopped. You know the kind.

"So, Morrison, where are your pajamas and teddy bears? Isn't that what little kids usually do when they come to the drive-in at bedtime?" Danny slung his arm around Marcy but she pulled away. Marcy looked surprised to see us both.

"Paul?" She looked a little scared. Danny stepped in front of her. "Get lost, Morrison. Marcy's my girl." He pushed her toward the snack bar. They disappeared in a swirl of people coming and going. I didn't know what to do. Back at the Chevy, I found Louie and Faye making out in the back seat like crazy. I felt like crying.

"Ace, what the hell?" Louie looked like he wanted me to get lost. I told him what had happened. "So go pound the loser, Ace."

"You said not to, didn't you? I mean, you said Marcy wouldn't like that."

"Changed my mind. Lay him out and bring her back her and have a beer. And Ace? Give me your glasses. Break those and you won't see nothin'."

"I've got to wear them or I can't see what I'm doing, Louie."

"Better get in the first punch then. Don't back up or nothing sissy like that. Just charge in and whale on the prune, got it?" That was Louie for you, giving instructions from the back seat of the Chevy on how to pound a guy while making out with the hottest girl in Montana. Faye's blouse was unbuttoned. I saw her skin around a white bra. I headed back to the snack bar, mad as hell that if I didn't pound Danny, I'd get on Louie's wrong side. Danny Mulligan scared me but it would be worse telling Louie that I backed off from a fight.

I scuffed my tennis shoes in the rough gravel outside the snack bar. It smelled of overcooked hot dogs. I thought of Max taking it to that Tucker bully with a barrage of punches. Max was more like Louie than me. So was Blue. Yet here I was, getting tips from Louie. It made me proud. I balled my fists to fight for Marcy, for my girl. I stood alone outside the snack bar half hoping that Danny was still inside and half hoping he wasn't. Now that the movie started most people had gone back to their cars.

A flickering orange neon light that read CONCESSION bathed over me. I felt cold and kind of mixed up. Should I be home painting model cars with Blue? Then I saw Danny. He was breathing all over Marcy, balancing a carton of popcorn in one hand and grabbing at her like nobody's business with the other. She tried to push him away. He laughed and pinched her butt. That was it for me, all right. I threw everything I had at his leering face. He barely saw it coming. When my fist connected somewhere in the vicinity of his nose, he gave a cry and snapped backwards, showering popcorn over his falling body. He lay in the gravel holding his face and sobbing. I stood there for a second, ready to belt him again, but he stayed down. I hoped Danny didn't have an older brother. I'd have to go interrupt Louie while he was getting it on with Faye. He wouldn't like that.

"Paul, what the hell?" Marcy didn't look too pleased.

"He has no right to treat you like that, Marcy. You're my girl."

"You broke his nose I think!"

"He asked for it." A man with long sideburns and a part in his hair as wide as the Clark Fork River was kneeling over Danny, who was crying like a girl. My hand hurt. I'd socked him good. "Let's get out of here." I led Marcy through the maze of cars until I found the Chevy. Try finding a black Chevy in the dark, unless it runs you down like Louie tried to do that night after the spring dance. "Don't look in the back seat," I whispered to her. We opened the driver's door and slid behind the wheel like I owned the car. I guess in a way I did, or at least I felt like it. Louie and Faye rustled behind us.

"You pound him, Ace?"

Marcy started to turn, but I stopped her. Who knows what she'd see back there. "Well," Marcy bragged, "Paul knocked him flat with one punch. Just like that."

Louie slapped me hard on the shoulder. "Expected nothing less of you, Ace. Help yourselves to the beer." The rustling started again. I turned up the speaker. There was Jimmy Stewart, talking about the Civil War. "Shenandoah" looked like a good movie. Marcy put on a pair of glasses to watch.

"When did you get those? Jeez, Marcy, glasses?"

"This summer, just for seeing far away." She pulled my glasses off. "Let's see how you do, Paul." She pulled off my glasses and waved them around. She even threatened to throw them out the window.

"Hey!" When Marcy was done messing around with my glasses I popped a beer for her but she wouldn't drink it. I downed it myself, figuring I impressed her by doing so. We watched the movie until the gunfire started and then made out. I tried feeling her up but she pushed my hand away. My fingers fell on her bare leg, cool in the night air. We kissed some more. Then I drank another beer before it dawned on me I'd have to go back to the snack bar to pee.

"My parents will wonder where I went," Marcy fretted. She looked in the rearview mirror to check her lipstick. Marcy was a looker, I'll tell you that, but different from Faye. I'd bet she could get ten boys staring at her at once but they'd all know not to mess with her. Marcy hadn't learned to push boys away. Danny knew that before I socked him.

"So whassa you tell 'em?"

"What?"

"Whassa you tell parents, Mawcy?"

"Why are you having trouble talking, Paul?" She shot me a scowl of disapproval. "You drank too much. My dad gets like that at family reunions. So I told them that I saw some friends from school. I lied to them and if they find out I'll be in big trouble." She nodded toward the beer on the seat beside us. "I'd drink one of those if I wasn't worried about my parents catching me. Maybe two." She leaned close to my ear. "Maybe I'll let you feel me up, would you like that, Paul?"

I reached for her blouse. She pushed my hand away again. "Sometime when we're alone," she whispered. "That's what I mean." She must have reconsidered because she took my hand and pressed it to a puckish mound under her bra. "Just this once," she said, holding my hand tight to her chest with hers. "My parents will kill me if I don't get back."

Louie spoke from the depths of the back seat. "Good idea. You two get lost. Don't come back 'til I say so." After we climbed out he locked the door behind us. Marcy kissed me, slipping me the tongue. Then she grabbed the front of my shirt. "Don't leave me again, Paul. I know you're hurting and all mixed up but I like you a lot, okay? Call me tomorrow." She disappeared into the rows of cars, her ponytail bobbing. Dizzy from the beer, I watched Jimmy Stewart talking to somebody's grave. "Martha," the tombstone said. My mother's name. The scene made me think of Mom kneeling at Dad's grave at Hillcrest Cemetery. I felt a wave of shame for lying to her. Now I was drunk again.

*I don't even know what to say to you any more, Martha. There's not much I can tell you about this war. It's like all wars, I guess. The undertakers are winning. And the politicians who talk about the glory of it. And the old men who talk about the need of it. And the soldiers, well, they just wanna go home. I guess you're not so lonely any more, with Ann and James and Jacob. And maybe the boy. You didn't know Ann, did you? Well, you'd like her. You'd like her, Martha. Why, she and James are so much alike, they're just*

*like... no... no... we were never that much alike, were we Martha?*
*We just sorta grew alike through the years. But I wish, I wish I*
*could just know what you're thinking about it all, Martha. And*
*maybe it wouldn't seem so bad to me if I knew what you thought*
*about it.*

Suddenly I felt like going home. I had to pee, too. Louie
was lost somewhere behind the fogged windows of the
Chevy with Faye. The car started to shake. I felt my way
through the dark to the bushes at the back of the drive-in,
careful not to trip into the barbed wire fence along the Clark
Fork River. It was easier peeing back there in the sagebrush
than walking to the bathroom at the snack bar. Danny might
be laying low for me if he wasn't still bawling like a baby. He
was the type. When I was done and zipped up I walked
around a bit, hoping to see Marcy again. I was cold and
lonely. The movie was about done. All the actors on the
screen were shot or crying. I wondered what war was all
about. Dad had told me about a place called Vietnam. He
figured it was the next big war for our country. I'd seen
headlines about Vietnam in the *Montana Standard*. I didn't get
what Vietnam had to do with Deer Lodge.

Some of the cars started to leave. I thought I saw Marcy
but it was too dark. The moon was a sliver. Even the stars had
gone to bed. Maybe the morning would bring frost. Frost on
the grass, on summer's last days, on Dad's grave. I stood near
the Chevy, shaking, with Louie nowhere in sight. A yellow
beam from a flashlight flickered around me an instant before
a big hand clamped on my shoulder. I turned to see Charlie
Mitchell, one of the town cops. I knew Charlie from the
lumberyard when Dad teased him about throwing old ladies

in jail. Light from the movie screen danced on his silver badge. My mother wouldn't be happy.

# Mom

*I was reminded of how* one person can hurt another from an encounter in *Little Shepherd from Kingdom Come* when Major Buford turned his back on Chad for wearing blue instead of gray. Chad's decision violated everything the major held sacred. I'm the first to admit that Chad's loyalty to the Union had little to do with my situation as a budding juvenile delinquent. It's just that hurting someone close to you hurts even more when you do it for the wrong reasons. I was coming to understand how literature relates to life. After Charlie delivered me to the custody of my mother, who looked ready to kill, it took her an hour to stop crying. I kind of hoped that old Charlie would hang around, at least long enough to drink the bottle of soda that Mom offered him, but Charlie meant business. He took off his hat and raked his flabby fingers through his crewcut.

"Sorry, Martha, I'm late to rattling doors downtown. I'd best get to gittin, I'd say." Charlie hitched up his gun belt and gave me a kindly look. The gun on his hip looked bigger than life. Just above the lip of the holster I could see the trigger, curved and black, waiting for a squeeze of an index finger. Just the thought of Charlie having authority to pull that trigger on someone scared me. "Son, your dad and I went back a long ways. Lost my own father when I was about your age. I know what's eatin' you but lying to your mama ain't gonna bring him back, hear?" He came close and patted my shoulder, an odor of onions wafting from his mouth, before he walked out to the black squad car and drove into the night.

Mom sent me to stew in my bedroom while she moped in the living room. The house felt lonely and empty. I was sure her crying was as much for Dad being gone as for her brat of a son. I was hoping she didn't smell the beer. Charlie sure did. After he found me at the drive-in he put me in the back seat of the squad car. He gave me a lecture about disobeying parents but said drinking beer was even worse because I was just a kid and if I didn't get a grip I might wind up in the reform school at Miles City. "I've got a good mind to take you to jail until you sober up," he said, but I think he saw I got the message. He let me move up front with him and drove me straight home. "I catch you with beer again and it's jail for sure, Paul." Then, "How old are you, boy?"

"Thirteen, fourteen in October, sir."

"Who bought you the beer?"

He almost had me there. I made up another lie. "Some people had their trunk open. I saw a can and took it." Charlie's face told me right away that he didn't believe a word.

"Happened to have a church key in your pocket, did you? Or was the beer sitting there open?" It was more of a statement, like he didn't expect me to answer. "And another thing, how did you get out to the drive-in? Don't tell me you walked, no kid today walks three miles anymore."

"A friend took me."

"Who is this friend?" For a second I thought of making up another story. Charlie's expression told me I'd be wearing coveralls in Miles City, making license plates or whatever they did, if I didn't play straight with him.

"His name is Louie. He's been helping me deal with things since Dad died."

"By buying you beer?"

"I never said that."

"Uh-huh." Charlie, by now turning the squad car down the road to the old farmhouse, shot me a sideways glance. I looked away. I was in big trouble. Mom had switched on the front porch light over the concrete stoop. The grass needed mowing. I'd been putting it off for a week, making excuses that I was having trouble starting the mower. Dad would never stand for that. He rebuilt mowers until they purred. Mom accepted my excuse because she didn't understand the mysteries of his shop in the barn.

Charlie pulled the patrol car to a stop. "How well do you know this Louie, son?" He was silent for a moment. "I know he gave you a hand with those Tucker boys. That was good. Supplying beer to young boys isn't. I think you're a little mixed up about things right now."

Maybe Mom intended to torment me with all that emotion in the living room while I sat on my bed inspecting a model Ford Fairlane that Blue and I made in sixth grade. It was duo-tone, red and blue, although I didn't remember ever seeing a Fairlane painted those colors. I trusted the painting to Blue even though he had the cast on his arm after old Betsy bucked him off. He got sloppy with the paintbrush. I thought of the Chevy, painted all black, and wondered why. Louie loved that car. It was hard to understand, Louie growing up with no parents. Was he really that much different from me? I missed Blue and Max. I thought about baseball, about the musky odor of a wet leather glove in summer rain, and after my mother quit her crying and went to bed, I fell asleep.

///// 

The story came out the next morning even before I got the third degree. I sat at the kitchen table in my pajamas. No bacon or eggs or pancakes this time. I made Mom forget about the day she saw Dad in the cemetery. She glared at me as I held my head over a bowl of cereal. Then she started in. After I told her I was going to see Blue, she went to the church supper. Imagine whom she saw there. Yes, Blue himself with his mother, and Blue you know is a responsible boy who goes to church socials with his mother. And no, Blue hadn't seen me. She got worried that maybe she misunderstood me. She called Max, talked to his parents, called Marcy's house and got no answer, drove the drag a few times downtown, waited outside the Rialto when the movie let out, scoured Milwaukee, Missouri, California, Texas, Kentucky and all the other streets in town named after cities and states, even went to the playground behind O. D. Speer School after the streetlights came on. Finally, after curfew blew at City Hall and the bells at Immaculate Conception Church chimed ten times, she called the *police*. She spit out that word like it was poison.

"Then, come to find out, you're escorted home in a police car with all the neighbors watching." Nothing bothered Mom more than other people thinking poorly of the Morrison family. She launched into one of her tirades and laid out the full emotional drama for me: her fear that I was dead in a ditch somewhere, kidnapped by who knows who, or taken to Butte by criminals who make me work in the mines while they play cards and drink whiskey and nobody ever finds me, while down at the clinic she listens to whispers as people gossip about our family, and when Sally grows up she will lead a life of crime because that's what she learned from her big brother. I admit Mom got me with that last one. I hated to think of Sally toting guns and robbing banks for a living. She was a brat but she was no Bonnie Parker.

Mom went on and on, blissfully not asking for an explanation, until Charlie's police car stopped outside the house, the red light on top again a beacon for nosy neighbors. She exhaled in exasperation. "Now what? This is bad enough, young man."

This time Charlie agreed to a cup of coffee. He eased his heft into Dad's chair at the kitchen table while I hovered over my soggy cereal, feeling worse all the time. I couldn't believe how much three beers made your head hurt.

Mom's demeanor changed. "What brings you back, Charlie?" She sounded composed all of a sudden.

Charlie got right to it. "Art Mulligan called me with a beef this mornin'. You know Art, a guard down at the prison, not a bad guy if you don't cross him. Says Paul here beat up his son Danny at the drive-in last night. You know the kid? Got problems for sure. No stranger to trouble, I admit that. But Art says Danny's nose is flat broke and claims Paul done it."

Mom stared at Charlie in disbelief. She grabbed the edge of the table as if to steady herself. She stared at my right hand, which held the spoon, and I realized it was purple and puffy. "Paul beat somebody up?" She looked at me from wells of sadness in her green eyes. "Paul?" Her tone suggested that I don't dare lie.

"He was hurting Marcy. I had to do something."

"Marcy? What in the world was Marcy doing there?" Mom looked like she wanted to cry again. "Charlie, we haven't had time to sort this out."

Charlie walked to the stove to pour more coffee. "Hope you don't mind me helpin' myself, Martha. Got used to the Morrison hospitality all those long years Frank had the lumberyard." He fell into an awkward silence. When nobody spoke, "Now this Mulligan kid. I'll bet half the boys in junior high school would like to lay him out like Paul did, knocked him flat on his back is what I heard. One thing to know. He's a cousin of them Tucker boys. We hear that family skipped but you never know. You hear from them Tuckers, you call me right away. They're a bad bunch in anybody's book." Charlie took a long swig from the green "Morrison Lumber" mug and set it on the counter. "Martha, I don't plan to make myself a nuisance around here. You got a good boy there. He's confused, that's my opinion." Charlie looked even bigger in the daylight. He was an old man who long ago lost the need to impress anybody. After he was gone, Mom tore into me. She marched me into the living room where she consigned me to one end of the couch. She absentmindedly picked up a *Better Homes and Gardens* magazine. She kept it on her lap, unopened, while I told her the whole story except for Louie buying beer. I figured I was in enough trouble already.

"What in the world would a seventh grader be doing with a high school boy out that late?" She gave me one of those glares before ruffling the pages in the magazine. It seemed odd, my mother thumbing through *Better Homes and Gardens* while I sat under the white heat from a pole lamp like a criminal in those detective programs on television. It was a gray morning and looked like rain. The living room was even darker because Mom hadn't opened the curtains. "You better have a good explanation for this, young man." She sounded hysterical. I felt sorry for her. I think it was dawning on her that with Dad gone she had to heap on all the punishment when I went astray. *I'm on my own now. Louie said so.*

"Mom, we were going to a movie. *Shenandoah* with Jimmy Stewart. It was about the Civil War, see, and —."

"You didn't have permission to do that. You lied to me. You met your girlfriend there. You got in a fight over her. And this Louie, I don't want you hanging out with him. He's too old for you. Who knows what else was going on last night that you're not telling me about. This is serious, Paul. Do you understand?"

"He's my friend, Mom. He looks out for me."

She crossed her arms, a sure sign of trouble. Her eyes shot daggers. "Your father was never sure about him and I'm not either. If you pull something like this again you'll be grounded for life and I'll have his hide. I mean it, Paul."

It was no use arguing. Mom kept me home for a month. I was to restrain from felonious behavior, earn top marks in school, never lie again and most repugnant of all, apologize to Danny Mulligan and mean it. Knowing he was a cousin to the Tucker boys, I was doubly glad for pounding him. After all that, Mom opened the curtains and headed outside to her garden. She paused at the back door.

"I hope that with all your escapades you haven't forgotten that Grandma and Grandpa are bringing Sally home on the train tomorrow. Get dressed and vacuum and dust the entire house and then clean the bathroom and check with me about everything else you'll be doing today. Got it?" Mom knew she was in charge again. Even so, I couldn't turn my back on Louie. Maybe someday I would be just like him.

///// 

School came the following Monday. Wearing new brown shoes that gave me blisters and corduroy pants and a shirt with a button-down collar made me sad. Autumn was like death all over again, at least until I saw Marcy in a red blouse and black skirt. Friday night's passion at the drive-in came back to me all at once. I stared at her in wonder. She smiled.

"Did you get in trouble, Paul? I really caught it for being gone so long when I got back to the car." She looked at me like we were in love. All day we traded locker notes scrawled on sheets of notebook paper. We had only one class together, which was fourth-period art. I used the time to sketch my impression of her. Her head looked too small but I made her breasts especially large and her lips red and sensuous like Faye's. I was having a great time until Miss Blankenship told us to leave our work on her desk. Everyone else had drawn Mount Powell's craggy peak as she had told us to do. She wouldn't recognize Marcy in the drawing except that I had written, "I love Marcy," in red letters on it. I hid my sure "F" in my science textbook and when the bell rang, scooted down the hall to shop class. We wore gray aprons that hung on pegs on the wall. Blue leaned over a table, measuring a board and ignoring me. Across the room, Max examined an array of woodworking tools. Blue was sore for sure. I waved at Max but he barely acknowledged me.

Blue finally came over to my house a week later to yell at me for being stupid. "You and me, we've been friends for a long time, Paul. It's like Louie is your best friend now. Max thinks so too. I know everything is changed for you" — he waved toward our house to show his reference to Dad being gone — "but I've got to tell you, what's the use of leaving us out?" He went on like that, brushing aside my observation that I still barely knew Louie. "We're not in his league, Paul. He's got a car, he's a fighter, look at that honey he runs around with. I'll bet she gives you wet dreams every night." That got us to talking about the night at the drive-in. Blue wanted all the details. It was just like him being mad one minute, talking like somebody's old man, and then hungry for details the next. He liked the part about the fight. It was a good thing Danny Mulligan was a freshman at the high school down the hill. At least I didn't see him around the junior high. He might be laying for me. The next day after school, since I was grounded for what seemed like eternity, Blue brought Max over to my house. Max wasn't sore for long. He told us a long story about dating the waif, holding hands, giving her a present he bought down at the Corner Drug. Blue made fun before bragging about making out with Rosie at the Rialto. It felt like old times. I didn't tell them about feeling up Marcy. It felt like a secret I wanted to keep.

Grandma and Grandpa stayed for a few weeks until they got bored. Grandma sat in the living room watching *As the World Turns* while she knitted. Grandpa paced around outside and sometimes strolled into town to watch people passing in cars, hanging laundry, delivering mail and walking dogs. A few times he went out to the barn to "check on things," as if being a guardian of it was required duty, but

I had come to know my grandfather as an impatient man. My mother was the last of six boys and girls from hardy Irish stock. Half of Montana descended from Ireland, I swear. You couldn't go anyplace without running into a Walsh or a Donnegan or an O'Neill. It's just that Mom's family came from North Dakota where Norwegians and Lutherans ran the show. If your name wasn't Peterson or Langrud or some variation you weren't part of the crowd. Grandpa didn't care. He said he missed his friends who met him every morning for coffee. He felt sad that Dad was gone. Grandpa was a lot like Dad. Maybe that's Grandpa stared out the window a lot.

"Your father is struggling with his own mortality," I heard Grandma tell Mom one night as they stood at the kitchen sink, Mom washing and Grandma drying. I didn't know what that meant but it sounded serious. Two days later we drove Grandpa and Grandma to the Northern Pacific depot. They had two big brown suitcases with wood trim on the edges. Mom had packed their red plastic lunch basket with sandwiches and fruit and filled their thermos with boiling hot coffee. We waited on the platform as the locomotive roared past, leaving Grandma and Mom to clutch their skirts and Grandpa to steady his fedora in the wind. When the train stopped white men in black uniforms and black men in white uniforms stepped from the train, blinking at the vestiges of the Old West surrounding them. Grandpa saw me staring. "Conductors over there" — he pointed to the black uniforms — "porters over there." Grandpa and Grandma hugged us. Mom cried. Within four minutes the train disappeared down the track, its red taillight winking in the dusk.

It was good to have Sally home again. She seemed confused that Dad was gone. I caught her looking at his jackets hanging in the hall closet. She caressed their sleeves with her small fingers. She told me about the month she had spent in Bismarck. She rode on a big paddleboat on the Missouri River. Our grandparents took her to the Twin Cities in Minnesota to see the state fair. It was full of farmers with draft horses and exotic breeds of cattle. Sally said the fair had a carnival bigger than she had ever imagined. She decided that the little one that came to Deer Lodge during the Tri-County Fair was a joke. I reminded her that we're a great deal smaller than Minneapolis and St. Paul.

I'd missed the whole thing. The Deer Lodge fair, that is. It didn't seem right going without Dad. He made a big deal out of driving down Main Street during the parade pulling the Morrison Lumber float with green crepe paper fluttering and Toby throwing bubblegum from a stack of boards. And always, on the Saturday night of the fair, Dad and Mom took us to see farm animals and after the sun fell over the mountains, to the midway of the carnival where neon lights tilted and whirled against an ink-black sky. We went together and left together. Sally got me to thinking about the fair. I wished I'd gone there with Marcy but it still wasn't right. *You're a man now, Paul.*

After supper one evening, Mom waved me outside beneath the giant cottonwood trees. "You've got a new job, Paul, for money. You can expect to work every Saturday for Toby down at the lumberyard." She saw my surprise but looked away. "You stick close to Toby. You need a man in your life. You work hard and come home hungry for a good meal like your father used to do." Mom left me standing under the tree. I watched her walk back to the house, still dressed in her starch-white nurse uniform. I wondered if we were hurting for money. She received an envelope from Uncle Don at the first of every month. She never left it with the rest of the mail but tucked it in her purse. Mom worked long days at the clinic. She was awake by five some mornings to fix our lunches for school. She ironed clothes in the kitchen long after we'd gone to bed.

The leaves were turning yellow by the time I started working for Toby. Everything was different. Edna had quit. Toby said that after Dad died Edna figured it was time to retire. He hired a new clerk, Lily Lundgren, who ran off with a cowboy singer named Eddie three weeks later. The first day I saw her she was all business and kind of bossy. She didn't allow me to hang out in the office like Dad did. It didn't matter because Toby worked me hard until lunch, even doing a little yelling to get me moving. Then he drove me downtown to the 4Bs restaurant for a hamburger and fries.

"You know, Paul, your mother's worried about you." Toby folded his immense height to fit on the round stool next to me. We sat at the counter next to old men in farm caps who banged away at their plates under a canopy of blue cigarette smoke. A couple of them leaned over to greet Toby. One of the men, his jaw full of whiskers, shook Toby's hand.

"I know."

"She doesn't want you getting into trouble."

"I know." The waitress behind the counter handed me a chocolate milkshake. It was swell of Toby to treat me.

"And what that means" — I could tell Toby didn't know much about giving kids the business — "is that you show up for work on time and do everything you're told and no messing around." I nodded my head. Then he got to the terms. "You give me eight solid hours every Saturday, you earn a buck fifty an hour, how does that sound?"

"I would make that much?"

"Sure as shootin', but you gotta earn it. Understand?" That's how it went. Toby ate his own hamburger without too much talking. He didn't ask at all about Louie. I was missing Louie to tell you the truth. He had avoided our house since the night at the drive-in. I figured Charlie had told him to stay away.

September started fresh but began to show its age. Leaves turned brown and fell. The wind brought October's chill. I was stacking boards in the warehouse one Saturday morning when Charlie came looking for Toby. They stood at the patrol car gesturing. Charlie pointed to his right arm, tracing a big finger across the upper portion. He climbed into the car and drove away. Toby came inside shaking his head.

"It's Hack Face O'Hanlon, Paul. He's deader than a doornail." He looked at me, his eyes swelling with concern. "The old buzzard got drunk on some cheap whiskey he keeps up there and fell into the saw. That big blade he uses to split timbers. Took his arm clean off and —." Toby stopped, probably sensing he'd told me too much. "No use in saying more."

"How did —?"

"His nephew found him. That's what Charlie said. That friend of yours, Louie Moretti."

Four days later, right after school, Toby took me to the wake in Butte. He'd clipped the obituary out of the *Montana Standard* and held it in his hand, squinting at the address, as he drove us through the winding streets and head frames in the mining district. He turned north up a steep road to a cluster of sagging houses barely arm's length from one another. "Welcome to Walkerville. Rows of company houses everywhere," Toby said, parking on an empty lot littered with broken glass and a few old tires. Nearby, a pair of bib overalls and two white bras as big as the Berkeley Pit fluttered on a clothesline behind a house that looked like it hadn't been painted for a hundred years. A gang of boys sauntering by gave us the hard eye. Toby saw that I was nervous. "They won't bother us, going to a wake and all. Used to hate coming over here when I played basketball, though. They'd jump us when we got off the bus." He climbed out of the pickup. "Lock the doors just in case."

Louie's Chevy was parked right in front of the house. Men with stooped shoulders mingled on the front porch, a covered affair, shingles missing, stretching from one side of the house to the other. Some of them held bottles of liquor. I stuck close to Toby. "Does somebody live here?" I whispered to him.

"Louie's sister, I think," he replied, making no effort to lower his voice. He pushed the screen door open with an ear-splitting creak just as a comely black-haired woman in a yellow dress greeted us. I knew right away she was Louie's sister. She welcomed us with a kind, "Come in please," but it was her eyes, deep brown pools of mystery, that lured us into the house. While Toby stared at her, searching for words, I found Louie leaning against a dilapidated stuffed chair in deference to a shaggy old cat that was sleeping in it. He held a glass of sloshing amber liquid.

"Glad you came, Ace. Damn cops tell me I can't hang around with you no more."

"I didn't mean to get you in trouble."

"Hell, it happens. I ain't nobody you want to know anyhows." His voice sounded strange. Then I realized he was drunk. "Wanna see the body, Ace?"

"What do you mean?"

"Uncle Jimmy, laid out as stiff as one of them logs he cut. C'mon, take a look." Thrilled at the stories I would be telling Blue and Max, I followed Louie through a succession of rooms toward the back of the house. There, on top of a door laid across two sawhorses was Hack Face, dead as you please, pale and shriveled. Somebody had drawn a sheet over his chest and the remains of his right shoulder. His head rested on a faded green pillow from the couch. His eyes were closed, his wild gray hair combed, the familiar stubble shaved away from his ruddy cheeks. I hardly recognized the old man. The door didn't look too comfortable even for a dead man. "You shoulda seen it, Ace. Not a pint of blood left in the old cuss. Live by the saw, die by the saw." An open bottle of whiskey rested on the door next to Hack Face. "We didn't want him feelin' left out of the party," said Louie, who lifted the bottle with unsteady hands and tried to pour himself another drink.

"Here, let me help." I filled Louie's glass about half full.

"You first, Ace. Drink to the dead." I looked toward the kitchen, a lean-to affair at the back of the house. Toby stood with his back to me, talking to Louie's sister and a sallow man with a drooping mustache. I swung the glass to my lips and sucked in a mouthful of the whiskey until my throat caught fire.

Louie laughed while I choked it down. "Hell, Ace, that's to Uncle Jimmy." He slapped me on the back hard enough to knock me over. I would have fallen but he grabbed me and pushed me back toward the front of the house. More men had arrived. They all looked tough and edgy, much like Hack Face before he died, but worn and ailing just the same. Some of them coughed into dirty handkerchiefs. They stood around cussing about the mines and the Anaconda Company. I could see that Hack Face had been just like them. It was easy to see why he wanted to get away from them, too.

It was getting dark. We walked to the street. "You ever seen the lights on Butte Hill at night, Ace?" Louie eased up on the hood of the Chevy, bracing his feet on the bumper. I did the same.

"I've never been to Butte at night, Louie." He offered me another drink of whiskey but I nodded no. I was feeling warm all over. If Toby found out I'd be in trouble for sure. Mom didn't want me to come to the wake except Toby told her he'd keep me out of trouble. I looked down on the city. The Mile-High City is what they called it on KXLF-TV. Butte seemed bigger than life. A sea of lights blinked below us. The mighty head frames over the mines stood like gallows against the twilight.

"Somethin' I gotta tell you, Ace." He wore his black leather jacket that made him look even more like Elvis Presley. He pulled the collar tight against his throat. "You asked about my mama and old man. Ain't nobody else who cared much to know about them. And so you gotta know that I shoulda been in the car with them. Maybe me and my sister both. We got no right to live when they got creamed like that. If only they had taken this car —."

"What car?"

"This car, damn Ace, the Chevy. This was their car, brand new off the lot, and I was messin' around with the keys that morning and lost them, and so they took us to school in the old Plymouth that was ready for the junk heap and on the way home the engine died on the tracks and the train came and —." Louie's voice collapsed into sobs. He wiped his eyes and slapped his hand on the Chevy. The glass of whiskey slid off the hood onto the road and broke.

"What, Louie, what happened?"

"Don't you get it, Ace? I killed my parents!" Louie jumped off the Chevy and ran behind his sister's house. I found him in the weeds, lighting a cigarette. Hack Face reposed through the window as men stood around him, talking and gesturing. Louie took a long drag. "Hell, they hardly know Uncle Jimmy."

"Louie, your parents, how could you have known?"

"Shoulda been me, I knew that all along. Reminders all over the place, them, your old man, Uncle Jimmy. That's why you can't hang around with me, Ace, you might be next."

"And the Chevy?"

"Yeah, especially that. It was their car. It's all I know of them anymore."

"You have your sister."

"She has that sorry ass husband."

"You have Faye."

"Yeah, I got Faye."

"And me."

Louie stared at me in the dark, sizing me up. "And you. You're more of a man than most I ever seen. Never forget that, Ace."

We stood there in the wind, watching the stars, until Toby came from the house calling for me. Night draped like a suffocating cape over Butte. I wanted out of there. "Coming!" I called to him.

"Remember somethin', Ace." Louie turned toward me, a pool of light from the window casting shadows under his eyes. "Nobody will lay harm to you if I can damn well help it. You belong with the livin'." He pulled me to him with one mighty curl of his arm before pushing me away. I left Louie, groping my way in the dark to find Toby. He stood on the sidewalk holding the keys to his pickup. "I got a little carried away with the whiskey in there, Paul. You drive. But for heaven sakes don't tell your mother." Toby fell asleep after I pulled onto the highway, shifting into fourth and feeling the power of the big eight pull us into the night. I thought of Louie all the way home.

# Toby

*The Minnesota Twins went* to the World Series that year. The day that Sandy Koufax pitched for the Dodgers, Mr. Arnosen played the radio in algebra class. That was the second game of the series, when the Twins won five to one. My hero Tony Oliva doubled for the Twins, driving in Zoilo Versalles and starting a late rally. I sat closest to the radio, which Mr. Arnosen thoughtfully left on medium volume on his desk near the back of the classroom. I think he wanted to hear the game as bad as the rest of us except that he felt obliged to satisfy our daily educational requirements. He mangled at least five pieces of chalk trying to explain integers to the twenty-two of us sequestered in four rows of desks. I barely paid attention. All I could hear was the roar of forty-eight thousand fans in Met Stadium in Minnesota.

Marcy and I broke up for a week or so after Mom grounded me. Then I slipped a note into her locker atoning for all my faults. It was a bold step but love takes its course, you know, and girls don't like disappointment. To celebrate we went to a movie at the Rialto where she let me unbutton her blouse halfway down. It was all very exciting except that most of the movie was filmed in daylight, meaning there wasn't a dark corner in the theater. Marcy buttoned up quick.

She held my hand tight, though, acting like she really cared. She didn't fool me. She didn't want me messing around.

Blue was heavy into Rosie until she dumped him for Danny Mulligan. Blue wanted to find Danny and pound him. I suggested once was enough. Then again, maybe Max should do it. Max would pound Danny into dust, except that Max was in love with Peg and cared about little else. He confessed to us that he might want to marry her someday. Blue rolled his eyes at that one, Max and the waif in wedlock. I admit it was hard to picture.

I knew I should stay away from Louie Moretti. Whatever it was that drew me to him was fateful. On a dare from Blue, I went looking for Louie and flagged him down on Main Street to ask for one more ride in the Chevy. Willfully ignoring my mother's stern warning would prove the greatest mistake of my young life.

It was an hour after sunset in October, two days after the Twins lost the World Series to the Dodgers in seven games. Louie pulled to the curb and swung the passenger door open. His face, barely visible in the dashboard lights, revealed nothing. He struck a match as I climbed into the Chevy and for a moment I remembered the night he chased me after the school dance. He scared me in a way I couldn't understand.

"Out for a walk, Ace?" Louie inhaled hard from a glowing cigarette.

"Where are you going, Louie? I mean, with your uncle gone?"

He started the Chevy down the mile-long drag, a small-town Main Street nearly empty except for pickup trucks parked outside a collection of bars, their neon lights blinking in the dusk. A few cowboys leaned on parking meters, beers in hand, watching us. When Louie gunned the Chevy they shouted and waved. I had no idea what I expected him to say, or why I again lied to Mom about going to hang out with Blue. I was missing Dad. Soon curfew would blow at City Hall.

"Louie, can I drive the Chevy?" I spoke the words before I thought them. At least I think I did. He steered onto a street at the edge of town and stopped. Summer was long gone and it was a cool evening, hinting of frost. Leaves had begun to fall. I hated this time of year, when the town felt naked and dead and school was back in business.

"Ace, the answer is that I'm going no place at all."

"You can come stay at my house, Louie."

"Thanks, Ace, but you don't get my drift. Hell, you're as lonely as me and ain't nothin' on the road ahead for us. Not me, maybe not you. Get it?"

He settled back on the seat, his boots braced on the dashboard, as I rolled the Chevy through the gears and felt its power. Louie seemed disinterested, maybe distracted, his mind somewhere else. I watched the gravel road ahead of me carefully. *He doesn't care that I'm not even old enough to drive.*

"Where should we go, Louie?"

"You're at the wheel, Ace. Hell, you decide."

We rumbled through the outskirts of town where houses were sparse. The night had arrived. Clouds obscured the moon and stars. Rocks from the road clunked under the fenders. Louie stared out the side window, lost in thought. I put a little more gas to the Chevy, pushing it to about thirty, when a hunched dark figure loomed in our headlights. He turned on his cane, his old man's face showing alarm, an instant before I hit him. He crashed onto the hood of the

Chevy as I hit the brakes and in a few horrifying seconds our worlds collided. His eyes stared at me through the windshield before he slid onto the road.

I remembered little else, except for Louie yelling at me to run and never look back. He shoved me off the seat and slid behind the wheel in my place. "You were never in the Chevy, Paul!" A hot odor of blood wafted over the crumpled form on the ground. A porch light flicked on down the road. I ran furiously into the night, gasping with disbelief, as if I was trying to run from myself and every bad memory that had haunted me. I don't remember how I got into my house without encountering my mother, or how long I lay in my bed cringing into my pillow over the ghosts of my first teenage summer. I had killed a man. I was just a boy. Why didn't I listen to my only parent? Why couldn't Dad come back to show me how to catch rainbow trout and throw a curve ball?

Louie took the heat for killing the old man. Charlie the cop, quoted in the newspaper, said his name was Oscar. He was a bachelor, eighty-four years old, a retired prison guard. He had a bad habit of wandering roads at night in dark clothing. "It was an accident," Charlie told the paper. "We didn't find any negligence on the part of the driver, Louie Moretti, who stopped right away and rendered aid to the victim."

Soon as the word was out, Blue and Max raced over to my house. "So how fast do you think he was driving that Chevy?" Blue pressed, his eyes seeking confirmation. "To the floor, I'll bet."

Max looked sad. I knew he was thinking about his brother. We talked for hours, just like always, first about

Louie and then about girls, sports and dumb kids in school. Everything had changed for us. We knew it.

The old man's death felt like a bizarre dream to me. A nightmare. In my sleep I saw him squeezed against the windshield, pleading with his dying eyes. Mom noticed me acting strange but assumed it had something to do with missing Dad. Mixed up as I was, I began more and more to picture Louie hitting the old man. I hadn't killed him. Louie did. The guilt ebbed.

I buried my memory of that night, much like I buried Dad and all the other pain from my first teenage year. From the start I came to believe that I never drove the Chevy that night, that the old man didn't die but walked on, kept hobbling to wherever he was going, watched the moon from the sidewalk, thanked the Lord for his good life and eased into his bed to sleep before waking a few mornings longer. From the start, I took Louie's advice. I never was in that car.

Louie disappeared from my life until a month later when I received a letter postmarked in San Diego, California:

> *Dear Ace (Paul),*
> *Joined the Marine Corps. Ain't cut out for school and I know it. Guess you ain't surprised. Then there was that trouble figured time to go. Wanted to tell you in person but too late now I enlisted thinkin what the hell do it. Faye cried when I told her but this is the way it is and who knows maybe I turn out a better person when I get out in a few years and this is what I have to do. Got nothing going in my life and know it. Sorry about that sob scene when you came to see Uncle Jimmy dead and gone we all have our problems and you have yours. When I left for basic training*

*my sister drove me to the bus depot she cried you can picture it. They cut my hair boss me around askin for trouble dont you think. Somebody will get his sorry ass kicked. Tell your mom sorry for any trouble I just see life different. Now a favor to ask. Go to Butte get the Chevy park it in your barn keep it shined til I come home. I fixed the front. Feel bad for that man. For you too, all you been through you know what I mean. Your the one I trust.*

Your friend, Louie

It's a good thing I was busy in school and in love with Marcy or I would have flipped. The evening after I received Louie's letter I went behind the barn to smoke a cigarette. In my investigations of Dad's shop I found his cigarettes hidden in every nook and cranny. Every time I looked for a tool I found another crumpled pack. I can't say that I liked smoking much except after Dad's funeral when I was looking at my cousin Susan's boobs when she was lighting up. I stood in the alley, humped against the chill off Mount Powell, to take a long drag in Louie's honor. That's how I felt about him and what he did for me. I didn't cry when I read his letter but felt a need to smoke. Louie would say, "Ace, act like a man."

I let Mom read the letter. She put on her glasses to read it, put it down, read it again. I watched her face but she didn't react to the "you know what I mean" business at the end. All she said was, "Well, maybe this is a good thing for him, moving on from what he did to that old man. I'll see if Toby can help drive the car over from Butte. We've got room in the barn." She gave me a hard look. "You won't be driving, Paul. Don't even think about it. Louie will live with that man's death for the rest of his life."

On a Sunday afternoon after church, Mom and Toby and I drove to Butte in her station wagon. Louie's sister seemed happy to see us. She invited us inside for coffee. It smelled good enough, reminding me of those Saturday mornings at the lumberyard, but she made me a mug of hot chocolate without asking. Some adults figure junior high kids don't drink coffee. Mom sat gingerly on the faded green couch right next to the pillow that was propped under Hack Face's head when he was dead and laying in that back room for everybody to see. I wasn't going to tell her. She didn't like Butte and I didn't blame her. It was a much bigger and dirtier city than Deer Lodge. Butte was a pair of ripped overalls caked with mine dust and dried blood.

"My name's Elaine," Louie's sister was telling us. "Elaine Sokolokovich. Now I know that's a mouthful but that's Butte, you see, everyone from these foreign countries mixed together like stew." Elaine, it turned out, was an Irish name given by her mother, also Irish. "She was Colleen, but my dad, he was Italian and he named my brother Louie to keep the Italian in the family, you see?" Mom looked mildly interested, probably worried that she was imposing on Mrs. Benedict back in Deer Lodge who was looking after Sally, but Toby stared at Elaine like he thought she was somebody special. She was a looker, all right. She sat in the tiny living room on a wooden chair dragged from the kitchen, a tattered apron tied around her blue dress. Every minute or so her deep pools of eyes shot fleeing glances at Toby. She looked like a rag doll, but a beautiful one, full of expression and good looks that made me wonder why she lived in this shack up a muddy road with hardly a penny to her name. If Louie resembled Elvis Presley, she was Natalie Wood, no kidding.

"And so my husband," she continued, "he tries hard to find work but the mines aren't hiring right now and he went down to Park Street this afternoon to play poker or I know he'd want to see you." Was it my imagination that Toby looked angry for just a moment? I remembered the sallow man leaning against the stove during the wake for Hack Face while Toby and Elaine stood close in conversation, ignoring him. "Josip Sokolokovich was his given name, you see, but we call him Joe." Then, maybe for Toby's benefit, "Louie never liked my husband. I tried to raise Louie best as I could, you see, but I'm only five years older and don't know much about that kind of thing. You see, Joe —."

She stopped and looked at the floor, where a threadbare rug failed to hide the gnarled wood planks. Elaine turned to Toby. "It's been a tough life for me and Louie, hope you understand."

We went outside to start the Chevy. Elaine handed Toby the keys. Their fingers touched just a little too long. I noticed it and so did my mother. Elaine pulled her ragged sweater tighter against her throat. "He don't want it sitting out here on the street where somebody messes with it, you see." She turned to me. "The boy knows why this car is important to my brother. Take good care of it. We're grateful." Toby hopped into the Chevy, his eyes on Elaine. He gave her a long wave and left, while Mom and I scrambled into the station wagon to follow. Elaine stood on the porch of the sad little house watching us go. I wondered if she was all that different from Louie.

/////

The first snow came late that year, unusual for Montana. The sky grew heavy and dark that morning. The temperature dropped, a few flakes followed, and by early afternoon the snow fell deep across the Deer Lodge Valley. The principal ordered the country kids to head for their buses. Fully half of the junior high school trudged outside into the white swirl, girls in their knee socks, boys in their fall jackets. I was in health class, sitting next to Max, who waved forlornly through the window at the waif's backside while she climbed aboard a bus headed south to the farms and ranches. It was pitiful seeing Max that way. Half an hour later, the principal canceled classes. Teachers stood in the halls, yelling at us to get a move on. "A full foot already," one of them told anyone who would listen. A parade of parents arrived at the school, spinning tires in the deep snow. A few pickups arrived with chains clattering on the rear wheels for traction. Marcy and I huddled outside the front entrance to the school, marveling at the winter scene. "We can give you a ride home, Paul."

"I've got to find Sally. She didn't wear boots." Marcy kissed me and ran off to her mother's Buick. I walked across the playground, snow filling my new black loafers, to O. D. Speer School, where Sally waited. Sally looked at me with big round eyes and grabbed my hand. "Will Mommy come get us, Paul?"

"Doubt it, pumpkin. She can't get away from the clinic when they've got patients and all." I carried Sally piggyback all the way home. She was a small nine year old but felt three times heavier by the time I saw our house through the swirl of snow. Good thing I was stronger than ever from helping Toby buck boards down at the lumberyard. I was almost five foot ten, tall as Dad. Mom kept measuring me with a yardstick she found in the barn. She kept a record of my height with pencil marks on the orange wall below the clock. I staggered to the back door, which we never locked, and Sally reached down to turn the knob. Although mid-afternoon, it was already gloomy and cold in our house. We took off our sodden socks and shoes and put them on the heating grate on the kitchen floor to dry.

"Paul, what are we supposed to do when it snows?"

"Play in it, I guess."

"I mean, do you plan to carry me all the way home every time we have a storm? Daddy would be waiting with the pickup."

"Things are different now, Sally. Until I'm old enough to drive we'll have to wade through snow."

"How old do you have to be? You're almost fourteen."

"Sixteen to get a license."

Mom called from the clinic to make sure we were home. I described the hike from the school in deep snow. "In God's name I don't know how we're going to manage without your father," she told me before hanging up. I sat at the kitchen table watching the white curtain outside when the mailman emerged into view, his blue uniform barely visible. He reached into the leather pouch slung over his shoulder. Moments later we heard a clunk at the front of our house when he dropped the lid on the mailbox. "Probably more sales circulars," Sally said from the couch where she was intent on writing in her journal. She was one of those kids who never stopped writing stories and reading books.

I found one letter inside the mailbox. It was addressed to Mr. Paul Morrison, General Delivery, Deer Lodge Montana. *"Dear Ace,"* it began. *"Aint no use writing a long letter but I'm*

*OK. Every day about the same here Marines don't care smart from stupid everyone in it together. You learn there way or highway, get it? Some showoff from Chicago thought he was a real hepcat tried to push me around. I pounded him behind the billet thought you would like that. Sergant made me dig cigaret butts out of the dirt all day for messin up that cat. Hell I could be in Butte in the mines diggin and fightin so no different."* Louie went on for another page talking about the firing range, the mess hall and a pretty nurse named Simone who gave him a shot in the butt when he came down with the flu. He asked about the Chevy and wrote how he was being trained for the infantry. He didn't mention the fatal accident at all. I reread the letter several times, trying to picture him writing it. Then I pulled *Little Shepherd of Kingdom Come* off the shelf and began reading it from the first page.

Chad in uniform, now Louie. I couldn't imagine Louie taking orders from anyone. I didn't know anything about the Marines except what I saw in the movies. I asked Toby, who said he didn't like the Marines much because he served four years in the Air Force, but he said everyone knew the Marines were the toughest outfit in America. "Your friend Louie, you won't recognize him next time you see him, and I don't mean just that they took the scissors to him. He's going to look different and act more grown up. You'll see what I mean."

I wondered about Toby's interest in Elaine. It was probably none of my business, but he mentioned Louie a lot all of a sudden. The Saturday after the big storm Toby asked if I'd heard from Elaine. We were inside the warehouse, clearing out room for a new load of lumber from the mill in Missoula. Two mice ran through the sawdust.

"No, why would I?"

"Well, I'm thinking maybe she called to ask about Louie's car in the barn."

"I haven't heard from her. Isn't it long distance to call from Butte?" Toby didn't reply. He looked sad and walked off in that long lope of his, snapping the tape measure on his belt. I think he liked Elaine but didn't know what to do, her being married and all.

I called after him. "Toby?" He turned, looking hopeful. "Why don't you give her a call and let her know the Chevy's just fine?"

"That's an idea, Paul. Maybe I should. If I can just remember how she spelled her last name, you know, one of those Butte names and all."

"Why don't you go over there and tell her?"

Toby toed the sawdust with his boot. "Well? You think I should?"

"She's probably wondering about the Chevy."

"I don't reckon I should go alone. You know." Toby looked a bit sheepish. I'll bet he was at least six foot eight, a high school basketball star grown into a middle-aged man, but at that moment he looked all kid. "Want to ride over? Tomorrow, I mean."

And so we did. Mom raised her eyebrows when Toby told her why we had to drive to Butte. I saw her do it, and so did Toby, but he didn't try to explain the flimsy excuse for seeing Elaine. I'm sure Mom knew what was up. She liked Toby. The tall balding man was good and honest like Dad. Finally she said to him, "I'm sure Elaine would want to know." Toby and I walked to his pickup, buried to the hubcaps in snow.

"I'd sure like to take the Chevy," I told him.

"I know."

"But isn't the snow —."

"Not if we take it careful like, Paul. But I'm thinking we better not because it wouldn't look good taking a chance with that hot rod on slick roads. Not after what happened with that old guy Oscar. I'd sure like to drive that Chevy again. That kid's got power galore going under that hood."

We crept over to Butte on an icy highway that looked like a mirror. It got bad enough that Toby pulled off the road. "Got to turn the hubs to get four-wheel drive or we aren't going to make it. Damn glad we didn't take the Chevy."

"Louie would kill us if we wrecked it."

"I know."

Butte's streets were plowed better than our streets in Deer Lodge, but the higher on the hill we went, the worse the traction. "Got to be two, three feet up here," Toby said. "Good lord, looks like the North Pole without Santa Claus." All the little mining houses, which I remembered as dilapidated and dirty, now were welcoming places, homely faces peeping out from caps of snow. At first I thought no one was home when Toby edged his rumbling old pickup against a drift outside Elaine's house. Then a hand nudged a shade aside in the front window. I glimpsed a dark bundle of hair and knew it was Elaine.

We stomped the snow off our boots on the wooden porch. I thought Elaine would open the door but we had to knock. When silence greeted Toby's second knock he turned away. "Guess maybe no one's home?" He looked disappointed. *Toby loves her but he's not even admitting it.*

"I saw her at the window," I told him. He knocked again. Finally, Elaine opened the door.

"What the hell?" I heard Toby say. I was afraid to look. One of her eyes was black and swollen shut. She traced a finger over a gash on her upper lip, wiping blood away. An ugly purple bruise covered her left cheekbone. She pulled her robe tight around her neck to hide the swelling but I saw it and so did Toby. Some of the injuries looked old and some new. I'd never seen anybody so worked over, not even Blue after the Tuckers attacked us. Elaine was living with a wife beater.

Nobody spoke. Then, from Toby: "Who —."

Elaine propped herself against the doorframe. She looked nothing like the beautiful young woman I'd seen a few weeks earlier. She held her body like it hurt all over. "He's out of work, frustrated. With Louie gone he don't try to hide it anymore."

I've never seen Toby so mad. I'd never seen him mad at all. An old timer down at the lumberyard told me nobody, ever, would break Toby's rebounding record at Powell County High School. "You oughta seen him back then. Carved out space under that basket like a one-man army. He was a good kid, 'cept when he got on that court in that Wardens uniform he got mean ugly to the other team. Best damn basketball player that ever went to this here high school. Bet you the shirt on my back he could have taken Wayne Estes one on one. Go ask him."

And so I did. Toby shrugged and walked away.

Elaine tried to keep Toby out of the house but he pushed against the door and it swung wide open, its rusty hinges squealing in protest. Toby charged inside with me chasing right behind him. Elaine stood crying, clutching her frayed robe around her shivering figure. Toby towered over her, clenching his fists. I'd never seen him that riled.

"Where is he?" he demanded. Toby even scared me a little, acting like that. He was plenty mad and Elaine knew it. She pointed to the kitchen at the back of the house. Only then did I see Joe standing in the pale light. Toby charged past Elaine through the room where Hack Face had laid dead. A second man stepped into view beside Joe. I felt cold and scared. Elaine reached for me.

"His brother," she whispered to me.

I expected Toby to hesitate but he didn't. The brother threw a flurry of punches at Toby, knocking his cap off, while Joe tried to jump him from behind. Toby snatched Joe like he was kindling wood and threw him against the brother, knocking both of them to the floor. Being young and stupid and remembering the Tucker boys, I ran to help Toby. He pushed me away. I fell hard against Elaine, who held me tight. Joe sprung from the floor with his fist clenched. He looked mean all right. He took a wild swing at Toby's head and missed. Toby decked him with a sickening smack to the face. The brother charged again. He hit Toby in the face and chest until Toby knocked the man to his knees with a giant roundhouse powered by years of bucking heavy lumber. Then Toby hit him again and again, swinging one long arm and then the other. Blood splattered on the grimy window panes. After the brother fell unconscious on the floor Toby laid into Joe. He was whining against the stove, spitting teeth.

"You want to beat a woman?" Toby swung his big elbow to hit Joe in the face. I heard a thud like two heavy boards colliding. When Joe buckled Toby punched him hard in the gut. Joe slumped to the cracked linoleum. He grabbed his face and bawled. Toby turned to Elaine and took her in his arms and hugged her. Some message, unspoken, passed between them again. I knew then that she was coming back to Deer Lodge with us.

///// 

Louie wrote me a letter to say he survived boot camp. He was coming home on leave before going to a place called Camp Pendleton, where Marines were trained to fight in Vietnam. *"Don't worry, Ace. Don't mean nothin. Marines call it a shit hole. Hell, don't know nothin about that and who cares any way just another war where Uncle Sam gets stoned."* I wondered what he meant. I showed the letter to Blue and Max who made fun of me. They said everyone in school knew what it meant. Blue rode me the worst. "You planning to become a priest, cowboy? Or maybe a nun? Ever heard of marijuana?"

Louie came home from boot camp just before Christmas. He rode the Greyhound bus all the way from California. It was a few days before the wedding. I don't know how Elaine got out of her marriage to Joe. It happened fast, and I can say for a fact that I've never seen Toby that happy. I wondered if Joe and his brother were gunning for Toby but Toby said nah, they couldn't fight their way out of a paper bag and were cowards to boot.

Toby and Elaine took me to meet Louie at the bus station down at Hotel Deer Lodge. I wanted to drive the Chevy but Mom would have nothing of it. She even made me wear a tie. Toby acted like his old responsible self again. He bought Elaine a new dress for the occasion. She looked like a million bucks all spiffed up without the bruises and cuts. All she brought from Butte the day of the fight was a satchel with some clothes and a family photograph taken of her when she was a girl. Louie was in it too.

The bus arrived at the hotel two hours late. Reeking of diesel fuel, a million bugs splattered on its windshield, it clattered to a stop. "I hope he didn't miss his ride," said Elaine, her eyes scanning the crowd for her brother. She squeezed against Toby's tall frame.

Fourteen passengers later, Louie marched off the bus. I had to look twice. His sweeping black mane was gone. His neck looked bigger. "Louie!" Elaine cried. She ran to kiss him. Toby stood back. I edged behind Elaine, waiting for my turn, until Louie snared me with a strong right arm.

"Ace, damn I swear you look taller. Maybe smarter too, but how would I know?" He gave me a strong hug before pushing me away. I was glad for that. My family wasn't the hugging type. He looked at Toby, who towered above all of us. "My new brother in law, huh, sis?" Louie gave Toby a good look. "Heard what you done to the wimps and I'm grateful." He offered his hand. Louie didn't waste any time letting you know where you stood with him.

Reverend Bartlett married Toby and Elaine on a Saturday afternoon at the Presbyterian Church. It killed Toby to close the lumberyard on his best sales day of the week. I asked Toby what Dad would have done. Toby smiled, seeing what I was getting at. "What the hell," he said, pleased that I led him out of his predicament. Toby asked that I be his best man, maybe because I'd watched him beat Elaine's previous husband to a pulp. I reached to the back of my closet to find the suit I'd worn for the seventh grade dance. Blue and Max wore theirs, too, although they looked too big for their clothes. Max was a beast. He lifted transmissions all summer helping his dad overhaul cars. Marcy came in a pink dress. She promised to kiss me in the alley behind the church after the wedding. Faye drove over from Anaconda in a car that was invented before peach pie. It was worth going to the wedding just to see Faye in a dress. It was a green chiffon affair that showed plenty of leg and cleavage. All the men and boys stared.

The wedding was about what you expect with lots of promises and kissing. Louie walked his sister down the aisle. He looked, well, different. She was a queen in white. After the reception at the hall next door, after Toby and Elaine left for their honeymoon in Coeur d'Alene over in Idaho and I kissed Marcy in the alley about fifty times and we listened to Max declare his love for the waif until we couldn't take it anymore, Mom and several other church women set to cleaning up what remained of the party. It looked like an all-night endeavor that involved scrubbing every square inch of the place. Blue and Max drifted home after hearing curfew blow at City Hall downtown. Louie motioned to me to bring Marcy. We followed him and Faye outside where we sat in the Chevy and revved the motor until it blew heat.

We made out until my lips hurt. Louie and Faye mashed down in the front seat. I was sure they'd do more than that later. Marcy pushed her tongue into my mouth. I wasn't too hot about fooling around with her the way Louie did with Faye. I liked Marcy too much. My mother said good girls don't get carried away. She said junk like that all the time. After we listened to at least fifteen songs on the radio, Louie spoke up. "So, Ace." Louie turned from the front seat to look at me. His neck rippled with muscle. He looked a whole lot different with most of his hair gone, including the curl in front.

"Yeah?"

"So Toby kicked that sorry ass Joe and his brother to hell and back?"

"Yup." Marcy slid her fingers across my leg.

"Gonna tell me all about it some time?"

"Yup."

"Busy back there, Ace?"

"Yup."

After the wedding, Mom changed her tune toward Louie. It helped that Louie worked at the lumberyard all week so Toby could take Elaine to Coeur d'Alene. Mom admired hard work. She took sandwiches and pie to Louie at lunchtime and sent me to the lumberyard after school to help clean up. The night before Louie went back to the Marines she had Louie and Toby and Elaine over for supper. Mom made Dad's favorite meatloaf. Louie minded his manners. He even helped me wash the dishes afterward. We stood at the sink, this bigger boy and me, while Mom took coffee to Toby and Elaine in the living room. He didn't say much until, "You gotta good home, Ace. Never forget."

When we finished, the talk out in the living room drifted to the war. I didn't know much about Vietnam except what I saw on television. It had nothing to do with Deer Lodge. We didn't learn about it in school either. Everything in the history books was old. Mom, sensing where the conversation was going, steered Sally off to bed. "Don't know what's next for me, tell you the truth," Louie was saying. "We do what we're told, Marines do our thinkin' for us you know."

"You going over there, you think?" Elaine looked worried.

"Sure, maybe, life's full of surprises ain't it?" Louie didn't want to bother her about it.

Toby lit his pipe. "From what I hear, those commies want to take over the world. Got the Chinese and Russians behind them. It's a damn mess over there in Asia, just like in Korea with commies coming from the North. Doesn't hurt to have some of our men in Vietnam to scare them off."

Mom, a good Democrat, spoke up. "President Johnson doesn't want to get us in too deep. You can bet on that."

Elaine turned to Louie. "They tell you anything about this?"

"They tell us how to fight."

I jumped in. "You already knew how to do that, Louie." He smiled and rubbed his hand over his buzz cut. I thought back to his letters. "What's it like in the Marines?"

"Lots of yellin', Ace. Runnin', chin-ups, taking rifles apart, puttin' them back together, shoutin'." Louie lit a cigarette. Mom handed him an ashtray. "Thing is, I feel good about it, Ace. Feel like I got a purpose, just don't know what yet."

Toby nodded. "Know what you mean. After I joined the Air Force they sent me to Korea to keep the commies under control. Idea was, they invade the South again and they'll aim for the United States next. Something to be said for defending our country."

"Is that what Vietnam is?" Mom asked. "Defending the country? Seems like it's a long ways from here. The Pentagon says right there in the *Montana Standard*" — she pointed to the Butte newspaper folded on the end table — "that we're sending more troops. In God's name I don't know why."

253

"Won't be long," Toby said. "Those Communists will turn and run like sissies when they see our boys charging them. Right, Louie?"

Louie nodded. "Damn right, we'll kick their sorry ass before you know it."

"Louie, your language." Elaine looked embarrassed. Seeing her there, happily holding hands with Toby, I wondered why she had stayed with that dismal man in Butte so long.

"Sorry, sis." Louie coaxed a final puff from his cigarette, exhaling blue smoke. "I ain't scared. Ain't been scared of nothin' my whole life except amountin' to nothin' and that's the worst it can get. If I go, what the hell, somebody's gotta do it."

Later that evening, when all the talking was done in the house, Louie and I walked outside to the barn to check on the Chevy. It was cold and more snow had fallen. Our breath rose in clouds. The moon was big and foamy like a tub full of cream. Naked tree limbs in the moonlight reminded me of Halloween. Louie pushed me into the dark barn before I could flick on the lights.

"Watch out for ghosts, Ace!" He laughed, making monster sounds. I found myself clinging to Dad's old coat that hung near the door.

"Geez, Louie, you scared hell out of me."

He turned on the light. "Somebody oughta, Ace. Now look there. You got that Chevy dressed up in fine style." Louie ran his hand over the gleaming black body. "You done just what I asked. Been hot roddin' the Chevy when your momma wasn't lookin'? Hell, I would." Louie didn't seem to want an answer. He edged around the car, looking it over like it was new off the lot.

"Louie? How come you haven't driven the Chevy since you came home?"

I thought he might be thinking about Oscar. I watched Louie's face but he didn't show any reaction at all. "Can't say, Ace. Been busy, I guess. Besides, I had Toby's old truck to drive 'round." Louie opened the passenger door and popped the glove compartment open. He slipped the photograph of his parents into his shirt pocket.

"How come the Chevy's black, Louie? I mean, I've been wondering for a long time. It looks different in that picture." I pointed to his pocket.

"Wasn't always that way. Came from the factory in what they call two-tone, red over white. Picture that, Ace. Matched the interior. Can you see your old friend Louie ridin' in the back in short pants?" He hesitated. For a second that far-off look came into his flashing eyes. "And you wanna know how it got to be black, dontcha Ace?"

I eased on top of Dad's old yellow stool and waited. Louie's shoulders slumped. "I ain't never told nobody this, Ace, 'cept Elaine knows. All this talk about fightin' in Vietnam, hell, ain't right to keep secrets anymore. What I said in the house that I ain't scared of nothin', well, I have dreams, see? Not dreams but nightmares. Ugly damn stuff, trains smashin' into cars, my parents all ripped apart." Louie leaned against the Chevy. He looked at the concrete floor, then at me. "This was no couple of times, Ace. Every night I see them, lookin' back at me. Know where I am? Standin' outside the car watchin'. Watchin' them suffer and die in that smashed up old Plymouth. They look back at me with hollow eyes. I hear them callin' for me, parents callin' for their damn little whiny kid who killed them. Back door of the car is hangin' open. I see a body on the seat. I know it's me but how could that be, here I am standin' outside watchin' my parents die. I know it's wrong what happened. Wrong as hell. Ace, gotta tell it to you straight, *I shoulda died there too.*"

His last words came in a whisper. He slumped against the Chevy, his big hands pressing against the fender. He was as broken as I had ever seen him. For an instant I could see that little boy in him.

"But you weren't with them that day, Louie. It wasn't your fault." I heard my voice pleading with him.

"Every bit my fault. I told you why, Ace, me losin' the keys to the Chevy and them drivin' that damn old Plymouth with the carburetor problem. Damn dream haunts me so bad I wake up screamin' sometimes. Uncle Jimmy used to slap me silly in the middle of the night. Told me to get over it, they was gone, I was alive. I never believed him. Ain't right that I lived. I know it ain't right. And the Chevy —."

"You painted it?"

"Smart kid, Ace. Saved my money, got a paint job. I was your age when I did it. Started drivin' then too. Ain't nobody said I was too young. Painted that car black and parked it on the train tracks and waited. Waited for what I deserved. Smoked a whole pack of Camels once. Damn train never came."

"Louie, the old man —."

He looked at me now, his eyes full of sorrow. I felt closer to him than ever. "It wasn't your time, Paul. You didn't kill him. It was me, just as sure as I killed my parents, I was payin' for what I done to them. Payin' by killin' that old man and havin' to live with it. Yeah, your hands were on the wheel of that Chevy that night but I was drivin', don't you see? Every bad thing that ever happened belongs to me for what I did."

I wanted to flee the barn but I felt stuck to the stool. Louie lit another cigarette. Silence fell over us like a blanket. Louie had opened a big door to my emotions. I was afraid to look beyond it. Finally, "Louie? I've been having bad dreams too."

He looked up. "Tell me, Ace."

"I see Dad laying on the floor over there after he fell off the stool. The sky is dark and the sun is gone but he's there and I see him and I know he's dead. His eyes are open. I know he's talking but I can't hear him. He's looking at me, holding out a handful of change. And then there's that man on the road, bounced right onto the hood of the Chevy, and he's looking at me because it was me, not you, who killed him —." Bile rose in my throat. I jumped off Dad's stool and flung it against the wall. It smashed against his tools, knocking pliers and hammers and saws clattering to the floor. I heard screaming. Only when Louie locked his arms around me did I realize I was hearing my own voice.

/////

Louie returned to San Diego a few days after Christmas. A Chinook blew from Canada to melt the snow into cold puddles. Clouds hung black over the mountains but no rain came. Louie reached for his wallet. "Had a birthday a ways back, didya Ace?"

"Fourteen, can you believe I made it this far?"

"Had my doubts, Ace." He pulled out a fresh twenty-dollar bill. "Happy birthday, Paul. Don't spend it all in one

place. Paul's a good name, even you'll always be Ace to me."
Nobody had given me that much money, ever. I felt the
slippery paper of the new bill as we stood around looking
uncomfortable. I didn't want Louie to go. Something about
him felt solid, trustworthy, even if he might bang me around
sometimes. I decided right then that I would show more
appreciation to Sally. Everyone needs a big brother. When the
bus arrived Elaine cried. Toby looked grim. He shook Louie's
hand before leading her away.

Louie tossed his sea bag into the baggage compartment
while the driver hollered for passengers to climb aboard. I
grabbed his jacket to give him a swift hug, my throat so thick
with emotion that I couldn't speak. "Somethin' happens to
me, Ace, that Chevy's yours. Hell, drive it to my funeral." He
laughed and slapped me on the shoulder. I watched the bus
disappear down Main Street.

# Tate

*We had a crisis on the first day* of 1966 when the waif dumped Max. He wouldn't come out of his bedroom for three days. It was something about expectations. She told Max he wanted too much of her. He told her she didn't want enough of him. Blue and I tried to console him but he sat on his bed and rocked back and forth and cried. We'd never seen Max blubber. He wouldn't eat even when his mother made his favorite chicken and dumplings.

"It just ain't fair," he repeated about 12 times. "You guys got girlfriends —."

Blue interjected. "Rosie dumped me too, remember?"

"You didn't love her."

"How do you know? Maybe I never told you the private stuff."

"Paul has Marcy."

"Well, Max, she told me to get lost until I pounded Danny Mulligan."

"Now you're making out down at the Rialto all the time."

That got Blue to bragging. "Behind the church at Toby's wedding, don't forget. I think Paul gave her the tongue."

Max couldn't be consoled. "I hate you guys. Get lost." And so we did. We knew it was bad business when the girl you loved dumped you. Truth was, Blue forgot about Rosie two days after she said goodbye. Now he was dating a sophomore girl named Debbie Peterson. Blue, with his handsome good looks, got any girl he wanted. It was different with Max. He went around with his belt about a foot too long, swinging off his blue jeans like an extra appendage, while the overalls he borrowed from his dad were way too baggy to impress girls. Max and his old man didn't make much money from automobile repair, I was sure of that. In the summer, weeds around their house grew knee high. The Jorgenson family paid most of their attention to grooming Kenny's grave at the cemetery. In the last days of summer Max and Blue and I had ridden our bikes down the narrow asphalt road to that haunting place to make sure nothing had gone afoul. We stopped at Dad's grave, too, and my best friends looked away when I cried. It wasn't far from where Oscar was buried. That's what Mom told me.

Big flakes of snow floated under the streetlights when Blue and I left the Jorgenson's house. Winter gathered around our little town like a parka. The night fell still in Deer Lodge. Hardly a car passed.

"Think he'll be okay?" I asked Blue, who wore a long yellow stocking cap that hung halfway down his back.

"He'll be all right. Bet you a dollar they are back together in a week."

"So Blue? How come girls get us shook up? I don't remember this happening last year."

"Damned if I know, Paul."

We walked in silence for a few blocks to Milwaukee Avenue, where we stopped on the corner. The snow, heavy and soft, muffled sounds. Our voices sounded like words spoken in cotton. A car schuffed past like a fast-moving sled. I was glad Blue was there. It felt quiet and sad and for an instant I thought of Dad, buried in silence under this white carpet.

Blue looked toward his house. "Suppose the folks have dinner waiting. Funny thing, us getting older and all." He sounded like an adult all of a sudden.

"Blue?" He turned to look at me. "I feel kind of mixed up, all these people dying and leaving. I don't want to grow up feeling sad all the time." He stepped close. I saw concern in his blue eyes.

"Paul, I don't know why people go. I'll bet Max is more upset about his brother than his girlfriend. And your dad —."

"I can't stand it I miss him so much." I felt my throat stiffen.

"I know. I wish I could bring him back for you."

We hugged and said goodbye. Blue tromped through the snow to his house, two bedrooms and a bath with shutters behind a picket fence. I headed out to our old house at the edge of town, breaking a trail through fresh snow. Mom said it didn't make sense to rent it anymore. "Maybe we'll move to North Dakota," she said one afternoon, scaring me. Tonight she would be fussing at the stove, steaming the kitchen windows with whatever she was cooking for dinner. I missed Dad but I missed Louie too. Both were lost to me in ways I didn't understand.

///// 

Louie's latest scrawled letter from Camp Pendleton described a nightmare that made gym class seem like a nursery school. Dragging fellow Marines through sand on the beach. Running in place like maniacs. Charging up a steep hill with packs heavy as your great aunt. Fighting, fighting, fighting. Shooting, loading, shooting. *Tell you what, Ace. Don't figure you wanna join Marine Corps unless you wantin your ass kicked every day, nobody sobbin for our sorry souls here let me tell you say hi to Elaine and Toby he not a bad guy glad there happy."*

When Mr. Fulton, my social studies teacher, assigned us to write book reports about a current event, I decided on Louie and Vietnam. Don't ask me why. It seemed like the obvious thing to do.

"You better do a whole lot of study about Vietnam, then," Mom told me in that declarative way she had about her. She sent me to the city library on Missouri Avenue to read newspapers and magazines. Miss Lettman, the librarian, was overjoyed that an eighth grader would invest his free time outside school hours to learn about an international event. She brought me stacks of magazines she said would make me an enlightened citizen. It felt a little bit scary, just me and Miss Lettman and all those books. Her perfume smelled like dying lilacs. A ticking clock echoed through the big old Kohrs Library below portraits of dead guys like George Washington and Abraham Lincoln. I tried to picture President Johnson wearing a white wig like Washington or a black beard like Lincoln. After school the next day I brought Marcy who got the old librarian remembering Mark Twain. Such a brain, that Marcy Kersher. While they talked about Huck Finn and Tom Sawyer, I read about Vietnam.

Turns out the American preoccupation with Vietnam started when President Eisenhower was in office in the 1950s. It was a Cold War thing. President Kennedy sent advisers to tell the South Vietnamese what to do. President Johnson, after he was re-elected in 1964, got worried about Communists running amok from North Vietnam and sent more troops. I couldn't imagine Vietnam's jungles and rice paddies. I'd never been to Wyoming or Canada. Going to see my grandparents in North Dakota, somewhere east of Deer Lodge beyond the big mountains, was an expedition. Tell me I'm stupid. Louie going to Vietnam was about as remote as somebody going to the moon. Some of the big city newspapers that Miss Lettman dug out of the back room showed pictures of Vietnam. The natives didn't look like anybody I knew. Who knows why we wanted to get involved in their business.

"It's politics," Marcy explained to me when I walked her home. "We need to stop Communists before they take over the world like Hitler tried to do in World War II. President Johnson thinks we can help the South Vietnamese defend their country. That's all there is to it."

"Where do you find out these things, Marcy?"

"I read, silly." She rolled her eyes. I confess that before I knew Louie I spent more time checking sports scores than reading world news. This talk of Louie maybe going to Vietnam really shook me up.

A few days after I handed in my report, Mr. Fulton asked me to stay after class. He was a skinny man with black glasses that gave him raccoon eyes. Everybody was afraid of him because he subscribed to news magazines like U. S. News and World Report and quoted facts about current events that made our heads spin.

"Paul, this is an excellent report. I wanted you to know that." He handed it to me with a big B+ scrawled in red ink in the corner. "I couldn't give you an A because of the bad language. We don't like students to swear in junior high school."

"But that's how Louie talks, sir."

"And how far did this Louie go in school?"

"He didn't graduate, sir, but —."

"But nothing, proper grammar is important if you hope to go very far in this world, young man, and it's time you learned that."

With that, I tuned out Mr. Fulton. I thought of Louie dragging fellow Marines across a sandy beach. I pictured them holding onto his ankles, his lungs burning for air, as he struggled to pull them forward. To save them. When I told Miss Lettman about Louie joining the Marines she pushed her glasses higher on her nose and walked along the shelves until she found two books about an island in the Pacific Ocean named Iwo Jima. I'd heard men talking in the barbershop about Iwo Jima. They got solemn and one cried. "He fought there," the barber told me with no small reverence after the other man left. "Yes, son, he survived combat in the worst battle the Marines ever fought." Miss Lettman bustled over to the table where I had spread my notebook and pencils. "Read these," she said. "Then you will understand your Louie."

I spent hours in Dad's recliner, the vinyl worn from the evenings when he nestled there to smoke his pipe and watch television or read books by his favorite Western author, Louis L'Amour. The Christmas before he died I gave him three new books. When Dad got going on a book he wouldn't stop. I guess I was much the same because I read the whole Iwo Jima story in two evenings. It was a bloodbath for our side in the beginning, the most Marines ever killed in a single battle, but we won in the end. I thought of veterans in Deer Lodge who threw a wreath off the bridge into the Clark Fork River on Memorial Day. Now I understood why the man in the barbershop cried.

I wrote Louie a few letters. I knew he didn't want to hear about girls in the junior high school and fart jokes between classes. *He was dragging Marines through the sand.* I wanted to thank him for his sacrifice but the truth was, I didn't know how. "Hope you're doing fine, I am too," I wrote at the bottom of my letters. I knew it was lame. Somehow I knew Louie would understand. *Act like a man, Ace.*

The papers were full of war news when Louie wrote again. He'd written "Vietnam" at the top of his letter and circled the word in red ink. *"Hell, Ace, damn Commies don't know what they got comin. Going to kick some serious gook ass and then come home. Keep the Chevy humpin for me. Tell your mama she makes the best meatloaf in the world. I know a hunnert guys down here would kill for a meal like that hell some would kill anyway but that's another deal. I know you wanna be like me. Truth is I wanna be like you. Good head on your shoulders use it. Another thing turned 18 they call me a man now I get home to Montana how bout some cake and candles?*

*Your friend always Louie."*

I didn't hear from Louie for a month. The New Year promised some relief after everything that had happened in 1965. January wasn't finished before Blue started talking about eighth grade graduation and going to high school. Just as he predicted, Max and Peg got back together. They held hands every day before the bus hauled her away after school. She'd never be a pretty thing like Marcy or Debbie but she was kind to Max. I began to understand what he saw in her.

"Do you dig Marcy because she's a fox or because she has a brain?" Blue asked me. There he went again, looking for a complicated conversation. "I mean, why are you surprised that Max found a girlfriend?"

"I guess I like Marcy for both. And about Max, never thought about it much, Blue."

"I'll bet. Now Debbie and me —." Blue rolled into one of his rants about how boys and girls are different. Most of the time he was telling me stuff I already knew. Fortunately it was lunch hour and the bell rang. "We'll finish this after school," he told me as he warmed up his trumpet in the band room. I retrieved the big mouthpiece for the sousaphone from a drawer in the teacher's office. Mr. Klinnert kept it there because he didn't like kids fooling around with the sousaphone between classes. I slid inside the loop of the big instrument, which sat on a stand on the top deck behind the rest of the band. I didn't get to practice much. A sousaphone wasn't the kind of instrument you lugged home after school. Mr. Klinnert informed us we would spend the whole period practicing "Stars and Stripes Forever" and a few other patriotic songs. Boy, what a killer. *We're playing songs about flags and guns while Louie is shooting at the enemy.*

About halfway through class Blue clutched his stomach and bent forward and his trumpet clunked on the floor. Mr. Klinnert watched for a moment like he figured Blue was joking before he put down his baton. It would be just like Blue to pull a stunt like that to get the school talking. The music stopped but Blue's groans filled the room. "Bobby Taylor, what's ailing you?" Mr. Klinnert didn't know what to do at first. He knelt beside Blue, who whispered to him while the rest of us strained to hear. Mr. Klinnert raised his head.

"Might be appendicitis," he said to nobody in particular. I volunteered to carry the news to the principal's office. Walking down the hall between classes was a big deal. The hall was forbidden territory. Lockers stood silent. All the classroom doors were closed except for two. Once I alerted the principal that Blue was sacked over like a dead man, sparing no details about his groans of pain, I was sent back to my sousaphone with instructions to stay out of the way. Mr. Klinnert and the principal, Hank Smith, hauled Blue away. As soon as they disappeared down the hall, half-dragging Blue while he moaned and complained, we broke into corny descriptions of Blue's demise. Kids who sat closest to him in the horn section offered the most knowledge. Mr. Klinnert returned before the juiciest details were divulged. "Appendicitis," he repeated. "His father is coming to take him to the doctor."

That night, at the hospital, Blue scrunched in bed as if old Betsy had kicked him between the legs. "Did they have to cut off any private parts?" Max wanted to know. Blue looked alarmed. "You think —."

"He's just trying to scare you, Blue." I handed him a glass of ice water off the table beside his bed. "The appendix is a few inches away. I looked it up. You'd lose your privates only if the doctor slipped with the knife."

Max pressed on. "Have you looked, Bluesy? To see if anything's missing?"

Blue managed a groan of disgust. They had him wrapped in some weird gown that tied behind his neck. It resembled a bib for fat kids. Just then a nurse, a nun, came into the room. It had four beds but Blue was the only patient in there. An enormous white habit dwarfed her shriveled face. She looked like Red Skelton in his Clem Kadiddlehopper costume peeking out from the Zenith at home. "You boys scoot along now and let Bobby rest. He's going to feel sore for a couple of days." She pushed aside Blue's gown to get a good look at his incision. It was gross, all right. Max stuck out his tongue in revulsion. We beat it for the door while Blue laid there all cut up and half naked. I couldn't wait to tell everyone at school. Louie would like to hear about it too. He'd laugh his guts out.

We met Mrs. Taylor on the stairs. "Good of you boys to come. I was hoping Bobby would have company while I got dinner ready at home." She kissed us on the tops of our heads before breezing to Blue's room.

"Think they would tell him, Paul?"

"About what?"

"If the doctor slipped and cut off some of Blue's manhood?"

"We'd never hear the end of it."

///// 

Early in the *Little Shepherd* book, my hero Chad and his dog Jack fought the contemptible Dillon brothers and their mean dog Whizzer after a chance meeting in the woods. Chad and Jack won, but you knew it wasn't finished because the Dillons were a dirty and conniving bunch. I hadn't really forgot about that fight with the Tucker boys down on the river. It's just that I never expected to see them again. The Saturday afternoon after Blue's surgery I hauled the trash outside to the cans behind the warehouse at the lumberyard like I always did. An Edsel, fender missing and blue smoke chugging out the back, crept past me in the alley. I didn't recognize the occupants until the driver threw the car in reverse and Tommy's fat face leered at me from the window. The car was crammed with Tuckers. I saw at least one of Tommy's big brothers squeezed into the assemblage.

Tommy rolled the window down in a gush of cigarette smoke. "L-l-l-ook-y what we got here. O-o-o-ld four eyes." His stammering was worse than before. He still looked like a sneering gopher. Vapor swirled around his long yellow teeth in the freezing afternoon air. His head looked like the business end of a dirty broom, the same old Tommy. A door on the Edsel popped open. *Oh no. Not another fight.* This time I was alone. Louie off to war, Toby inside bucking boards, Blue in the hospital maybe missing some private parts, Max somewhere adoring the waif. *Just me all alone with the whole Tucker clan.* One of the Tuckers swung his thick legs out of the wheezing car and planted a pair of giant boots in the dirty snow. He was Tate, the oldest brother who had tossed me into the rocks. He looked bigger and meaner. *What are they doing in Deer Lodge? Didn't the police run them off?* I thought I was a goner. Tate looked me over like he was trying to remember. Then he stepped between me and the warehouse door.

"We got a bone to pick with yur buddy Elvis in black, fur eyes, the one who worked over my little brothers." The zipper hung loose from his ragged coat like a torn tongue. He wore a red stocking cap stained with oil and coaxed over his enormous ears. As he edged toward me I pulled a board the size of a baseball bat out of the garbage can.

"T-t-t-hink t-t-t-hat little ole pieca wood goina save ya?" Tommy chattered from the back seat. He sounded gleeful.

*What would Louie do? Pound him, that's what. He wouldn't back down.* Tucker spit a stream of tobacco juice. It fell in a

Kevin S. Giles

sickly brown puddle at my feet. He smiled through stained teeth. I hoped he didn't know that I pounded his cousin Danny Mulligan. I wouldn't live to tell the story. "That buddy yurs got lucky jumpin' my brothers from behind. We gonna square up with him real good. Where he hidin?"

"Hurry up!" a woman yelled from the car. Her fat face peered out the open door. She was gray and puckered around the mouth. I knew right away she was old lady Tucker.

I took a chance. "You supposed to be here? I hear the police are looking for you and all of them." I pointed toward the car. I was sure the woman heard me. She leaned farther out of the car.

"Now, Tate! Let's git!" The brother edged toward me, balling his fist.

"You asked about my friend in black. All I know is that he's looking for you. He said he wants another crack at the biggest one and then he'll work his way down to the runt." I looked at Tommy. The board felt like lead in my hands. Any of those Tuckers could pound me, even the mother. Dad told me once that she decked a pump jockey at the Esso service station when he missed a spot cleaning her windshield. She wouldn't pay the thirty-two cents she owed for a gallon of gasoline either.

Tate, indecisive, rubbed a grimy paw across his face. He wasn't afraid at all of the lumber I waved in his direction but his mother was a different story. So was Louie. "You tell him fur me the Tuckers come a'callin' fur eyes. We gonna catch him sooner later and whomp him good. We gonna have him beggin' like a little gurl." He stepped past me. Without another look he loaded his bulk into the Edsel. The low-riding heap groaned into gear, chugged to the street, and barely cleared the railroad tracks before disappearing to the West Side and I hoped out of my life.

After work I gulped down dinner and raced to see Blue. He was home from the hospital, propped on pillows on the couch, eating a bowl of chocolate ice cream and frowning at Lawrence Welk's champagne music. "Don't suppose they'll ever get somebody to play rock, do you? I'm thinkin' the Dave Clark Five. Imagine them playing 'Over and Over' with those bubbles flying around. Wouldn't that be a kick?" Blue was wild about the British Invasion ever since the Beatles hit the *Ed Sullivan Show* in 1964. He bought all the new records at Safeway with his allowance money. The albums cost two ninety-eight apiece. For me that was worth two hours of work at the lumberyard. I saved some of my money for dates with Marcy and some for Christmas presents but gave most of it to Mom to help buy food and pay the electric bill. I was no hero. It's just that Dad would want me to do that. I don't have much to say about Christmas. It came and went without a Christmas tree. None of us, not even Louie, felt much like going to the woods to cut one down. That was Dad's special event of the winter. On Christmas Eve, after we came home from church, Mom sat in the living room and cried. I can't explain how terrible it was opening gifts without Dad. Too sad for words.

About the time that Blue and I couldn't stand watching the champagne bubbles another minute, Max came to the door. He unbuckled his rubber boots on the porch, knocking the snow from them, before coming inside. Blue's mother didn't like snow on her carpet. It was a recipe for trouble.

"What, no *Gunsmoke*? I thought it was time."

"You're early, outlaw. Marshal Dillon hasn't drawn his gun yet." That was Blue, joking around. "Know what? I wish we had another channel in Deer Lodge besides the one from Butte. I got some reception one night from the Missoula station but the vertical hold wouldn't work. The screen just kept rolling."

Max seemed unimpressed. "Well, Bluesy, at least your family has a Zenith. The corners of the screen on our old Philco are turning black." Max turned to me. "Paul, think you'll ever get one of those falutin' color TVs we saw in the window at Gambles downtown?"

"Looked all green and purple to me. Like Martians invading Deer Lodge. Now wouldn't that be something."

Blue shifted on the couch. He held his side and grimaced. "Laying here all day I watch the news sometimes. More Marines going to Vietnam." He looked at me, waiting for a reaction.

"That's Louie, then." Blue and Max knew I was feeling down. I didn't talk about Louie much. To tell you the truth, I was worried for him. "The Tuckers paid me a visit today." Blue nearly fell off the couch. Max, fiddling with a dial on the television set, whipped around.

"Where!" they cried in unison. I told them about the encounter in the alley that afternoon. Neither of my best friends turned away from me even when the opening music of *Gunsmoke* began.

Blue whistled. "You could have licked them all, Paul. Whipped their asses and sent them off to Anaconda or whatever hole they crawled out from." Max stayed quiet at that. We all knew the truth. Blue was trying to make me feel better, that's all.

"I was worried," I told them. "They looked even worse than that day at the river, driving that beater of a car and all. That big Tate Tucker stuck his brown teeth right in my face like he wanted to bite my head off. What do they want with Louie anyway?"

"They talk big when Louie isn't around," Max said.

"Old Louie would wallop them for good, that's for sure," Blue said.

"Imagine how he'd smear them this time with his Marine training," I said.

That settled, we turned our attention to television. It didn't occur to me that the Tuckers might be hungry and out of luck.

///// 

In the evenings after I finished my homework I went to the ice rink down the street. Blue loved to skate but couldn't until he healed. Max tried a few times until he caught his skate on the ice and fell on his face, gashing his chin. Then he quit skating but came to the rink anyway. When it was dark and cold Max heaped logs on the bonfire until it showered sparks into the star-drenched sky. I think Max melted five feet of ice while he burned logs and dreamed about the waif. When Marcy wasn't being brainy, spending half the night studying for tests, she came to skate with me. We held hands while we glided across the rough ice in the dark, her mitten locked in my glove.

"Please don't go," she said the night of Valentine's Day.

"Not until nine thirty."

Marcy laughed in the moonlight. "Darling, I don't want you to go away."

"Why are you calling me darling? I'm not old enough for that."

"Will you stay with me, darling?"

"I told you, I don't have to go home yet."

Marcy laughed again. "Not tonight, silly, I mean forever. You'll be my grownup man and I'll be your lady and we'll get married and own a house and have kids."

"When does all this happen?"

"After we get out of college, of course. When I'm an English teacher and you're a doctor."

"A doctor? Science is my worst subject. I'm not too thrilled about blood either."

"You'll learn. You just have to apply yourself, Paul."

"That's what my mother tells me every year when the report cards come out."

"Well, see?"

"See what?"

"That makes two women in your life who know what's good for you."

"Great."

We skated in silence for a few moments. The air felt frozen and still as if time had stopped. The bonfire across the ice popped and sizzled. Max grinned with happiness. Peg's farmer parents had allowed her a rare evening in town. She stood beside Max, clutching his coat. For an instant I thought of Louie and how he must miss Faye. I stopped skating and pulled Marcy against me.

"If we have kids then that means we get to—."

She pressed her mitten over my lips. She came close enough to fog my glasses with her warm breath. "I know what's turning in your dirty mind but that happens after we're married, silly."

"We're getting married? We're only fourteen."

"That gives us time to plan, don't you think?" We skated in the tingling chill until the ten o'clock curfew blew at City Hall downtown. I admit I was feeling good about Marcy's marriage proposal as long as it involved sex.

"I'm late, Marcy. I completely forgot the time."

"Me too, Paul." We unlaced our skates beside the fire. The flames withered into glowing red embers. Max and Peg said goodbye and sauntered off, clinging to one another. Marcy tied her skates together and draped them over her left shoulder, one skate in front and one in back. She stepped close, pressing her lips to mine. It was a long, soft kiss, full of feeling.

"I'll never leave you," she whispered. She walked into the night toward home. Sadness washed over me, for Dad and Kenny, for the old man named Oscar, even for Hack Face. For Louie, as I remembered his nightmares of his parents broken and dead in a smashed-up car. Boys can get filled up with depressing thoughts if they're not careful. I looked at the fire, now dying itself, and cried.

A warmth settled over the valley overnight, a sign of early March. The incessant but soft wind sounded like a grandparent's kind lullaby outside my bedroom window. When I walked to school that morning water covered the ice rink. Our bonfire looked black and dead. The air felt warm and cold at the same time. Clouds bunched over Mount Powell to frown at the valley before racing south with the wind. Winter was far from over. Sure enough, by the time I walked home for lunch the Chinook was gone. Melting snow froze again. I walked slow, trying not to fall.

"So, Paul, what do you make of this?" Old Mr. Pearson stood at his front porch throwing sand on the steps. He didn't wait for my reply. He never did. Near deaf is what Mom said, bombed on some remote Pacific island called Guadalcanal during World War II. He was a distinguished veteran, she said, who deserved our respect. "Wait five minutes in Montana and the weather changes. Wait ten and it changes back, huh, boy?" Mr. Pearson gave me a friendly smile. I tried to imagine him younger, like Louie, dressed in a military uniform.

"Mr. Pearson, can I ask you a question?" He turned away, still talking. I walked closer and asked him again, louder this time. He heard me now. He lifted his head, his eyes full of history, ears perking to hear.

"What's that, boy? You speak up now so I can hear you right and proper."

I mustered the biggest voice I could. "Mr. Pearson, what happens to young men when they go to war?"

"When young men go to war?" He paused, searching, showing the wisdom in his lined face. "That's a mighty big question for a boy. I reckon that's a question somebody should have asked a long time ago, Paul. My thinking is that it changes them, most for the good, some for the bad and many, well, they don't live to know the difference." He saw the concern in my eyes. "Nothing anybody can do but pray they come out on the living side. Those young men, it's between them and the Big Maker." He pointed to the sky. "Why do you ask, boy?"

I told Mr. Pearson about Louie joining the Marines and going to Vietnam. I think he heard most of what I said. At least he listened and nodded. "Vietnam, you say. Full of commies. Don't suppose you know I was a jarhead too. A Marine like a lot of men around this town. Your friend Louie is doing right by this country. Don't fear for him, Paul. I never knew a Marine who wasn't proving something to himself by going through that hell. You tell him your neighbor Mr. Pearson said Semper Fi." He rubbed his reddening bare hands together. Then he waved goodbye and worked his way down the sidewalk to the back of his house, sprinkling sand from a Folgers coffee can like the ones Dad used to collect his coins for the boat. I felt sorry for Mr. Pearson. He lived alone. His wife died of cancer when I was in grade school.

The mailman arrived at my house when I did. "Something for you, Paul," and when he handed me the letter I recognized it right away. It was crumpled and dirty, like it had been packed out of the jungle. I tore into the house. *"Ace — don't know what I got myself into here,"* it began in a hurried scrawl, as if written in lantern light. *"In the jungle after dark all the time lookin for gooks don't tell Elaine. Walk through rice paddies gooks shot one Marine dead head blown clean off. Trouble is cant see em comin know what I mean pour lead out of this here cannon they give me shootin at shadows. Hidin everybody hidin. Some damn Marines wanna quit. I tell them come to Butte wanna see a real fight or my buddy Ace rippin up them Tuckers."*

I laid the second page of Louie's letter aside while I heated green pea soup on the stove. I wanted to savor every line before going back to school.

*"Some of these cats cry themselves to sleep. Git lonesome for Ma and Pa, see, all torn up about it and you wonder how hell Corps*

*failed them not to behave like men. Any them would ask I say aint no treat to have no parents but hell nobody asks. We eat slop out here sure would like some home cookin but you know how it is this aint no picnik. I wrote Faye she wrote back once thats it mad I enlisted madder than hell about Vietnam said she aint goin sit and worry about me no more. Makes me sad but what you gonna do. Aint got no time to mope. You see her you tell her Louie loves her yes I said it Louie loves Faye. My platoon goin on patrol tonight up the peninsula going to hunt down gooks. Ace let me tell you this aint no fun don't want you thinkin it is you behave yourself stay out of trouble don't want you wind up like me wonder what hell your life is all about got it? Be a good man hold your head up thats the one thing I want you to remember always Ace. Tell em Louie said so."*

*"Your friend forever Louie."*

I folded Louie's letter back in the envelope and stowed it in the top drawer of my bedroom dresser next to the others he had written me. I would write him after school if I could figure out what to say. Eighth grade wasn't much fun. Our teachers talked about how we had to work hard to prepare for high school next year. My first period after lunch was study hall. I wanted to write Marcy a locker note but spent the entire hour working algebra problems. I didn't understand why I needed to learn equations to measure lumber or change spark plugs. "Algebra teaches you how to think," Mom told me at least once a day. I knew she was right, but the truth is, I didn't care. I had my mind on other matters.

I felt a tap on my shoulder a few minutes before the bell rang to change classes. It was Mrs. Mulvane, the office secretary. She squinted at me through her big white glasses.

"Someone here to see you, Mr. Morrison." She pointed to the hall. I left my desk, book open and pencil worn to a nub, to investigate this unusual event. I first saw Elaine, her eyes red from crying. Toby braced her with his long arms. Then I saw the small yellow envelope.

# Elaine

*Now when spring comes* I remember green buds bursting in the golden willow trees and meadowlarks singing in the countryside. I think of a skinny Montana boy emerging in shirtsleeves after a hard winter, born into a reawakening as the earth renews. He marvels at the flight of bumblebees, inhales the heavenly aroma of purple lilacs and fresh-thawed earth, admires late snow that caps mountaintops high above the valley. He oils Grandpa's old baseball mitt, pumps air into sagging bicycle tires, digs with a shovel in the backyard to find earthworms for fishing. His friends Blue and Max come in their tennis shoes and patched blue jeans and summer t-shirts. The three boys sate their appetite for this freedom until night settles and they gather to trade stories under the yellow glow of corner streetlights until their parents call them home. Tomorrow will be another day, longer and warmer, dressed in its splendid green clothes. I think back to where my childhood lingers in a dusty corner of my brain, back to an inconvenient beginning to my teenage years. I think of that night of my first dance when my march to maturity began.

Oh, Louie, why? You left me when I needed you most. Didn't you hear my anguish? I hated you at first and held a

280

match to your letters. Then I heard your voice. "Ace, be a man." Now, so many years later, I preserve your last words to me in the metal box from my boyhood where I hid my baseball cards, news of President Kennedy's assassination, my best marbles from grade school that Max didn't win from me. The flame's ravenous lick left a brown stain to remind me how close I came to erasing your words. Boys do foolish things. Where would I be today without your letters? Was it my conscience that blew out the match? Or your otherworldly breath? A heavy burden, regret.

Did I ever know you? I understand now how it's possible to make the biggest impressions with the fewest words. From the moment I met you in 1965 you made me a man because I saw that you learned the hard way. Even in death you were a survivor. If only you hadn't died before I wrote my last letter. More than anything I wanted to say how you helped me after Dad died. You saved me after I hit and killed that man on the street and now you've traded your life for mine. I loved you. Will you forgive me, Louie?

///// 

After Elaine told me that Louie was gone I left school and walked all the way home. Just like that. Sadness fell over me as I sat alone in the barn, looking at the Chevy, trying to fathom the brief official message in the telegram Elaine had thrust at me. Louie's death made the local paper, the *Silver State Post*, the very next day. He was the first Deer Lodge man killed in Vietnam, the article said, although the paper didn't tell much about Louie's life except to note his kinship with Elaine and Toby. Elaine supplied a picture I hadn't seen before. It showed Louie glaring from under a crisp white hat, a Marine tunic buttoned over his hard neck. Louie still looked like Elvis, but now the modern version. His simmering eyes hid the grief of his lonely life.

As if the Chevy beckoned them, Toby and Elaine came to our house to plan Louie's funeral. Word got around. The good folks of Deer Lodge brought cake and stew from home and boxes of candy from the drug store. Marcy skipped school and sat next to me all day, holding my hand, guarding me from our mutual unspoken understanding that in Louie's death I also was mourning once again for my father and Kenny and everyone else who abruptly left my life. I didn't tell her about Oscar and never would.

She pressed against me, whispering. "I never took the time to know how much he meant to you and I'm sorry for that."

"I'm not sure I knew myself. When someone's alive there's always a tomorrow. And when tomorrow never comes —."

"Then you know?"

"Yes. You know how special that person was but you can't tell them, ever. It's the end."

Marcy shifted on the couch. She turned toward me with thought in her eyes. One of her Catholic moods was coming on, I was sure of it. "Or the beginning, Paul?"

"No, death is final."

"For that person's life on earth. But what did you learn from Kenny and your Dad and Louie? Maybe, even, from Hack Face O'Hanlon?"

I managed a weak laugh. "I learned that I hate whiskey. I'll bet Hack Face brewed that himself. But I get what you're saying. It just takes a while to figure out. Everything moved so fast after the dance at the gym. I felt like a kid then. Now I'm not so sure what I am anymore."

Marcy smiled. "I couldn't wait for the night of the dance. I wrote *Paul Morrison* in my notebook about a thousand times. My mother took me shopping for the best pink dress in Deer Lodge. If you had ignored me and danced with other girls I would have died." She winced at her unfortunate choice of words. "I'm sorry, Paul, I shouldn't have said it that way."

"You looked good in pink, Marcy."

"I'm glad you think so." She leaned over to kiss me on the cheek. "There's something I want to tell you, Paul. I mean, if something happened to me or you I wouldn't want this to go unsaid."

"Are you breaking up with me?"

"No, silly. It's just that, well —." She looked around the house. The adults were in the kitchen drinking coffee. "It's, well, I love you, Paul."

"You love me?" I never imagined hearing that from a girl — or telling her either. That was a huge step in dating, something I wasn't prepared to understand.

"I don't want to embarrass you. I just don't want to leave you wondering. Everybody needs something good to remember."

"I —."

"Do you the feel the same about me? We've been going together since the dance. You even got in a fight over me."

"Danny Mulligan?"

"You pounded him good."

I suspected I loved Marcy but I didn't understand why it was hard to tell her. I bent toward her with good intentions just as Mom walked into the living room. "Not here, not now," she said, assuming we were about to make out. Behind her came Elaine, pressing a tissue to her eyes. "I want to tell you kids about Louie, things you don't know."

///// 

The morning of Louie's funeral, I turned to Chad Buford for consolation. I opened the worn book, its covers creaking from use, and turned to the opening chapters. That's where Chad's Aunt Jane, the only mama he knows, dies. Chad discovers as a young boy what everybody learns sooner or later. Life is a solitary journey.

*It was the spirit of the plague that passed, taking with it the breath of the unlucky and the unfit; and in the hut on Lonesome three were dead — a gaunt mountaineer, a gaunt daughter, and a gaunt son. Later, the mother, too, "jess kind o' got tired," as little Chad said, and soon to her worn hands and feet came the well-earned rest. Nobody was left then but Chad and Jack, and Jack was a dog with a belly to feed ... "God!" he said simply. "I am not nothin' but a boy, but I got to ack like a man now."*

Thirty years passed before I opened *Little Shepherd of Kingdom Come* again. I'd misplaced my old book in a move to Oregon. I searched boxes in the garage for hours as panic washed over me. How could I be so careless? Then one day I opened the silver tin box where, carefully folded under Louie's letters, I found the English paper I had written about the book in seventh grade. After reading it I charged into my stacks of belongings with renewed determination. I found the book deep in a chest full of old newspapers that included alarming reports of President Johnson's escalation of the Vietnam War. Its yellowed pages held untold secrets about my life. Not even when I coveted it so in 1965 did I realize its enormous potential.

What made a boy a man? Was it the advancing of age, or the accumulation of memories, or the shaping of character? Or taking a position that hurt loved ones who disagreed? When the Civil War began, Chad broke the news of his unexpected decision to the kindly old gentleman of the South who had taken him from a mountain cabin in the Cumberland's, raised him on a well-fitted plantation, and sent him to the finest schools in Kentucky. The major had expected Chad to fight for the Confederacy.

*The hour had come.*

*"I'm going away, Major."*

*The Major did not even turn his head.*

*"I thought this was coming," he said quietly. Chad's face grew even paler, and he steeled his heart for the revelation.*

*"I've already spoken to Lieutenant Hunt," the Major went on. "He expects to be a captain, and he says that, maybe, he can make you a lieutenant. You can take that boy Brutus as a body servant." He brought his fist down on the railing of the porch. "God, but I'd give the rest of my life to be ten years younger than I am now."*

*"Major, I'm <u>going into the Union Army</u>. The Major's pipe almost dropped from between his lips. Catching the arms of his chair with both hands, he turned heavily and with dazed wonder, as though the boy had struck him with his fist from behind, and, without a word, stared hard into Chad's tortured face. The keen old eye had not long to look before it saw the truth, and then, silently, the old man turned back. His hands trembled on the chair, and he slowly thrust them into his pockets, breathing hard though his nose. The boy expected an outbreak, but none came. ... The boy knew he had given his old friend a mortal hurt."*

Had I disappointed my father? My mother? I took to Missoula's streets in the early 1970s to protest the Vietnam War. Looking back on that, I realized that my involvement in the marches that swept the nation started with outrage over Louie's death. It was grief all over again. My surviving parent, the Democrat, voted for McGovern. Staking a position during times of war can be a lonely path. After Richard Nixon resigned the presidency I became even more fervent in my belief that the war in Vietnam was a waste of human life.

You see, Blue died there too.

///// 

I drove the Chevy to Louie's funeral. The old car roared to life right away while Mom waited on the back porch. When I pulled alongside the house she opened the passenger door and climbed in and said nothing about me driving without a license. At that moment it seemed we had a new understanding between us. I wasn't a boy anymore. My childhood had evaporated somewhere in 1965.

Faye came to say goodbye to Louie. She wore a simple black dress. The makeup was gone. I couldn't help noticing that even in the midst of sadness she looked prettier than ever. She squeezed my hand and leaned close to whisper in my ear. "I hated him for leaving me and now I can't tell him how mixed up and wrong I was. Paul, what have I done?"

"I'd bet he's still listening, Faye." She bowed her head and cried. I didn't know her last name. She was Faye, a knockout even at a gravesite.

We buried Louie next to Dad in the cemetery below Mount Powell. Six Marines in dress blues marched Louie's casket to his grave. They folded the flag into a triangle. Elaine reached for it with shaking hands. After the Marines shot three volleys into the air, another Marine on the hill above us played Taps on a bugle. Mom told me later she was sure Dad was standing there with us. Kenny and Hack Face, too. She sure had a lot of faith. The minister, a Marine chaplain, spoke about duty and honor and serving God. His last sentence stuck with me: "Louie Moretti died a brave man, fearing no enemy, committing the ultimate sacrifice in service to his country."

As we walked from the gravesite I handed Elaine the keys to the Chevy. She pushed them away. "He wanted you to have the car, Paul."

"But it's yours. It belonged to your parents. I know what happened."

Elaine squeezed my hands between hers. Toby stood behind her, tall as a tree. "Then you understand how special a gift he gave you. It's what we have left of Louie." She wiped her eyes and looked toward Louie's silver casket, which sat alone now, awaiting its descent into a tomb of concrete and earth. "Take care of it like he did. That's what he would want, you see." I glimpsed Elaine's rounded belly when she turned away. Toby, a father. Imagine.

Louie died from "small arms fire," the Marines told Elaine. He was awarded the Navy Cross for his bravery under fire trying to save fellow Marines from enemy attack. It happened near a place called Quang Ngai City in something called Operation Utah. That's all we knew until several years later when Elaine received a letter from a Marine in Louie's platoon. The man, Seth McGregor, was a car salesman in California. "He was my buddy and looked after me," Seth wrote. "We knew we would see trouble but that firefight was the worst ever. The gooks opened up a machine gun on us and took half our platoon. I was hit in both legs. You're probably wondering how Louie died. He was dragging me out of the line of fire when the gooks shot him. *Dragging Marines through the sand*. It was bad and he didn't suffer at all. If he hadn't saved me I wouldn't be writing this letter to you today. I walk on artificial legs but I thank the Lord every day for Louie saving my life. I didn't know Louie had family until another buddy in our platoon sent me his obituary. We didn't talk much about family in Nam because it was bad luck. I'm sorry it took so long. Louie was a good man. Be proud of what he did." Seth enclosed two crinkled snapshots in his letter. One showed Seth and Louie with their arms over each other's shoulders in a muddy jungle camp. The other was the photograph of Louie's parents in front of the Chevy.

After the funeral we went for lunch at the church. Too few of us. Blue was there with his parents, Max with his dad, and the kindly old town cop, Charlie Mitchell. Faye came, Marcy and her parents, Mom and Sally, Toby and Elaine, Edna and a few others. Most of the townspeople knew Louie was a war hero. They also knew he killed Oscar, or thought they knew, and I figured they stayed away because of that. My secret ate away at me. When I couldn't stand it anymore I asked Mom if I could drive Marcy home in the Chevy. She lived only two blocks away.

"Don't get caught," she told me out of Charlie's hearing. "I'll catch a ride with Blue's parents. You go straight home and you park that Chevy in the barn where it belongs until you're old enough." That was Mom, giving me a little rope and pulling it back. With the funeral and all it hadn't yet occurred to me to press for more driving time but she knew I would.

Marcy sat beside me. The car rumbled, wanting more speed. We passed her house, both knowing what we were going to do. In a minute flat I was on the highway heading north out of town. "For Louie," I said.

"For Louie," Marcy answered.

We had renewed respect for Louie after what Elaine told us in the living room. After the train killed their parents, the bank took their house. They first stayed with Uncle Jimmy but he drank too much and disappeared on benders that lasted for days. Snow and rain fell on them through holes in the roof of the shack he called home in Butte. Sometimes Louie and Elaine slept in the Chevy. "That Chevy is what we had to remember our folks and it was the one thing we could depend on, that and each other," Elaine told us. She dropped out of high school to fold laundry at Silver Bow Hospital and mop the floor at an uptown bar after the drunks went home. That paid just enough for the little house in Walkerville. Louie started working at the Mountain Con mine was he was ten, doing small chores around the tender house after school. "He wanted to work and pay his way, you see, even when he was a pup." When he was fourteen he quit school, lied about his age and went to work in the mine tipping ore cars. "He didn't want me working in the bar no more," Elaine said. "He worked like a man to put food on our table. Uncle Jimmy come around now and then, offering to help, but Louie took pride in making do. Then I married that awful man that Toby beat up, and Louie thought there was nothing left for him to do. He came over here to stay with Uncle Jimmy on the mountain." Elaine dabbed at her nose with the tissue. "It's terrible, really. I don't want to sound like a wallflower, you see, but the truth is I wouldn't have survived without Louie. It makes me sick thinking of that little boy working at the mine. Nobody cared about us but Louie wouldn't give up. We were desperate, you see, so very desperate."

The Chevy took off like a rocket in flight, its front end nosing into the air like an anxious runner, eight cylinders thundering as we buried the needle at one hundred and ten. I muttered thanks for a dry highway and didn't ease up until we streaked past the old prison farm five miles down the road.

"I'll get in trouble for this, Marcy."

"So will I," she said, not a hint of worry in her voice. I drove casually back to town, watching for Charlie, who knew I was too young to drive. I pulled the Chevy to a stop at her house. She kissed me and slid across the seat to climb out.

"Marcy? I meant to tell you."

She turned to me, her eyes showing anticipation. "Yes?"

"I love you."

Mom beat me home. She yelled at me for being irresponsible and threatened to have Toby come take the Chevy away for good. I'm sure she knew why I did it but she grounded me for two weeks with no television anyway. She never fully understood my friendship with Louie but she knew grief. The Chevy stayed.

# Sally

*Years later, I stood on the covered porch* of our old house, feeling its emptiness. It was the morning of my mother's funeral. Storm clouds gathered over the Flint Range but whatever was brewing would merely freshen the valley on a warm October day. Threats of snow had given away to Indian summer. Sally came from the garden to hand me a rose, our mother's favorite. Frost had wilted its petals. "Mother protected her roses to the end. I don't know how she did it, evening after evening, shielding them from cold air until she got too sick to make a difference. Even keeping them growing, how did she do it? Shielding, always shielding, wasn't that Mother's way?" Sally looped her arm around me. My sister was all grown up, consumed with causes and ideas, filled with dreams and wonder, finding peace in all things. She was a confirmed hippie, built on grains and vegetables, exhibiting the family's slender side. Sally had inherited our mother's youthful beauty. She brushed her red curls from forest green eyes and looked up at me.

"You didn't kill her, Paul. I know that's what haunts you. She was sick and dying. Her heart went bad and then came the drinking, so much drinking. It was Daddy, you know. She never got over him being gone. She's with him now, don't you think?"

"Sally, do you remember how it was? Before the trouble?"

"I remember the four of us at the kitchen table. Mother setting out the best meal she could muster out of that pantry, Daddy smelling like sawdust, you getting teased about girls. It was good, like that flower you're holding, and it bloomed and faded before I was ten." Sally, a writer of growing repute, spoke in lyrical sentences. She knew a great deal more of my past than I expected of her. She held me close while we stood silent for a moment, finding solace in the great mountains to the West. It would be our last time together at the old house. We had spent the week loading memories, good and bad, into boxes before we turned over the keys and said goodbye to the place. The yard had fallen to weeds and the barn needed a coat of paint. Our mother had clung to life there and I was rarely around to help.

"Remember, Paul, how I asked you so many questions when we were kids? You always had an answer for everything. You got into some trouble and fell into heartache but you also had dreams. I hope you haven't forgotten the pleasures of life, Paul. The good people, the good things that made you a man. Daddy and Mother and Louie and Blue and Max and Toby and so many others, don't forget what they did for you."

I looked at the smiling kind woman comforting me, taller than anyone would expect from the Morrison clan. She was all I had left of my family. "I'm sorry I was gone from your life for so long, Sally. I won't do that to you again."

We buried my mother after a hard rain swept over the cemetery. It brought a wave of late autumn wind off the mountain, but not cold enough for snow, and about a hundred of us stood in the soggy dead grass and prayed. She disappeared into the wet ground beside Dad and Louie as my sister wept and the old Presbyterian minister I had known as a boy shook with palsy as he tried to read scripture. When everyone had gone I looked down at my mother and said goodbye to her the best I knew how, much as I had done with Dad all those years ago, my head full of confusion and regrets. I touched his headstone. Was he waiting for my mother? *Hello Martha, welcome home.* I turned to the other grave next to Dad. "Louie Anthony Moretti, USMC, Killed in Action ...," I said out loud, averting my eyes from the finality of what was printed there. I swear it was Louie, right then, who steered my gaze to a fourth grave across the cemetery. He spoke inside my head somehow, telling me to face my past. I knew who was waiting there for me. I sank to my knees and begged Louie for forgiveness. The rain fell again.

## /////

I had dodged this moment since that night of the accident. This was why I had come back to Deer Lodge. I had put my mother in the grave because of it, just as I had done to Louie. Secrets bring a terrible toll. We never forget our haunting memories. The other grave was in the Odd Fellows section beneath a small headstone that had gathered moss that obscured the inscription. Chiseling at the letters with a key to the Chevy, I finally uncovered what was noted there. Oscar Robert Dunne was his name. "Died October 28, 1965." That's all that was left of Oscar, a name and date, and my own deep guilt at killing him.

I hated the Chevy for it, hated Louie for taking the blame, hated the world for letting Dad die in the middle of what should have been the best summer of my boyhood. I even blamed Oscar for choosing to shuffle across that dark road the very instant I pushed the gas pedal farther to the floor. Somehow I had eluded my conscience for all those years. Now, finally, there was no escaping it.

I talked to Oscar, underground in his eternal sleep, hardly fitting on the day of my mother's funeral. Nothing seemed right anymore. I told him I was sorry, hearing the words wash out of me into the cemetery silence hovering over a thousand others just like him, lying prone in their Sunday best under tons of earth and a carpet of decaying leaves. I admitted what I had done, pleaded for Oscar's forgiveness. My secret was buried in his grave, fouled with my youthful indiscretions, awaiting my maturity to dig it up. How had I come to accept his death as yet another calamity in my young life? To talk myself into believing it was Louie who hit Oscar with the Chevy? To watch Louie go off to war in a damp jungle and die because of it?

They said Oscar died on impact. They found his cane in the ditch fifty feet from his caved-in body. He died of internal injuries, it was determined, but only years later when I went to the library in Butte to look up old newspaper clippings did I discover that. He had retired as a tower guard from Montana State Prison after thirty-one years. He never married and had no survivors, at least nobody remembered in his obituary. His parents had come from Ireland. Louie's name was there, too. "Louie Moretti of Butte, the 17-year-old driver ...." Just as I already knew, the police chief described Oscar's death as an unfortunate accident. Louie had been alone in the car, the police said. *And Louie took the blame and it haunted him into a firefight in Vietnam and he died with my secret.*

At the police department that afternoon, I found a young officer leaning against the wall, reading a newspaper. Two cells, both empty, stood open. He heard my footsteps and looked up. "Help you, sir?" He didn't look much older than me, and I wasn't yet thirty.

"I was looking for the chief. I have a crime to report."

He tossed the paper on a chair. "That's me. Chief Davis. You were expecting somebody older?"

"Maybe older than me, I guess. What happened to Charlie?"

"He died a few years back, before I took this job."

Motioning off the chit-chat, he reached for a pencil and a clipboard. He was all business, I could see that. A rusty fan whup-whupped on his desk. "So about this crime?"

I told him everything I could remember about Oscar's death. He showed no reaction and never wrote anything. Then I told him how I met Louie, and my father dying, and Louie dying, and now my mother. The chief looked at me in disbelief and tossed the clipboard onto his desk.

"Let's get to the rub of it. You're telling me that you were behind the wheel of a car when you were thirteen and killed this man? And ran? And your friend Louie took the rap for it?"

As I nodded he leaned over to pull open a drawer on a gray filing cabinet. "I know the case, Mr. Morrison. It took me awhile but I found it in a box in the basement after somebody came in here last fall to ask about it. Don't suppose you want to know who that was?" Chief Davis held the yellowed file open for me, pointing to a signature I recognized right away.

"No, she didn't —."

"She did, Mr. Morrison. She thought something was wrong and came down here to the office and asked to see the file. She said it had troubled her since you were a boy. Oh, and we require anyone who looks at a file to sign it for the record." She had written "Martha Jane Morrison" in her familiar looping handwriting. She had dated it, too, October 28, 1980. *She remembered the anniversary of Oscar's death.*

"Did she —?"

"Think you were driving the car? She could see from what we have in the file that it was this friend of yours, Louie Moretti. She hoped in her heart it wasn't you. Frankly, there was nothing in this file to confirm her suspicions. The investigation didn't amount to much and maybe Charlie didn't ask all the right questions. I've seen better police work in my young career but I know better than to pass judgment on a cop who knew this town inside and out. Whether Charlie knew … well, this case is now sixteen years old and the presumed driver is dead. And sadly, your mother, too."

The chief closed the file. He suddenly looked weary. "It won't surprise you, Mr. Morrison, that most of what we do around this town is chase barking dogs and break up bar fights. I have one officer on patrol at any one time and sometimes they quit the job out of boredom. I come from a small town myself — Stevensville over in the Bitterroot Valley, heard of it? — and when I found out Deer Lodge was advertising for a police chief the idea of working here didn't seem all that foreign to me. In three years I've never had a serious crime. No murders, nobody robbing Safeway with a gun, nothing really bad. This case, with Oscar Dunne, it's bad, but it's also old as Mount Powell out there."

"Are you going to arrest me?" I began, but he waved me off.

"I could throw you in one of those cells for manslaughter and we could have a trial and maybe put you in prison, but that's presuming we could get around Montana's statute of limitations. Maybe you could clear your war hero friend Louie and own up to your mother and stand tall for what you did. Sound right? Here's the problem, Mr. Morrison. Even if you're telling the truth, there's nobody left to corroborate it. Your word against nobody's. You were a boy. This happened so long ago I had to blow dust off the box downstairs. Mr. Dunne's death was an accident, fair and square. The file says so. We're between county attorneys right now, so I'm making a decision all by my lonesome that I'm not going to send this case to some hotshot lawyer over in Helena to make something out of. I'll bet you've paid a thousand times for whatever you did. You coming here to own up might be justice enough. In fact, I'm convinced of it. Now go home and put this behind you."

I couldn't believe what I was hearing. "My hurting over this makes me sick. I killed them all, chief. I came here to confess. My mother —"

He slapped the file shut. "This is going back to the basement. You know, I had some problems too when I was a kid. That's why I'm a cop. Neither one of us has much mileage on us but we've already traveled a long road. What would your parents have wanted if they were sitting here today, listening to you?"

From out of my memory came their voices. Dad, in his shop. Mom, at the stove. "I can hear them say it: 'Be a good man, Paul. That's how you'll pay your debt.' "

Davis held out his hand. "We're done here. Nobody will ever know about this conversation if you never give me reason to bring it up. Good luck, Mr. Morrison, and goodbye."

I went to my rented Jeep Cherokee and drove home to Oregon through a sudden blizzard that filled mountain passes with snow. There was nothing left to do but get on with my life.

# Faye, again

*Now, in my forty-seventh year, I look back* on the heartbreak of my first summer as a teenager with a mingling of utter fascination and befuddling sadness. Calamity enters our lives without invitation. Death clobbers us with a big hammer. The optimists say that loss builds character. I'd rather see my father alive, an old man now. Louie, too, grown and married with kids. Old Oscar, dead of natural causes instead of the terrible way I sent him to his grave. My mother, spared of my mistakes. Kenny and his prom date, alive and smiling and lifting the mantle of grief from their families. Jimmy O'Hanlon, turning his back on whiskey and dangerous saw blades.

Death hastens maturity, yes, but so does life. I never shed my hurt for those days past, but as the young police chief helped me understand, I put my guilt to better use. From those roots of sorrow sprang an adulthood of unimagined happiness, even as I spend my days helping people understand why life evaporates in an instant. I didn't sell lumber, as I always had supposed, but instead studied psychology to become a grief counselor. Some of my clients are boys and girls whose parents died suddenly. Some are older people, older than me, who lost their sons and daughters and friends in Vietnam. Stick with what you know, my father often told me.

I never forgot about the Tuckers and their poverty. Tate went to prison for killing somebody in a fight over money. Word was the middle one, Tony, made something of himself and owned a grocery store in Wyoming. I looked up Tommy Tucker in Anaconda. When he opened the door at a sagging house near the smelter smokestack I was surprised to see him stooped and emaciated. Tommy wore the face of a slow, befuddled man. He fussed with a stained undershirt. A hand-rolled cigarette drooped from his lips. If not for the gopher teeth I wouldn't have known him. I took Tommy downtown for a meal at the café. He shoveled away two hamburgers and three orders of French fries, washing them down with coffee and about a gallon of chocolate milk. He barely spoke. Seeing Tommy was something I had to do but it wasn't pleasant. Back at his house I handed him five twenty-dollar bills. He took them without thanking me and went inside. I considered the door closed on the Tuckers for good.

Marcy and I went steady until our sophomore year in high school when her family moved to Kalispell. I saw her a few times after that. We wrote letters but time took over. Deep into our junior year, she sent me a final letter. It took her two pages to reveal that she had found a new boyfriend who, surprise, had this big idea of becoming a doctor. I never went all the way with Marcy.

A few weeks after we graduated from Powell County High School in 1970, when the soft evening light spilled over the mountains, Blue and I loaded the Chevy with fishing equipment and headed north to the Little Blackfoot River. At last I was a legitimate driver, fully licensed. We still went to the Clark Fork, sometimes on bikes, but we had become men and often ventured farther from our little hometown. The Chevy would take us where we wanted to go. We stopped off the gravel road to Beck Hill and climbed through barbed wire fences as flitting chickadees greeted us from the golden willows along the river. We waded through the tall grass, laughing about the time we got drunk on Louie's beer in the mountains, when Blue suddenly dropped his fishing rod and raised his arms to the mighty pines around us as if embracing the wonder of Montana. He looked upward, seemingly in prayer, while the cool shadowy air gathered around us. I stood quietly, watching him as a man, remembering him as a boy. He lowered his arms, ending whatever reverence had come over him, and told me in his most matter-of-fact tone of voice that he had enlisted in the Army.

For a moment there was silence between us except for the chickadees and the babble of the Little Blackfoot over rocks and the whine of truck tires far away on the highway to Helena. Finally I mustered the words. "You can't do this, Blue. There's still Vietnam. We're not talking about fighting the Tuckers."

"We've got to end it, Paul."

"Can't the war end without you? Haven't enough Americans died in that mess? I mean, Louie —."

"He died like a Marine. In many ways he was the best of all of us. Thing is, Paul, I can't judge my life by his. We grew up in this little town thinking it was the whole world. We're not kids anymore. We know it's different for us now. Deer Lodge is a dot on the map and I want to know what else is out there for me."

"So I'm supposed to feel good about you maybe going to Vietnam?"

"Should I wait until I'm drafted? Next time those jokers on national television spin those little ping pong balls with numbers on them, I'll be one of the first, don't you see? It's the way things go. You, being a college boy next fall, will have a student deferment. What about me?"

"There's still time for you, Blue. We can room together at the university in Missoula. You could study girls and in your spare time track down Miss O'Leary."

Blue laughed. His perfect teeth glistened in shafts of sunlight falling through the trees. "She's probably a hundred years old by now."

"That didn't worry you before."

"I was desperate for a girlfriend."

"Like that's ever happened in your life. You had a million of them."

"And a million more are waiting for me too, don't you think, old friend?"

"Blue, I don't want you to go."

"I need to make something of my life, Paul."

"You already have. Captain of the debate team. National Honor Society. Valedictorian of our class. Bucked off Old Betsy. Punched in the nose by Tommy Tucker. Shall I go on? You don't need to prove anything to anybody, especially to yourself. Blue, you can't do this. Please?"

Blue put his hand on my shoulder like he often did when he saw I was distressed. He was taller than me and almost fatherly at times, knowing the void in my life and trying to fill it best he could. "I know you're worried about me after what happened to Louie. Funny thing is, Paul, I don't feel afraid at all."

"You're so much like him, you know. More than me, more than Max, you're most like Louie in ways that never occurred to you."

Maybe it was fate that swept Blue into a soldier's uniform. He never knew fear. Such open-eyed courage was difficult for me to understand. I tended to plot alternatives in my life while Blue charged straight ahead. He was a born leader, born to possibilities beyond my imagination, blind to his own fate. I never fished with Blue again. He was one of the last American soldiers to die in Vietnam. He stepped on a land mine on his nineteenth birthday. Blue was the best friend I ever had, more than Max, even more than Louie.

Max made first-team all-state in football at Powell County High School. We roomed together at the University of Montana. While I discovered beer kegs and hard-rock bands like Iron Butterfly he played offensive tackle for the Grizzlies. Max had become a giant of extraordinary strength. He stood head and shoulders above me, a beast with wild blond hair, but he also stood with me. Nobody gave me trouble when Max was around, especially after we got word that the Viet Cong had killed Blue. Friends circle the wagons. Neither one of us wanted to face death ever again. I think Max played football more for Kenny than for himself, fulfilling his parents' dreams of what his brother could have achieved had he denied that reckless surge behind the wheel. After two years, homesick and failing most of his courses, Max dropped out of college and came home to Deer Lodge to open an auto repair shop. A few months later, he married Peg. I no longer call her the waif. She's a wonderful doting wife who helped

Max overcome his deep grief for his brother. They have three daughters. Their boy looks just like Kenny.

Eleven years after Dad died, when Sally packed and left home for college, Mom began dating a man named Steve who came to the clinic with a broken arm. They got serious but eventually parted because she couldn't let go of my father. She led a sad life, never quite moving beyond his heart attack and the grief that engulfed us. I guess she discovered that lost love runs deep. My mother's nursing job ended after she was caught smelling of alcohol. The stunning cheerleader in the high school yearbooks, the diligent and loving wife and mother, drank herself to an early death. The day she died she resembled a much older woman than her fifty-one years. Sadness weighs heavy on a broken heart.

Sally became a professional writer. She bought a log house in the Flathead Valley in western Montana where she would sweep that curly red hair from her eyes and bang stories into her word processor while her golden lab, Dusty, snored on the plank floor. Her latest book, "Heartstrings and Other Threads of Life," is getting good reviews. Maybe you've heard of it. Sally remembers little of Dad but she's a survivor of those sad and lean years growing up without him. It's better to write about what you know.

Elaine and Toby raised three sons. All of them played Wardens basketball. They had Toby's height and Elaine's grace. The oldest one, Louie, was a striking likeness of his fallen uncle. Toby helped Elaine shrug off the misery of her early life. He was her salvation. She was his, bringing light to a lonely man's existence.

It might surprise you that I married Faye. Hooking up with her wasn't about Louie at all, although I've considered that possibility over the years. She disappeared after his funeral to what I expected would be a bleak existence in that shack on the hill above Anaconda. Eventually I forgot about her. Five years after I confessed my crime to the Deer Lodge police chief, I was attending a mental health conference in Seattle when a striking woman in a red dress touched my arm. We wore name tags but it was her face that I recognized first, except the heavy makeup was gone.

"Faye, how did you—."

"I wouldn't have recognized you in a million years. No glasses anymore and now you're all grown up, Mr. Morrison."

"I still go by Paul."

"And I still go by Faye."

Faye was a woman of uncommon beauty but of humble roots. It took her eleven years to finish college, paying for books and tuition from her tips as a waitress. Funny how life works out. Like me, Faye was a clinical psychologist. We went to lunch and talked for two hours. After Louie died in Vietnam, she managed to graduate from high school, studying while her father nodded off in his alcohol-fueled stupors. Her mother had abandoned them when Faye was a young girl. Faye never knew why her mother left, but eventually took the same course, packing a bag and fleeing after her old man pulled a gun on her in a drunken rage. She told me a story that rivaled my sorrowful young life and in some ways was worse. By Sunday, when the conference ended, we had made plans for her to fly to Oregon to see me the following weekend. The teenage Faye who dazzled me as Louie's girlfriend had matured into the adult Faye sitting next to me in seminars listening to presenters talk about the emotional complications of unresolved grief. Her sophistication left me grasping to understand how she had overcome her bleak lot in life. The professional Faye wore a gray business suit. She swept her sumptuous brown hair back in an office-friendly bun. The red lipstick and heavy eye-liner had disappeared somewhere in the past, replaced with subtle makeup that allowed her natural beauty to charm a room. She wore studded earrings that hinted money. Faye had become a woman who knew what she was all about.

"Tell me about Louie," Faye said as the conference ended and we clicked our briefcases shut. "I mean, you haven't mentioned him this whole weekend but we both know his death had something to do with us meeting like this after so many years." A wave of grief flickered in her eyes. I was sure she had seen the same in me. "Paul, maybe Louie was built to live a short life. Do you ever think about that?"

I suddenly felt conscious about my Brook Brothers suit, and my red necktie, and my gold watch that sparkled in the sun. "Sometimes I worry that I've changed so much that I'm not like him at all anymore, Faye. What would he think of me today, dressed like this? He would say, 'Ace, I'll pound you if you get to braggin' you're too big for the rest of us.' I go see him, you know. The cemetery is a lonely place for the living. I see Louie and my parents and somebody else I'll tell you about sometime. I go see them all, but it's Louie I talk with the most."

Faye looked up at me. I had grown so much taller than her. "We both have lives filled with loss, Paul. You know that he loved you, right? I didn't understand why he was hanging around with a thirteen-year-old kid that summer but it's clear to me now. You were his promise. You were his future. You would remember who he was and why he mattered and that's the best any of us can hope for in life. He saw much of himself in you. You were his little brother, a boy who needed him, and he needed you. Do you see it, Paul?"

"Is that why we're wanting to see each other next weekend, Faye? To keep Louie's memory alive? For both of us?"

She looked uncertain, but only for an instant. "We can't change our troubled pasts, Paul. The people we lost, the confusion, the regret. You know that as much as I do. We can find comfort on the road ahead. If we didn't know that, we wouldn't be grief counselors, helping people move on with their lives. You can't spend a lifetime being the clueless boy who throws rocks at passing cars. I worked hard to find respectability in my life. Look at us, Paul, all grown up now."

The afternoon sky loomed blue and big, and for a moment my mind drifted back to Montana to lazy summer afternoons as the Chevy sat gleaming in the mountain light. "I loved him, you know. I still do."

"I know, Paul. So do I. Now let's look forward, shall we?" She leaned up and we kissed. I couldn't wait to see her again. Faye taught me there's more to life than death. She survived a hardscrabble existence to make something of herself. Sometimes the people we knew as teenagers stand with us until the end. I've been married to Faye for fifteen years. We named our older son Frank, after my father. Bobby is our second son. We call him Blue.

Louie, were you a boy or a man? Dad barely met you, and yet he recognized a conflict inside of you. I know now that you were both of those people. Even today, with all of my professional training, I can't grasp the depth of your pain when that train killed your parents. Your loss was immeasurable. You were old even while young, your life already full of gathered burdens. Remember that first night when you scared me and I stole your car? You were bigger and crazier than what I could understand. It was 1965 and I was thirteen years old. I think back to how that dance brought me that first sweet touch of adolescent love with Marcy Kersher. When I look at the sky on a cloudless night I see stars and a moon that look the same now as they did then, yet on our mortal earth, yesterday is history. Or is it?

I have your Chevy safely stowed in my new garage. You'll be happy to know I clean the spark plugs now and then and wax your car until it gleams. It's still black, by the way. Yes, it's yours, now and forever. I see you behind the wheel, the cigarette dangling from your lips. "Ace," I hear you say, "don't cream the Chevy or I'll pound you." Well, Louie, the engine still purrs like a kitten but these days I don't push this marvelous memory of you past seventy. We cruise your Chevy on Sunday afternoons, Faye and the boys and me, but don't think for a minute that we're raising hell. I'm a good man, Louie, much like Dad and much like you.

Oh, Louie, there's something else. I save my spare change in those big red coffee cans. They're filling up fast. You never know, maybe someday I'll buy an Evinrude.

# Acknowledgements

*I'm reminded that fiction* is a compilation of everyone a writer knows, or knew, or simply observed. It's also the sum of a writer's experiences. Quite by accident I fell into an email exchange with several of my childhood friends that lasted years. The only qualification for participation was endurance and a deep memory. Together we reached into the past to rediscover our youth. That journey inspired me to write this fiction. Thanks to all of these lifelong friends, the Hooligans from Deer Lodge, Montana.

*Special thanks to my* wife, Becky, who encouraged me through long winter nights of writing and the ever-frustrating revisions, and who chose the title for this novel to save me from my first inclinations. Craig J. Hansen and Dave Ruch guided me through early drafts, as did my brother, Jeffrey Giles. Jim Peacock inspired some fresh new directions to the story. Hillorie Giles-Brauch helped me prepare the manuscript for publication. Thanks to all my kids and grandkids: Heather and her Jim, Harmony and her Jim, Hillorie and her Dwayne, Haylie, Kazin, Kimberly, Seanna, Liam, Kyleigh and Kayde. Together they make my writer's soul complete.

CPSIA information can be obtained
at www.ICGtesting.com
Printed in the USA
BVOW00s2146211016

465679BV00001B/34/P